Shifter Chronicles
Birds of Prey
Bear Claw
Eye of the Tiger
Coyote's Kiss
Wolf Pack

Anthologies
Caught in the Middle: Magical Ménage

Collections
Bite Me!: Savage Love
Summer Seductions: Summers' Girl
Cloaks and Daggers: Vampire Hunter

What's her Secret?
Last Call
Designated Alpha

PACK BALANCE

Dedication

For Pam, aka assistant, aka big sister. Thank you for
all your support and everything you do for me.
Thanks for being my traveling buddy and partner.

Chapter One

"Stop! Police!" Cooper Grainger shouted as he followed his suspect down the fire escape.

Of course, the idiot didn't stop. Instead, the skinny moron glanced over his shoulder at Cooper, stumbling when he saw how close Cooper was. His eyes widened almost comically, and if Cooper wasn't trying to intimidate the man he would have laughed. At six foot tall and a solid mass of muscle, Cooper felt like he was chasing down a kid instead of the thirty-five-year-old junkie. The drugs and alcohol Kenny had consumed most of his life had taken a toll on his physique. He couldn't have weighed more than a hundred twenty pounds. He was severely underweight.

"Come on, Kenny!" Cooper yelled. "You know I'm going to catch you."

They were almost at ground level. The four flights down hadn't affected Cooper but Kenny was rasping and panting. Cooper stomped down in his black, beat to hell combat boots. He wore his usual uniform of faded jeans and a black T-shirt. Tonight he'd included a tactical vest, just in case someone decided to take a shot at him.

He knew his appearance sent fear into the men and women who were dragging his city into the gutters. He used it to his advantage as often as possible and the full impact when dressed like he was added to his dangerous stature. The creeps that he'd been dealing with lately needed a good scare. Cooper was determined to bring them all down.

"You're just making this harder on yourself," Cooper shouted at Kenny.

"Screw you, Grainger!" Kenny screeched. He turned his head again, causing him to miss the next step. Kenny shrieked as his arms flailed, and he went crashing down.

Cooper slowed, watching him fall. It wasn't far enough to injure Kenny, but it would put an end to his stupid escape attempt.

Cooper stopped following and stood with his hands on his hips as Kenny lay sprawled on the ground at the feet of his partner. Josiah Burns looked up at Cooper with a familiar smirk.

"He ran?" Josiah asked in his deep southern drawl.

"He ran."

Shaking his head, Josiah reached down and hauled Kenny to his feet. "Really, man? Every time?"

"I didn't do nothing," Kenny claimed, but his eyes were darting all around nervously.

Cooper had worked too long in the narcotics department of the Clear Creek, Missouri Police Department not to know the signs of a lying suspect. "Three dead." Cooper stepped closer to where Josiah was holding Kenny up. "We want to know what new shit has hit the streets."

"I don't know!" Kenny wailed. "I swear!"

WERE CHRONICLES
Volume Five

Pack Balance

Pack Investigator

Pack Law

CRISSY SMITH

Were Chronicles Volume Five
ISBN # 978-1-78651-953-5
©Copyright Crissy Smith 2016
Cover Art by Posh Gosh ©Copyright April 2016
Interior text design by Claire Siemaszkiewicz
Totally Bound Publishing

Published in 2016 by Totally Bound Publishing, Newland House, The Point, Weaver Road, Lincoln, LN6 3QN, United Kingdom.

Totally Bound Publishing is a subsidiary of Totally Entwined Group Limited.

"Then why did you run?" Josiah asked, shaking him.

"I see cops and I run. It's like...built in," Kenny claimed.

Cooper met his partner's gaze. The look that passed between them was one that had been practiced over many years. Kenny wasn't being completely honest and they both knew it. While Josiah just had a really good ability to read people, Cooper used his wolf shifter senses to pick up on the signs that Kenny was showing and trying to hide. The nervousness and desperation was a bitter scent to his nose. They'd busted Kenny many times over the years, and while he did always try to escape, he was more anxious this time. Sometimes Kenny even gave them tips. The fact that he hadn't even hesitated before taking off told Cooper a lot.

He growled, leaning his face closer to Kenny's.

"Okay, okay. Maybe I heard some stuff," Kenny said as he held his hands up. "But I don't have nothing to do with any of it."

Cooper didn't bother correcting Kenny's grammar. Kenny was actually more together than most of the poor souls that had given their lives over to drugs. "Why don't you tell me and I'll decide how *involved* you are."

"Sure, man, I'll do that," Kenny promised.

Cooper didn't like the way his eyes rolled from side to side. Breathing deeply, he concentrated on the scents around him. Not an easy thing to do with the stink of the dumpster mixed with piss and vomit from the back of the bar.

There... He could smell someone approaching. He jerked his chin at his partner. "Backup?" Cooper asked Kenny.

Kenny's eyes widened even more and his jaw dropped open.

"Let's go," Josiah rumbled as he jerked Kenny to the side of the building and away from the weak alley light.

Cooper turned toward the sound of careful and slow steps. Crouching down, he prepared himself for a fight if needed. The two men that stepped out of the shadows farther down the alley were not strangers to Cooper. He stood to his full height and crossed his arms over his chest. It looked like he and Josiah would have more of the locals to interrogate. He cut his gaze to the side and smiled at his partner. Josiah smirked while shaking his head. He knew how much Cooper wanted to let loose on these two. The last time they'd had them in their sights, they'd slithered through like the snakes they were. Human snakes — not the shifting kind.

"Well, well, well," Kade Montgomery said with a sneer. "If it isn't our favorite narc cop."

"And two of my favorite all time losers," Cooper replied back.

Kade and Jordan thought they were tough shit. He and his partner had busted them numerous times. Jordan's entire family were involved in a number of illegal activities. Every member of the Bradley clan was in and out of jail and Jordan was following in their footsteps with vigor. Cooper had tried to help the youngest Bradley. He'd hoped that by giving Jordan someone he could talk to and offering him a hand in getting out of the hard life he led, the kid would be able to make something out of his future. It had become clear quickly that Jordan had no intention of changing his ways. He wasn't just mixed up in the family business. He loved it. Jordan was a bully and enjoyed drugs and hurting people.

Jordan Bradley sniffed. "I've been waiting for this day a long time." He bounced on his toes while he spoke.

Cooper wasn't intimidated. Even if he hadn't been a shifter, which he was, he was sober, trained and ready. "Yeah? Me too."

Jordan rushed him, but Cooper easily sidestepped and using Jordan's momentum, pushed him farther away. Jordan skidded several feet down the alley. Cooper twisted in time to catch Kade's arm as Kade threw a punch.

Tightening his fingers around Kade's wrist, he caused Kade to cry out as he yanked him forward. Cooper made certain not to crush the bones in his grip. He snarled into Kade's face. Kade paled before starting to shake with fear. *Oh, this is great.* Kade and Jordan hadn't known he was a shifter. Cooper grabbed the collar of Kade's shirt before launching him into the brick wall right next to his partner. Josiah had Kenny on his knees with his hands cuffed behind his back. Josiah bent to secure Kade, grinning at the whining kid. "It didn't hurt that much," Josiah taunted Kade.

Cooper was hit in the back. He grunted but remained on his feet, so he turned and glared at Jordan. It would take more than Jordan's strength to knock him down. Spinning, he swept his leg, catching Jordan by surprise. A yelp sounded just before Jordan hit the ground. Standing over him, Cooper scowled. He hadn't even worked up a sweat. Jordan's head had slammed into the cement and he was moaning.

"You'll be joining us at the station," Cooper said, as he rolled Jordan over. He placed his knee on Jordan's back, allowing him to reach around and pull out his cuffs.

"This isn't over," Jordan said, before grunting as Cooper tightened the bindings.

"Oops," Cooper laughed. "Too tight?"

"You're going to be sorry," Jordan warned.

Cooper yanked him up and spun Jordan around.

"You don't threaten me," Cooper snarled. "I will tear you apart."

"Try it!" Jordan taunted. "You don't know what you're up against this time."

That was interesting. He'd get Jordan back to headquarters and try to get a little more from him. It couldn't hurt. Maybe Jordan was just running his mouth, but maybe not. Cooper pushed Jordan forward to meet up with his partner and the two other prisoners.

"I called for a couple of cruisers," Josiah told him.

"Good." Cooper took hold of Jordan's shoulder as Josiah and he led their perps out of the alley toward the front of the club.

Night Moves was a popular local hangout that was doing good business on a busy Friday night. Music blasted out of the open door, mixing with the sounds of cars whizzing by.

Cooper was getting a headache, all the noise and commotion joining together to make his head throb. It had been a long day. Hell, it had been a fucked up two weeks since the first young shifter had been found in a dark alley from a drug poisoning. Cooper and Josiah were running themselves ragged trying to find who was responsible and make sure no one else died. It wasn't a simple task.

Clear Creek was the biggest city in five counties. A lot of the neighboring residents migrated there on the weekends. Sadly, the numbers included young adults who were looking for a party. It was a dangerous time for anyone to be experimenting with drugs in the city.

Cooper had wanted to work in the narcotics department of the Clear Creek Police Department since he'd first been a patrol officer at the young age of twenty. When he had driven a cruiser, he'd watched good people lose themselves in pills and other drugs. A man or woman who had smiled at him the week before or said a friendly 'hi' had turned into someone completely different under the influence. He'd wanted to help those people. Now, fifteen years later, he was fulfilling his dream but he was feeling helpless, instead of like he was making a difference. In the last five years, drugs had flooded in to his city. The current popular illegal substance was the worst he'd ever seen. For some reason, the mixture that was circulating was deadly to shifters. The lab hadn't figured out what was being put in the drug that was poisoning the shifters, so Cooper and Josiah were determined to find the source fast.

He halted Jordan at the curb in front of the bar as two black and whites pulled up. The cop car sirens and lights drew attention from the club goers. He ignored the onlookers so he could keep an eye on his suspect. He and Josiah had taken a chance in hunting down Kenny but it appeared to him that Jordan might be the key to finally catching a break. He gripped Jordan's shoulder as he leaned down close to his ear. "We'll be talking soon," he warned Jordan.

"Whatever," Jordan muttered.

Cooper wasn't buying his tough guy act. For one thing, he could feel Jordan tremble under his hand. For another, Jordan's voice shook slightly.

One of the uniformed officers approached and Cooper pushed on Jordan to get him moving. Officer Grant nodded to Cooper. "You want him booked?"

remained cowering as the two wolves stalked toward Cooper.

In an instant, Cooper had been howling and his body had started to change. It had been both horrible and frightening to watch as his clothes had torn and his body had reshaped itself. She'd wanted to close her eyes. She hadn't wanted to watch anymore. Instead, she'd witnessed Cooper's full transformation from human into a wolf shifter.

Of course, she hadn't known that was what they called themselves back then. It wasn't until a month later when the announcement had come from the Wolf Council and other shifter organizations that they were real, did she start to understand that what Cooper could turn into wasn't just a fairy tale. No, the man she loved was half animal. And she was a horrible person who had darted into the alley as Cooper had fought two beasts and ended up running from him. The only thing she'd done right that night was when she had grabbed the young woman to take her to safety.

As she'd yanked her to her feet, Julie's gaze had met Cooper's. Eyes that were so familiar to her had widened in surprise. She'd run then, sprinted out of the alley with her hand wrapped around a stranger. Police lights and sirens in front of the restaurant had been all she could see. She'd collapsed into the arms of the first uniformed officer she'd seen. There was no way to explain what had taken place.

Lucky for her, she hadn't had to. Josiah had shown up and taken over the scene. Julie hadn't talked to him, but she'd been able to see the worry on his face every time he'd glanced her way. By the time Cooper had stepped out of the alley, Julie had thought she'd lost her mind. If only things had been that simple.

"Assault on an officer and interfering in an active investigation," Cooper stated. "Have him taken to one of the interrogation rooms as soon as he's done." Cooper could use the charges against Jordan to hopefully persuade him to give up the information Cooper and Josiah needed.

"You got it." Grant gripped Jordan's arm and pulled him toward the squad car.

"Shit!"

Cooper turned to his partner when he heard Josiah curse. Kenny was leaning to the side, and Josiah was trying to keep him up while Kenny was convulsing. Cooper rushed over to them and grabbed a hold of Kenny's arm. "What happened?"

"He just started to seize," Josiah told him.

He helped lay Kenny down on the ground. Kenny was sweating and appeared almost green. His small body jerked, so Cooper placed a hand against Kenny's chest to keep him down. A few officers had run over to offer their assistance also. Cooper glanced up at the closest. "Get an ambulance here," he ordered.

"Yes, sir."

As soon as the officer grabbed the mic from his shoulder, Cooper returned his attention to Kenny. Damn, he didn't know what the strung-out man had taken. He leaned close and took a big whiff of him, hoping to pick up on a scent that could help Cooper determine what mixture Kenny consumed. All he could catch was dirt, piss and stale cigarettes. That wasn't going to help. He didn't know how long it'd been since Kenny had showered or taken care of himself. Like a lot of the junkies around town, Kenny didn't have a permanent address. He just crashed wherever and whenever he could. It made tracking down Kenny harder but Cooper had known that Kenny would show up at the bar eventually, which was why he and Josiah had been staking it out.

Josiah held Kenny's head straight as the seizures finally stopped. He looked up and caught Cooper's gaze. Cooper could read his partner well. Even though Kenny could be a pain the ass, he was also just a guy who'd hit a rough patch. Josiah wanted to help him, and Cooper was at a loss at what to do.

"Ambulance is five minutes out. They were on another call a few blocks away that didn't require transfer to the hospital, so they'll be right here," one of the officers said.

Cooper nodded. They'd get Kenny medical treatment. After, maybe he and Josiah could finally talk Kenny into getting the help he needed. They'd tried before and Kenny had always resisted, but they had to get through to him. Kenny wouldn't last much longer on the streets.

The ambulance pulled up to the curb at the same time as a news van. *Fuck, I really don't want to have to deal with the media.*

"Step aside."

Cooper froze as he heard the command. No, it couldn't be.

He raised his head and standing right in front of him was Julie Sullivan.

He swallowed hard when his gaze met hers. She was in the process of bending down when she spotted him. For several moments neither one of them moved. Cooper wouldn't have been able to if someone had been shooting at him. Memories flooded his mind as he took in the beautiful human in front of him.

"Coop," she whispered, and he felt her words like a caress over his body.

"Hey!" Josiah grabbed his shoulder, yanking Cooper out of his shock. "You okay?"

Cooper pushed himself away from Kenny, Julie and the entire scene. He climbed to his feet, refusing to look back.

"Cooper?" Josiah stepped in front of him. Cooper didn't know what his partner saw on his face but he frowned before glancing in the direction of where Cooper was looking. "Julie?" Josiah's mouth dropped open.

Cooper would have laughed if his heart didn't feel like it was going to pound out of his chest. His partner was just as shocked to see Cooper's old lover as he was.

"Hi, Josiah," Julie said quietly. "What's this guy's story?"

His partner glanced back at him. Cooper raised his eyebrows and tilted his head slightly in the direction of Julie. He needed Josiah to take care of this. Cooper had to get away from her so he could get himself under control. Just hearing her voice was screwing with his body. His cock was hard, his pulse raced and the wolf side of him wanted to howl. The itch under his skin was starting, like when he needed to shift.

"I think Grant needs you," Josiah told him with a wink.

Cooper managed to grunt before he rushed off, taking the excuse of talking with the officer even though he knew Josiah had made it up. He walked fast, avoiding the numerous cops and onlookers who milled around. Now that the excitement was over, hopefully the public would take off. He spotted a quiet, shady spot against the building and had to keep himself from sprinting to it.

He placed his fist against the old brick as he lowered his head. Cooper drew in a deep breath through his nose then exhaled from his mouth. He repeated this several more times before he felt that he finally had control of himself once again. Turning, he placed his shoulders against the building and looked over to his partner and the one woman he'd never thought he'd see again.

She had her back to him now, so he could take his time looking her over. Julie had always been on the tall side for a woman. She was five foot seven, which matched his own height well. Tonight, she had her long brown hair braided down the back, the end reaching a few inches from her pants. She wore the usual Clear Creek EMT uniform of black cargo pants and red T-shirt, but she didn't look like the other paramedics Cooper was used to dealing with. No, she was unique, special, and once, a long time ago, she'd been his.

* * * *

Julie brushed her bangs out of her eyes as her partner Shawn Hargrove took the front of the stretcher to lift their patient into the back of the ambulance. She didn't want to look behind her, but she just couldn't resist. Cooper Grainger. She hadn't thought that she'd run into him so soon after returning to Clear Creek and her old job. No, if she'd known that tonight would be the night that she'd see him again, she'd have prepared herself better — she scoffed — if that would have been possible.

"That was awkward. What'd he say to you?" Shawn asked her as she followed him into the vehicle.

Realizing that she needed to get out of her own head and start thinking about her patient, filled her with guilt. Sure, the guy on the stretcher was stable for now, but she had a job to do. "Nothing," she answered her partner. That was the truth, wasn't it? Cooper hadn't spoken to her at all. The hurt and pain in Cooper's eyes told her volumes, though.

"I'll finish taking his stats and you can get us out of here." She really, really wanted away from this scene.

Cooper had looked good, but then, he always did. There was so much that she wanted to say. Little by little, she'd been forming a plan. The first move had been returning home. She knew how badly she'd hurt him. God, he still might never forgive her, but she had to try. She'd returned to work just that week. Okay, so she was a coward. Julie should have gone to Cooper the minute she'd gotten back into town. The chances that he wouldn't want anything to do with her were high, but she had returned for him. That had to count for something. Now they'd run into one another and she hadn't been prepared. *Crap!* She'd screwed up again.

Shawn frowned at her while he walked backward to leave the ambulance. He hadn't forgotten that she'd skipped out on him either. It would be easier to gain Shawn's forgiveness, though. Shawn knew what had happened and although he was disappointed in her, he understood. Shawn would be on her side. That's what friends were for. Josiah had been just as surprised as Cooper to see her, but he'd recovered more quickly. He'd given her all the information he could on her patient before turning his back on her. That had hurt. At one time she'd considered Josiah one of her best friends. Of course, that had been when she and Cooper were together and before she'd hurt Cooper so badly.

"You sure you're all right?" Shawn asked, as he stood by the open doors.

Julie lifted her head and peered past him. Just her luck—she could see Cooper and Josiah huddled together on the sidewalk with their heads close together. What were they talking about? Her? Maybe. But both men were dedicated cops, and chances were their attention might have gone right back to the case they were working. Cooper could have moved on already. He might be settled down with a woman who accepted him. Julie wanted to be that woman and hoped it wasn't too late. She could have stayed away but she'd never stopped loving Cooper. She didn't think she ever would. She had to get him back before he forgot all about her and what they'd shared. Her timetable had just jumped forward. She needed to talk to Cooper. She shook her thoughts from her head. "Let's get out of here."

Shawn nodded before he slammed the doors closed. Julie looked down at the patient on the stretcher. He was resting comfortably for now. They needed to get him to the hospital so they could find out what drugs he'd taken. She wasn't sure whether or not he was a shifter or a human. That wasn't something that was noticeable unless the shifter wanted it known. She had plenty of experience with that.

How could she have known Cooper for so long, slept beside him and started making a life with him when he'd been keeping such a huge secret? Had she missed the signs, or had Cooper just been so good she hadn't stood a chance of realizing he was keeping something from her?

She didn't have the answers any more now than she did a year ago when she'd left. Trying to make sense out of anything that had happened that night long ago was like banging her head against a wall. It didn't matter anyway, not really. That was what she'd decided and why she'd come home.

In her heart she knew Cooper was still the same man that she'd fallen in love with. She just had to accept that there was a huge part of him he'd left out.

The engine started, and she braced herself on one of the hand rails. As the ambulance merged with traffic, headed for the hospital, she went to work on recording the information on her patient. His first name was Kenny and he was homeless. He was also on some kind of illegal substance. She slid the blood pressure band around his arm and turned it on. As that test was running, she checked his eyes, nose and mouth. The familiar routine of taking care of someone in need relaxed her. It didn't matter to her whether or not this man was good or bad, homeless or rich. What was important was that she could help him.

His blood pressure was good and everything else was normal. There wasn't anything else to do except watch him and make sure he was safe during the ride.

She took a seat next to the stretcher and glanced out of the two small narrow windows at the back of the ambulance. She couldn't see the bar or cops any longer. They'd moved away from the area and closer into town. She was getting farther from Cooper. That thought make her ache.

It had been two weeks since she'd packed up her things and driven her old Jeep toward Clear Creek. Her brother Garrett had been happy to put her up in Kermit for the time she'd stayed with him, and she felt a little guilty about leaving him alone again, but she'd finally gotten the courage to follow her heart. A year ago when she'd showed up on his doorstep, she'd only been planning on staying a week or so. A week had turned into a month and as she'd struggled to understand what had happened with Cooper, she'd grown comfortable in her brother's home. But it was when her father had told her and Garrett that he might have cancer that Julie put off leaving for a while. Two months after she'd arrived, she'd taken a part-time job as an EMT. She'd wanted to be close to her parents when they had doctor visits and at the end, the chemotherapy. The EMT position at least allowed her to make money while she was in Kermit.

Her brother worked at one of the fire stations and had put in a good word for her. It had been nice spending so much time together and they'd grown closer than ever. Garrett had never met Cooper, although her parents had when they'd visited Clear Creek for the previous Christmas. That had been two weeks before she'd run away.

The health scare had brought the entire Sullivan family closer. Luckily they'd caught the small tumor in her dad's stomach early and after twelve treatments, he was on the road to recovery.

She'd been so relieved that her father was going to be okay. She'd even debated about staying in Kermit, but she couldn't get her mind off Cooper or the events that had sent her running.

They'd been on a date when her entire world was rocked. Cooper had held the door open for her as they'd left her favorite Italian restaurant. She'd heard a muffled scream, not really placing it for what it was until later. Cooper had pushed her back into the restaurant yelling at her to call nine-one-one. She had, but she'd also followed him into the alley. There, what she'd seen still gave her nightmares. Two giant wolves had cornered a woman at the end of the dark alley.

Julie had watched in horror as Cooper ran at the two animals, yelling at them. She'd wanted to shout at him to shoot them, but she hadn't been able to make a sound. The woman who'd been screaming had

Chapter Two

Cooper rubbed his fingers over his forehead. The headache that had started a little while ago was now pounding and making him sick. He paused outside the room where Jordan was being held.

"We don't have to do this now," Josiah said.

They did though. Cooper couldn't let this hot lead in the case go just because he felt like his entire world was falling apart, again. "I'm fine," he lied.

Josiah shook his head. "At least take some aspirin, you stubborn fool." He held out a packet to Cooper.

Grateful, Cooper took them and tore open the package with his teeth. He popped two pills in his mouth and used his coffee to wash them down. At least that took care of one of his problems. He didn't even want to think about what the reappearance of Julie into his life meant—not that he expected to see much of her. Julie had obviously returned home and hadn't gotten in touch with him. He'd tried. God, he'd tried so hard to explain things after he'd shifted that night. If he could do things over again, he would share his secret with her as soon as he realized that he was in love with her. Instead, he'd done what he'd always done and kept the other part of him hidden. Only his partner had known he could shift into a wolf, since that had been before the shifters had gone public. And Josiah had figured it out after them working together for a year, catching small signs that Cooper hadn't known he was showing his partner.

"She's back." Josiah leaned closer as he lowered his voice. "That has to count for something."

Cooper snorted. "Does it?" It was the question he kept asking himself and now that he'd said it out loud, Cooper felt like an idiot.

"She didn't have to come back," Josiah pointed out.

"Her home is here, her job. That's why she returned," Cooper said.

"I think you're wrong. You were so shocked from seeing her that you didn't really see her," Josiah told him.

Cooper frowned. "That doesn't even make sense." He relaxed against the wall and took another drink of his coffee. It was bitter and scorched but he didn't expect anything different at the police house.

"She watched you," Josiah said. "As you walked away, she didn't take her eyes off you. And there was longing, regret and a spark of hope. You know I can read people, and Julie is not over you."

The ache in his heart seemed to grow bigger. He wanted to believe his partner, but he wasn't sure he could make it through another heart break. "Fuck, I need to shift."

Josiah laughed. "Well, let's get our interrogations started so you can do that."

Cooper drained the last of his coffee then tossed the paper cup into the nearby trash can. "Okay." He pushed himself away from the wall and strolled to the door. He opened it and saw Jordan with his arms folded on the table and his head down. Jordan didn't even look up when they entered. Cooper slammed his hand down right next to Jordan's head.

Jordan popped up and if he hadn't been handcuffed to the metal ring in the table, he'd probably have fallen.

"You're sleeping?" Cooper asked with disgust. "Really?" Did this kid not know how much trouble he was in?

Jordan scowled back at him. "Can't say your place is very entertaining, so there's not much more to do."

Cooper had to give Jordan credit for trying to remain tough. The punk didn't have a decent bone in his body. He was probably proud to have been arrested — something to add to his street cred. Cooper shook his head and sat directly in front of Jordan. As he'd discussed earlier with his partner, Josiah stayed back against one wall with his arms crossed over his chest.

"I hate for you to tell others I'm not a good host, so why don't we get started," Cooper said. "You're facing some very serious charges."

"And you'll fix them for me?" Jordan sneered.

Cooper shrugged. "You help me and I help you." He leaned forward. "You're in serious shit, Jordan. There is no one here to help you. We've got your buddy Kade. Kenny is under police guard at the hospital. One of them will talk. So why don't you do yourself a favor and don't waste my time."

"Talk to you? I'm not a narc!" Jordan exclaimed.

"Assault on an officer," Cooper reminded him. "You'll do time for that. Is that what you want? Go to prison when all you have to do is answer some questions?"

"I'm not telling you anything," Jordan said. "I'll be a hero in jail and you know it. You will just help my reputation."

Cooper glanced over his shoulder at his partner. "Guess I owe you a hundred bucks."

"Yep, and don't try to get out of it this time."

"I can't believe he didn't talk," Cooper stated as he stood.

Josiah stepped closer.

"Of course," Cooper continued. "That doesn't mean I can't make the others think he did. I wonder what Kade will give me if he thinks Jordan rolled."

Josiah laughed. "I'm not taking that bet."

It was the oldest trick in the book. Cooper was taking a chance, but he figured Jordan really didn't want to be known as a snitch. "We'll let Kade leave first, if he cooperates. That way he can start the rumors about Jordan before Jordan even gets out."

"Fuck you!" Jordan yelled. "No one will believe I ratted."

Cooper had been making his way to the door. He glanced over his shoulder at Jordan with his best surprised expression. "Sorry. I forgot you were here."

"You're such a dick," Jordan said.

"Well...yeah," Cooper agreed easily. "Now, what were you saying?"

"I'm not saying shit," Jordan replied.

Cooper grinned. "That's not what I'm going to tell Kade — or Kenny, when we talk to him. I hear that he's almost ready to be released from the hospital. Maybe Kade won't give you up to the neighborhood but Kenny doesn't have any loyalty to you." Cooper mixed enough truth in to cover his lie. And he could lie to a suspect. He had no idea how Kenny was doing. He'd asked Grant to check into Kenny's condition and hadn't gotten word back yet. He did know that if Kenny survived, he wasn't Jordan's lackey like Kade. He'd have no problem spreading rumors where Jordan was concerned. Kenny was only friends with the person who could get him drugs at that moment. He only looked out for himself.

"You can't tell people I talked to you. You'll get me killed," Jordan told him. His voice wavered slightly.

Perfect.

Cooper shrugged. "The thing is, I don't really see that as a bad thing. You're a drug pusher and I've spent a lot of years putting people like you in jail. But you just get out again." He turned to his partner. "This idea is sounding better and better."

"I'm going to hurt you one day," Jordan spat at him. "You think you're so tough. Well you won't be when me and my boys get done with you. You've been making lots of enemies on the streets. I won't even have to pay to have you messed up. The boys will do it for free."

Oh yeah, he had Jordan scared. The only way he'd be so stupid as to say that to Cooper while in custody was if he was about to shit himself in fear. Well, Cooper wasn't going to put up with that crap. He was a damn good detective and he would *not* back down, especially not to some punk who needed a good ass whooping.

Cooper used his shifter speed to hurl himself at Jordan. He picked Jordan up by his neck. The chain attached to the cuffs made it impossible for Jordan to fight back. Although, even if he hadn't been restrained, Jordan stood no chance of hurting Cooper.

"I told you before not to threaten me!"

"You can't put your hands on me," Jordan shouted. "I'll sue you and this entire city."

Cooper snarled but released Jordan. Jordan fell, missing his chair, and landed on the floor. The chain rattled.

"Try it," Cooper dared. He whirled around and knew that his eyes were glowing. His wolf was close. Too much had happened and he was hanging on to his control by a thread. At normal times he could bring portions of his wolf out and use the animal side of him to intimidate others but at that moment, his wolf was surfacing on his own. After the night he'd had, his wolf was itching to be released. He needed to shift soon.

"Let's go see what Kade has to say," Josiah said.

He followed his partner to the door, but paused to glare over his shoulder. Jordan had climbed back in his chair but the young man was pale and shaking. Cooper narrowed his eyes. "You'd better pray Kade doesn't roll over and we still need something from you."

Jordan didn't respond, but Cooper saw him swallow hard. They'd let Jordan sit and think about his future while they tried their hand at breaking Kade. Cooper truly did hope that Kade wanted to talk. The longer the interrogations took, the bigger chance that a shifter was out there digesting a drug that would kill them.

Cooper let the door slam behind him before he leaned back against it.

"You have to get yourself under control," Josiah told him.

He nodded. "I know." A few more hours and he'd be able to go home and spend some time as his wolf. He just needed to catch a damn break in the case.

"I'm going to grab us some cold drinks," Josiah said. "Why don't you take a few minutes? I'll meet you in front of Kade's door. He's in C."

"Thanks, man." Cooper patted his partner's shoulder.

Josiah walked off, heading toward the break room. Cooper watched him go. He was lucky that they'd been assigned to one another. Josiah was more than his work partner. He was Cooper's best friend. He pushed himself off the door and strolled down the hall. When he reached the men's room, he passed another officer and nodded in greeting. He didn't want to talk to anyone just then, so he hurried by.

Lucky for him, the restroom was empty as he walked up to the sink. He braced his hands on the cold porcelain while leaning close to peer into the mirror. His eyes had returned to normal but he had dark circles under them. His dark hair was shaggy and he really needed to get it cut. Basically, he looked like crap. The long hours he'd been putting in showed on his face. Not the best time to run into Julie again. He snorted. God, he couldn't believe he'd seen her after all this time. She'd looked so good too. Why couldn't he get past his attraction to her? He knew it was more than physical and that what he felt for Julie was true. A part of him wanted to rejoice at her return. If she was close enough maybe he could win her back. The other side of him was terrified. Cooper couldn't go through another heartbreak if Julie didn't want him. But now was not the time to worry about his love life. He had to stop thinking about her. He had work to do.

He turned on the cold faucet before lowering his face. He cupped some water and splashed himself. The chill felt great against his heated flesh. He repeated this action several times before turning off the water. He grabbed a paper towel from the holder on the wall and patted his face dry, feeling better. He just needed to keep his attention where it belonged. It shouldn't be too hard. Julie had left him. Found out what he was and ran. He needed to remember that.

With new resolve, he turned and strolled from the restroom. Josiah stood outside the interrogation room on his cell phone. When he spotted Cooper coming, he said a few more words then hung up.

"Anything on the case?" Cooper asked as he joined his partner.

Josiah shook his head. "No, I was just making a date for later."

He slapped his partner on the shoulder. Josiah was a lady's man and never short on female companionship. Cooper used to enjoy going out with him and watching Josiah use his slick moves on women. That was before Julie. Once he'd hooked up with Julie, he no longer cared about anyone else. After, he couldn't go back to one-night stands. Not when he'd learned how it felt to have someone at his side to share his days and help him through the tough cases. He was lucky that Josiah and Julie had bonded as friends very quickly, since both of them were such important parts of his life. It had hurt Josiah when Julie had taken off, too. Every time Cooper had tried to call Julie and had gotten her voicemail, Josiah had been at his side, telling him that she would come around. At first, Cooper had believed him but as they days had turned into weeks then months, he knew he'd lost something special.

"Ready to get this over with?" Cooper asked.

"Yeah."

* * * *

Two hours later, Cooper really wanted to strangle someone. He slammed his fist on his desk. "Nothing! Neither one will tell us shit," he griped to Josiah.

"At least we can hold them tonight. That will give us time to plan our next move," Josiah said calmly.

"We need to get a warrant," Cooper said. "I'd bet anything that they have some of those drugs in their place."

Josiah sighed. "You know we don't have enough for a judge to sign off on a warrant. I've put some feelers out, so I'll make a few calls. You knew they wouldn't talk."

He had, but that just pissed him off more. He saw Officer Grant hurrying toward him. Hopefully the young cop had some good news. As Grant got closer, Cooper's gut felt heavy at the expression on Grant's face.

"I just got off the phone with the hospital," Grant said as he joined them. "Kenny is going to be okay."

Relief washed over Cooper. Maybe they were going to finally catch a break. "That's good."

"However, he doesn't remember anything before forty-eight hours ago," Grant told him.

"What?" *No, this can't be happening.*

"The docs say that whatever Kenny took wiped out his memory. He'll recover, but there is no telling if he will remember what he took or where he got it."

"You got to be fucking kidding me," Cooper grumbled.

"The hospital did match it to the same drug that is killing the shifters," Grant continued. "The new element of memory loss wasn't in the old samples, so the doc thinks someone is playing around with the ingredients."

Josiah bumped his shoulder. "That could mean they weren't targeting shifters. A mistake made during production? The poisoning and overdoses are just a tragic side-effect? Maybe they're trying to make it safer?"

Grant shook his head. "No, the unknown component that was found to be deadly to shifters was doubled in this batch."

"Shit!" Cooper's stomach cramped and he felt like throwing up. There were some sick people out there.

"Sorry, I thought you would want to know right away," Grant said.

"Thanks, I appreciate all the work tonight," Cooper told him.

"No problem," Grant replied. "I was happy to help."

Cooper waited until Grant had left before turning to his partner. "We have to find those drugs. Jordan is involved. I can feel it."

"Let me see what I can piece together," Josiah stated as he sat at his own desk. "Maybe—just maybe—we can convince a judge to take a chance and issue a warrant."

At least they would be doing something. "What do you want me to do?"

"Get out of here." Josiah glanced up. "Oh, perfect timing, you have a date."

Cooper froze. Josiah was looking behind him. Cooper couldn't get his body to move. He didn't think his partner would set him up with Julie and not warn him. But what the hell was he talking about dates for otherwise?

"Glad you could make it," Josiah called out.

"No problem. I needed to get out of the office."

Cooper's tension left him so rapidly that Cooper went weak at the knees. He gripped his desk as his oldest friend stepped up beside him. Michael Riley had been his college roommate their freshmen year, both of them studying criminal justice—Cooper to become a police officer and Mike to start the long process of being one of the most powerful defense attorneys in the city.

Josiah and Mike had met through Cooper and had become good friends over the years.

So this was what Josiah had been up to earlier.

"I never said the date was for me," Josiah said with a smirk.

Cooper understood. Josiah had called Mike to take care of him. It was times like these that Cooper truly knew how lucky he was. Josiah always had his back.

"So, you ready, man?" Mike's hand came down on his shoulder.

Oh, he was so ready. "Thanks," he told Josiah. His partner only nodded in response. Cooper grinned back before turning to Mike. "It's been too long."

"I know," Mike said. "I've got a case that is driving me crazy. Can't seem to track down the one witness I need."

"I'm sorry." Cooper hadn't been a good friend the past year. He and Mike used to run together in human form every morning and as wolves, at least twice a week. "I should have checked on you."

"Don't worry about it." Mike slapped his back. "I was giving you space. I know how hard it was after... Well, anyway... I'm here now, so why don't we head out?"

"Sure," Cooper agreed. He'd find a way to make up his absence to Mike. He grabbed his phone and keys off his desk. When he passed Josiah, he clasped his shoulder briefly. His partner had known that Cooper needed someone to run with and Mike also knew enough about Julie to listen if he needed to talk. Josiah had driven them in to work that morning, so Cooper followed Mike to his Mercedes. The sleek silver car was way outside Cooper's price range but to Mike, the fact that it was a couple of years old meant that he wouldn't have it for much longer.

As much as the two men had in common, there were also several things that they were the complete opposite about. Mike clicked the remote, which chirped as it unlocked. Cooper pulled open the door and dropped inside. He was anxious to get where they were going.

"The park okay with you?" Mike asked, as he climbed in on the driver side.

"Yeah." It'd been a long time since he'd transformed and run in Pack lands. Every couple of weeks the Alpha invited all the wolf shifters to the park and they ran together. Cooper always looked forward to those nights. But that was something else he'd stopped doing when Julie had taken off. He just hadn't wanted to be around a bunch of people.

"So you want to talk about it?" Mike started the car as he spoke.

"Josiah told you?" It wasn't really a question he needed answered.

"You're on a case, called for an ambulance and Julie is there," Mike said. "That's about all I got from your partner."

It was enough. "Pretty much sums up my night," Cooper replied.

"If it was that simple, Josiah wouldn't have called me. Not that I mind, but I just want you to know you can talk to me."

"I do know," Cooper responded. He really was grateful for Mike's presence.

"So how'd she look?" Mike asked.

Cooper chuckled. "Just as good as I remember."

"Did you say anything to her? Ask her how long she'd been back?"

"No, I, uh...was shocked to see her," he admitted.

"No big deal," Mike said. "At least you didn't say anything that you'll regret. Do you know where she's staying?"

"Probably her house. I checked on it a few times but she had her partner looking after it. He never told me much but I could tell he wasn't any happier about her disappearance than I was. I kept hoping that meant she planned to return," Cooper said.

"Good, so you know where she'll be when you are ready to talk to her."

Mike had a point. Cooper could wallow in self-doubt or he could try to win Julie back. If that was what he truly wanted? Of course it was. He didn't want to be hurt again, but on the other hand, he was still suffering being away from her. "I won't let her get away this time," he stated it out loud to himself, not really speaking to Mike.

"That's the man I know," Mike approved.

He felt lighter already. Julie had fallen for him once. Sure, she hadn't known about his ability as a shifter but he was still the same man. If she loved him once, she could love him again. At least he had a better chance of convincing her to give him another try with her in the same city. He was done sitting back and letting the world pass him by. He was going to get his life back. He'd find out who was killing the shifters with their drugs. He was going to get his damn happily ever after. He just needed to find a balance in which he could love Julie and still be true to his wolf side.

Chapter Three

The ground beneath his paws was moist and soft. It had been far too long since he'd been in Pack territory and let his wolf out. The wind ruffled his fur as he used his incredible speed to race through the trees and fallen logs. Mike stayed at his side as the moon shined above them. The light even seemed to illuminate the path for him. Cooper felt free.

He was very lucky that he had such an understanding and compassionate Alpha. Instead of pressuring Cooper to run with the Pack, Alpha Jeremy had offered to listen to him and just sit and talk. When Cooper had confessed how much Julie's rejection had hurt him, his Alpha had told him not to give up on her. Cooper had just about given up on that advice.

With the reappearance of Julie in his life, he was glad he'd listened. Jeremy had been right once again. Cooper owed the older wolf shifter a lot. He'd taken Cooper into his Pack and was a true friend.

In the year that Cooper had been pulling away from the Pack, Jeremy had still kept in touch with him. His Alpha was the only shifter he'd run with in the last several months. It had only been a few times, but Cooper could look back now and see how his Alpha had been making sure Cooper was okay.

Mike bumped into him and almost sent Cooper into a stumble. He needed to just enjoy his time as a wolf.

He leaped over Mike, nipping playfully at his back side. Mike yelped before chasing after him. Cooper took off toward the small creek that was only a few yards away. Just as he reached the water's edge, Mike bumped into him, knocking him off his feet. He rolled to the side, before popping back up. Mike barked softly—what Cooper took as laughing—and strolled up to the creek. Cooper followed then lapped up the cool liquid, refreshing himself. He lay down in the damp bank, resting his chin on his paws. He'd needed this and already felt steadier for it. In the past year he could admit to somewhat punishing himself when not allowing his wolf this much needed release.

Cooper was done, though. He'd never before let humans or anyone make him feel less of a man for being able to shift—until he'd lost Julie because of his abilities. Seeing her earlier had helped clear his mind and how he'd been acting by not spending time as his wolf like he'd always done. If Cooper hid what he was, how could he expect Julie to accept him?

He closed his eyes and sighed. Cooper already had a plan forming on what his next steps should be. He'd let her shock wear off from running into him but by the weekend, he would track her down and make her talk to him.

There had been so many times he'd almost driven to Kermit to see her. It hadn't been hard to find her. Her entire family lived in Kermit and her partner had filled him in on everything else. He'd met her parents and was pretty sure they'd liked him. Then again, that was before Julie had found out what he was. After the shifters had gone public, he hadn't been certain whether or not that would help his case, so he'd stayed away.

Too much time had been wasted. Julie belonged to him. He had to man — or wolf — up.

* * * *

The long road that led to Cooper's house was so familiar that it made Julie's heart ache. She'd never lived with Cooper but she had spent more time at his home than her own while they'd been dating.

He'd picked a residence on the outskirts of town where the houses had more room between them than if he was in the middle of the city. There were also numerous trees and a wooded area around the back. When she'd started to date Cooper and had visited him for the first time, he'd told her that he saw so much hatred and the bad side of people that he enjoyed the solitude, being away from everyone. She'd bought his explanation easily. Now that she knew what he'd been hiding, so much more made sense.

Julie turned onto the smooth asphalt, following the driveway until she was in front of his cabin-style house. She parked and stared ahead. Julie had fallen in love with the structure and found it more comfortable than her own place. Even though the morning was dark around her, the outside lights illuminated the grounds and she could see that he'd recently cut the grass. The green, thick lawn neat and gorgeous. The flowers they'd planted together leading up to the front door were in full bloom.

She could still recall every detail of that long Saturday. The way the sun had beat down on Cooper's broad shoulders. The sweat that had dripped from his body that had made him look even sexier as he'd dug the holes to plant each delicate flower. After they'd finished and while they'd both still been dirty and wet, Cooper had taken her hard and fast in the entry of the house. Then again in the shower.

Julie shivered, remembering how Cooper's hands felt on her. She had to shake the memories from her mind as she turned off her car. There were no lights shining through the front windows. Cooper might not be home yet. It had only been a couple of hours since she'd seen him for the first time in a year but it was almost four in the morning. That was late to anyone's standards, except for the people who worked late shifts like her and Cooper.

He could still be at the station or he could be in bed. Maybe he was seeing someone else and he wasn't alone. Oh God, that thought made her want to puke. Maybe she was making a mistake surprising him. She should just go home and wait until she had a better plan. Cooper didn't like surprises.

No, I have to do this now. She hadn't expected to run into Cooper yet, but now that she had seen him, she needed to explain things. To apologize and tell him how wrong she'd been. Even if he was with someone else, Julie needed to set things straight between them. She'd been wrong, and Cooper deserved to hear her say the words. Even if there was a chance he could break her heart by dismissing her. It wasn't like it wouldn't be justified after what she'd done.

Her cell rang, causing her to jump. Julie had to dig through her purse to find the small device. Seeing her brother's name on the screen calmed her. He knew her schedule so his calling was a pretty regular thing.

"Hey, Garrett," she greeted.

"How's it going?" Garrett replied. "You get your man back yet?"

Julie had come clean to her brother. Had told him every detail of why she'd left Cooper. Garrett had surprised her by taking Cooper's side. Even before the shifters had come out publicly, Garrett had known all about them. He'd explained that he'd known a few from working at the firehouse. They were good guys and once he'd learned about their abilities, he'd never thought of them any differently than the other guys he worked with.

Julie had been shocked. But the two men that Garrett had told her about had been willing to talk to her about being able to shift. They'd probably helped her with her feelings for Cooper more than anyone else. She was lucky to have been able to speak with Tom and Steve so freely.

"I saw him tonight," she told her brother.

"How'd that go?"

"Well, it was unexpected. I was out on a call and the guy was one of Cooper's suspects. I didn't know until I came face-to-face with him. I wasn't ready," she admitted.

Garret's sigh spoke volumes.

"I'm at his house now," she said, before he could speak.

"Why didn't you tell me that first? I'll let you go."

"I'm not... I mean..." She didn't really want to confess she hadn't gotten up the nerve to see if he was home or not.

"You're sitting in your car?" he guessed.

Yeah, her brother knew her well. "Yes."

"Julie," Garret said softly. "You made the decision to return and try to get him back. You love Cooper, right?"

"I do."

"You're going to have to take a chance and talk to him," Garrett said. "You should have done it the minute you got back."

"I know," she replied. "It's just..."

"You think he'll still be angry?"

"I would be," she responded.

"Cooper's not you. You'll only find out if you actually talk to him, though. What'd he say when you ran into each other?" he asked.

"Nothing, he looked shocked and then his partner came up and Cooper left. He looked like he'd seen a ghost," she explained. "I could see the hurt in his eyes, though. I don't know if he'll forgive me."

"Maybe he won't," Garrett told her gently. "You can't know until you try."

"You're right," she admitted.

"So why don't you take a deep breath and go knock on his door?" he suggested.

"I will," she promised. "Did you need something?"

"No I just wanted to check on you," Garrett said quickly.

Too quickly. "Garrett?"

"Tom was hurt in a fire. He's in the hospital," Garrett said.

"Oh God! Is he going to be okay?"

"Yes but it still scared me," Garrett answered. "I'm not sure why, but for some reason, I thought that if anything happened to him since he was a shifter, he'd just be able to shift and be fine. Too many movies, I guess. But he's hurt bad. Steve is staying with him at the hospital. I feel so helpless."

Her brother had such a kind heart. He was a strong man and his job was hard, but Garrett was one of the firemen who truly believed in what he did. It would be hard for him to deal with a friend being so hurt. "I could come back for a few days," she offered. "Tom was very nice to me and I consider him a friend."

"No," Garrett said. "I want you to stay and talk to Cooper. Tom isn't even awake and he wouldn't want you to stop what you're trying to do."

"If you're sure," she stated with concern.

"I am," Garrett assured her. "I just left the hospital and needed to hear your voice. I was outside when the roof collapsed and I'll admit that I have never been so damn terrified in my life."

"Oh, Garrett." Her heart broke for him. "Maybe you could come here? Get away for a few days?"

She held her breath at the silence on the other side of the phone.

"I think I'd like that," Garrett finally said.

"Good," Julie told him. "You can come whenever you get a chance. I'll be able to show you around. I really love it here. I think you will too."

"Maybe I'll even get to meet Cooper," he said.

"I get it," she replied. "I'm hanging up."

"I love you," Garrett said.

"Me too, big brother. Me too." She ended the call, hoping that he really would visit. She missed him already and it had only been a week. While she'd always respected and loved Garrett, she now considered him one of her best friends. The only downside of moving back to Clear Creek was being away from her brother.

She knew she'd put off going to Cooper's door long enough. It had taken her a lot of courage to make it this far and if she had to come back, she knew her nerves would be worse. Okay, it was time to take the first step of trying to win him back.

She exited her Jeep and started forward. Not only were there no lights in the front but she couldn't see any farther in the house. His truck could be in the garage, so that didn't tell her anything. She passed the beautiful flowers she'd thought about earlier. Three steps up and she was on the porch. She could do this.

Cooper had the same white wicker furniture off to the side of the deck. Many nights they'd sat nursing a beer and just holding hands. Tears built in her eyes as she wondered if they'd ever have the opportunity to do it again. With determination coursing through her, she stomped up to the front door and knocked.

After a few minutes she pounded harder. "Come on," she mumbled under her breath.

Just as she fisted her hand for the third time she heard the sound of a vehicle approaching. Headlights washed over her as a Mercedes pulled up behind her. *Whose car is that? Cooper's new girlfriend's?*

Julie narrowed her eyes as she leaned forward to try to make out the occupants in the car.

"Looks like you have company," Mike said beside Cooper.

Looking at Julie standing on his front porch, Cooper wasn't sure he could get out of the car. He'd expected he'd have to track her down before they saw each other again. He was shocked to see her waiting for him.

"Go!" Mike pushed his shoulder.

Cooper glanced over at his buddy.

"You can't tell me you weren't going to track her down," Mike said.

"I was," he admitted. "I just..."

"If you don't go to her, you might lose your chance," Mike pointed out. "Again."

Cooper growled. "I'm going." His heart was pounding and his hands were damp with sweat. He jerked the handle of the car and pushed it open. Julie had started down the steps but paused when he stepped out of the car.

"Good to see you again, Julie," Mike called out.

Cooper peered over his shoulder into the car. Mike was leaning into the passenger seat to look out at Julie.

"Hi, Mike." Julie waved.

"Go home," Cooper ordered Mike before slamming the car door closed.

Mike honked before the vehicle took off. Cooper stood staring at Julie. Her light brown hair fell in front of her eyes and she brushed it back. Cooper's fingers itched to feel the soft strands once again.

"Cooper," she said softly, but he still heard it as clear as anything else.

"What are you doing here?" he asked, surprised at the huskiness he could hear in his own voice.

"Can we talk?" she asked.

He nodded. He strolled forward until he was directly in front of her. "Let's go inside."

Her smile was strained. "Okay."

It took every ounce of his control not to touch her when he passed by. If she was a shifter, there was no doubt that she'd be able to hear his blood pumping in anticipation. He pulled his keys from his pocket as he hurried forward. Julie followed behind him at a slower pace. He unlocked his door and pushed it open before he stepped aside to allow her to enter first.

She walked into his home, and Cooper vowed that one day she would be walking into their shared home. He flicked on the entry light so that she would be able to see, since he didn't actually need it. It was just something he'd always done for her. As Julie strolled farther into the house, he closed the front door and trailed behind her. She knew his place well, but she still looked back and forth like she was searching for something. Instead of asking questions, he continued to watch her. Julie walked all the way into the living room before spinning around.

"It looks the same," she commented.

He nodded, at a loss for words.

"I don't know why I expected your place to look different," she said.

"Why would I change anything," he finally spoke. "It's still my home."

"Right," she replied before she rubbed her hands on her jeans. "Can we sit?"

"Please." He waved to the couch. "Do you want something to drink?"

"No thank you."

He sat in the chair across from her.

"I'm—" she started before faltering.

Cooper didn't help her out. He needed to hear what she had to say before he could begin to convince her that she belonged with him.

Julie scooted up to the edge of the couch and gripped her hands together. Her head was bowed, but when she lifted her gaze and he saw the tears pooling in her eyes he gasped.

He started to rise to comfort her, but she smiled and held up a hand. "Cooper?"

"Yes?"

"I'm sorry."

He blinked and blinked again. For so long he'd prayed to hear those words when she'd first left him. "You're sorry?" He didn't know why he repeated her words.

"I was wrong, Cooper," she said. "And I am so very sorry that I hurt you."

Julie's words whirled around in his head, repeating over and over until he couldn't believe that he'd heard her correctly.

"I was scared and I said things that I didn't mean, and I ran away. I've never regretted anything more in my life."

"You were gone almost a year," he pointed out.

"But I'm back now," she replied.

"To stay?" he asked.

She nodded. "To show you that I still care."

He couldn't stay seated any longer. He paced away, taking his time to choose his words carefully. Could it really be this easy? Julie had come back for him? He reached the window and looked out into the back yard. His hands were shaking so he stuffed them into his jeans. He didn't want to mess up this opportunity.

"I know I don't have any right to ask this, but I was hoping you would forgive me," Julie said.

Cooper closed his eyes. Happiness spread through him.

"I'll do anything to get you to give me another chance," she continued.

"Stop," he ordered as he turned toward her.

She'd also risen and stood next to the couch. Her eyes had filled with unshed tears which make his heart ache.

"I forgave you the minute you returned. You don't have anything to make up for because I don't want anything from you."

"Oh." She stepped away.

He shook his head. "That's not completely true."

"What do you mean?" she asked.

"I do want things from you," he told her. "I want you to accept my wolf. I want to hold you in my arms again and kiss your sweet lips. I want you to love me like you did before, but this time forever. I don't want you to walk away ever again." He was out of breath when he finished.

The tears that threatened to fall dropped down her cheeks. "You do?"

"I never stopped loving you, Julie," he admitted.

"Me either," she whispered.

He moved quickly until he had his arm around her and was holding her tight. With his free hand, he brushed away the wetness from her face. "Then stay," he murmured to her. "We'll work everything else out but don't leave me again."

"I want to stay," she told him.

Cooper lowered his lips to hers and kissed her gently. She opened for him and her familiar taste exploded on his tongue. She tasted like dark chocolate and vanilla. He tightened his hold, pulling her chest flat with his.

Julie moaned into his mouth, and he swallowed the sweet sound. He gripped her waist and lifted her so she could wrap her legs around him. They'd been in this position before and Cooper would never tire of it.

"I want you," she whispered to him.

Cooper took several steps forward to the couch. He lowered Julie down and lay on top of her. He settled in between her legs, rubbing his hard cock against her.

"Yes," she hissed.

He pressed harder, loving the sounds he pulled from her. She moaned, long and low. He felt the sound all the way to his toes. He shuddered before he sat up and yanked his shirt over his head. She smiled as she ran her hand over his chest where the tattoo was that covered his heart, the small Celtic symbol for strength. She lifted her lips to trail kisses over the ink.

Cooper gripped the back of her head to hold her to him. She used her tongue to drive him crazy until his wolf was close to the surface and he was growling. He'd never been so near to losing control around Julie before. He wouldn't have dared to show any part of his wolf before, but now she knew what he was.

"I want all of you," Julie told him. "Don't hide the wolf from me—I accept him, accept you."

He was so in tune with his body that he thought he could feel his blood rushing through his veins. He grabbed hold of her shirt and pulled her up. She helped him tug it over her head. They frantically began to shed clothes, rolling off the couch, with her landing on top of him, naked. She straddled his waist and placed her hands on his chest. She reached back to grasp his erection.

Cooper groaned as her hot hand encircled his flesh. He pushed into her hold.

"Patience," she teased. She lifted up, positioning him at her damp pussy. All she had to do was lower herself and he would once again feel what it was like to be inside her.

"Please," he begged.

She smiled. Cooper's breath caught as she gave in and began to sink onto him. Her inner muscles clamped down and he shook with the effort it took not to thrust up. Inch by inch she moved until he was buried deep inside. Once seated, she dropped her head back but didn't start to ride him.

He let his breath out. "I need you to move."

"Yes." She lifted up slowly until the tip of his cock was almost free before she slammed herself back down.

"Oh God!" he cried.

He hadn't been with anyone else in the entire time that Julie had been gone. It didn't matter to him whether or not she'd had another lover. She was his once again, and that was all he needed to know.

Cooper gripped her hips hard and she rode him. Each time she rose and fell, her pussy was tight around his cock and it was difficult to keep from coming so soon. He lifted his head enough that he'd be able to lick a path between her breasts before he started to lick at her left nipple.

He drew the small nub into his mouth then bit down gently.

"Coop," she said with a whimper.

Instead of replying, he teased her nipple more then moved on to the other. Julie picked up her speed and dug her nails into his chest. He bucked up, driving his cock deep, while clamping his lips down again on her.

Julie rocked forward, lifted, came down, quicker, harder and faster.

She repeated the action over and over until she was breathing hard and he knew she was close to climax. Her skin was flushed and her eyes bright.

Cooper raised his hands to her breasts and thumbed her nipples.

"Uh!" she screamed and fell over the edge of completion.

She was so tight around his cock it was almost painful. He plunged up desperately until his seed filled her.

Julie fell on top of him and he held her close. Inside, his wolf was calm and he felt like everything was right in his world.

"I love you," he whispered and kissed her forehead. "It's crazy how much I love you."

Chapter Four

Cooper woke slowly but even before he opened his eyes, he knew where the feeling of contentment came from. Julie was back in his arms and they'd reconnected. She was his once again. He peered down at her enjoying the sight of her still sleeping. With her head on his shoulder and one leg wrapped around his, he could remember waking this way many mornings before.

The clock on the bedside table showed it was past eleven in the morning. So much had happened in the last twelve hours that he was still a little mystified Julie had been the one to come to him. He'd never expected it. He had been working on his own plan to reclaim the woman he loved. Instead Julie had walked into his arms more than willingly.

He brushed a soft kiss over her forehead, causing her to murmur something in her sleep but not wake. A wicked idea formed and he grinned. Cooper rolled her over onto her back and slid down her body, taking one nipple into his mouth and sucking. She moaned as she started to move her legs restlessly. He kept in his chuckle while he moved lower, trailing kisses.

"Cooper," she whispered.

He glanced up to see her eyes open and on him. "Good morning."

"One of the best in a very long time," she replied.

He lifted an eyebrow.

She laughed. "Yeah, that was corny."

"I don't mind," he said. "Are you on shift tonight?"

"Yes, night shift all this week."

"Me too. So I better get busy," he said.

Before she could respond, he gripped her thighs and spread her. He lowered his mouth to her wet folds and licked. She shuddered, so he continued lapping at her before he added a finger to open her up. Her flavor was stronger, but just as enticing, at her center.

"Don't tease," she begged.

He added a second digit while he clamped onto her clit. He pumped his fingers in and out until she was panting and shaking.

"Please, Cooper. I want you inside me," she cried.

Cooper lifted his mouth and peered up at her. Her face was flushed as she reached for him. He climbed up the bed until his mouth was inches from hers. She pushed herself up until her lips met his. As they kissed, she ran her hands down his back. Each touch felt like fire on his skin. Like she was branding him with her stroke. He gripped his cock to position himself at the entrance of her cunt.

"Yes," she hissed.

He pushed inside, filling her with one long thrust. Her inner muscles clamped around him. He groaned as he withdrew then plunged back inside. The link with his wolf opened as the animal pushed at him to mark Julie as their own. He drove himself deep, while dropping his mouth to her shoulder and sucking. Julie lifted her hips to meet each frenzied push until the only sounds in the room were her cries and the sound of their bodies slapping against each other. He lifted his head and stared into her eyes as he grew closer to release.

"Let go," he whispered. "Give yourself to me."

Julie screamed as she climaxed, the grip her body had on his pulling him along with her.

Spent, he collapsed on top of her. She brought her arms around his neck and held him close. "Perfect," she said quietly.

Cooper couldn't agree more. He carefully pulled out and sat back. A shower, breakfast and maybe another round before they both had to go into work sounded like heaven to him.

His cell phone rang loudly in the quiet room. He groaned but scrambled to find the annoying device. His jeans were in the doorway. He yanked out his phone, noting Josiah's name.

"What's up?" he greeted.

"I just got a call from one of our boys. I don't know how they did it, but Jordan and Kade made bail. They'll be out in an hour."

"Shit!"

"That was my reaction," Josiah said. "They shouldn't have even been arraigned yet. Somehow they got in front of a judge first thing this morning and the bail was set low. Something's off there, but it's already done. What do you want to do?"

"We need to follow them. They'll be trying to cover their tracks today," Cooper told him.

"I'll pick you up in half an hour," Josiah stated.

Cooper looked back toward the bed where Julie was standing and stretching. "Make that forty-five minutes."

Julie smiled as he hung up with Josiah. "I take it our morning is getting cut off early?"

He nodded. "Yeah, I have to go in early but I need a shower first. Join me?"

"Of course." She accepted the hand he held out to her.

"Make me one promise first?" he requested.

"What's that?"

"Come here after your shift," he said. "Hell, never leave here again. Stay with me."

"Are you asking me to move in with you?" she asked, her eyebrows drawing together. "Cooper, I love you, but I've been gone a year. Don't you think we might be rushing this?"

He shook his head. "Has anything changed? Are your feelings for me different now? We both know this is where we were heading when you left."

"Still…"

"Think about it. But for now, after work, come here," he pleaded.

She moved closer to him and cupped his face. "I will be here tonight. We'll talk more about the future later."

Cooper would take that. "Then let's shower."

She laughed and allowed herself to be dragged into the adjoining bathroom. Cooper released her to turn the knobs on and start the water. He tested the temperature, making sure it was hot enough for them. He motioned her in, never taking his eyes off her gorgeous body.

She stepped into the tiled stall, dunking herself under the two large showerheads. He followed behind, slipping his hands over her wet skin. When he'd first remodeled this area, he'd done so for the sole purpose of having a nice, comfortable and soothing place to wash away his worries after a hard day. After he'd begun dating Julie, he'd learned that he'd also made it possible to have combined showers with his lover. There was nothing like watching Julie with water cascading down her plump breasts to between her legs. Cooper grabbed a washcloth and soaped it up before running the cloth over her body. He washed her thoroughly, making sure to pay close attention to all her sensitive areas, like the soft skin below her belly button above her trimmed pubic hair.

He lowered down to one knee so he could suck up a mark while rubbing the washcloth against her pussy. Julie gasped as she gripped his shoulders. Cooper dropped the cloth and used his fingers to penetrate her. Julie rocked into his palm while shuddering in ecstasy. Since he knew he didn't have a lot of time Cooper had to get her off quickly. He added his mouth to his digits, dragging her climax from her with skill. He knew just how to touch her to make Julie fall over the edge.

Julie panted above him, and he waited until her legs had stopped shaking to stand up. He'd barely gotten his feet planted before she gripped his erection and started to pump. Each pull from her hand had him growing harder and desperate until his cock was once again ready to shoot. She used the exact amount of pressure and twist of her wrist to have him biting down on his lip as he came.

Fuck, that feels good. He wrapped his arm over her shoulder and positioned them both back under the water. Once they were clean he turned off the taps. Julie reached for the towels on the rack outside the stall, handing him one before wrapping the other around her body.

He wished he could take her back to bed and stay there the rest of the day — hell, or the entire week — but he did have to get to work. Now that everything was okay with Julie, he needed to give his attention to his case and saving all the other shifters. In truth, he should have already given all his concentration to the drug hitting the streets. Instead he'd been selfish and his mind had been divided. He watched Julie as she dried off. He didn't regret his actions, but he could now make up for his distraction and do his job.

"Why don't I make you some coffee?" she offered.

"That would be great," he said.

She smiled before she went to his dresser and pulled out a pair of sweats and a T-shirt. He hated her covering up that beautiful body but if he spent any more time staring at her, he wouldn't be dressed when his partner arrived. Josiah would love that. As she passed him to go out of the door, he caught her hand.

"If you hadn't come to me, I would have been at your door first chance I got. I just thought you should know," he told her.

Her smile lit up her bright hazel eyes. "I'm glad it was me that came for you. I want to prove to you that I want you just the way you are."

He cupped her face. "All is forgiven."

"No," she whispered. "But if I have to spend the rest of my life making up for hurting you, I will." She placed her palms against his chest. "I might have to get imaginative."

His body came alive. Those words had him instantly hard. She laughed then slipped from his grasp to continue out and down the hall. He turned his attention to dressing himself. He chose a dark pair of jeans and a short sleeve white T-shirt. He pulled them on before sitting on his bed to add his boots and socks. Once ready, he strolled into the bathroom and brushed his teeth. Everything complete, he hurried to the kitchen so he could spend the few minutes he had left with Julie.

She was right where he expected her to be, staring into a full cup of coffee. Julie had never been a morning person, which was why she'd always liked the late shift, working three in the afternoon to three in the morning, four days a week. Since his own hours were hard to determine, their schedules had never been an issue.

He stepped up beside her, accepting the mug she handed him. He placed a gentle kiss on her lips in appreciation.

"I talked to my brother last night. I asked him to come visit me," she said.

He leaned on the counter across from her. "A warning?"

She shook her head. "No, although he does want to meet you. My parents went on and on about you and I think he was jealous."

"I'd love to meet him as well."

"I'm going to try to talk him into moving here," she said. "I wanted to let you know."

"That would be great, having him here for you. I'd welcome him."

"Thank you."

The sound of a horn interrupted them.

"I have to go," he told her. "I'll see you tonight, though, right?"

"Yes," she confirmed.

"Okay." He set his coffee down before he wrapped his arm around her waist and pulled her close. He kissed her with all the passion inside him. When he released her, they were both breathing heavily. "Bye."

"See you later," she murmured.

He grinned the entire time it took him to collect his weapon from the locked drawer in his entry table. He pulled the door open and hurried out before he could change his mind and go back and ravish Julie.

He jogged to Josiah's truck. As he opened the passenger side, he couldn't help but notice his partner's wicked smile.

"What?" he asked as he sat.

"Whose car is that?" Josiah nodded toward Julie's vehicle.

"You know damn well."

Josiah laughed. "So she's back for good?"

"Yes," he confirmed.

"Good, maybe now you won't be such a prick all the time," Josiah said with a slap to his leg.

"Ha ha," Cooper replied.

Josiah put the truck in gear and started to drive away. "Seriously, I am so glad she's back. I couldn't be happier for you."

"Thanks," Cooper replied. "Also I wanted tell you how much it means to me that you were here for me this last year."

"Getting old. You're turning sentimental," Josiah noted.

"And you're still a jackass," Cooper threw back.

Josiah laughed, and Cooper joined him. They were all right. Cooper relaxed back into his seat. "So where we headed?"

"I figured we'd just follow them from the station," Josiah said. "I have the officer in booking watching for their releases. As soon as they are on the way out, he will give me a call." Josiah's phone started to ring. "Ah, there he is. Hello?"

As Josiah spoke to the officer, Cooper reached into the glovebox and pulled out one of the notebooks that

Josiah kept there. He took a pen from the dash and began to make notes. He'd need to note every location they visited today. Hopefully Cooper and Josiah would witness something to tip them off on what Jordan and Kade were up to.

Josiah hung up and glanced at him. "Good news," he said. "One of Jordan's cousins is there to pick the boys up."

"Who?"

"Lexis," Josiah told him with a grin.

"He's back?" Cooper asked.

Lexis Bradley was the worst of the entire family. The last time Cooper had heard his name had been when Lexis was arrested for murder. If Cooper remembered correctly, Lexis had been accused of killing an eighteen-year-old street kid who owed him money.

Since he didn't work homicide, Cooper hadn't been involved in the case, but because the Bradleys were so deep into drug running, Cooper always got a heads-up when they were involved in anything illegal.

"They couldn't make the case stick," Josiah said. "Their witnesses kept ending up dead."

"Damn it. Weren't they protected?" Cooper couldn't believe the district attorney would be stupid enough not to hide anyone attempting to rat out Lexis.

"They were in safe houses," Josiah corrected. "They just weren't safe."

"Fuck! We have got to get something on them."

"That's why we're doing this," Josiah agreed. "And there they are."

Cooper glanced through the passenger window as Josiah pulled up across from the police station. A black SUV with dark windows was idling at the front steps. Jordan and Kade strolled out of the front door, appearing not to have a care in the world. Fury raced through his blood. Those two kids were as evil as they came. It didn't matter who was hurt, as long as they made money.

Jordan slapped Kade on the back before he yanked open the door of the SUV. Cooper wanted to shift, run to the vehicle and tear all the three men apart.

"Calm yourself." Josiah's hand landed on his shoulder.

Cooper hadn't realized he was growling until Josiah broke him from his anger. "They're taking off."

"I'm following," Josiah said. He did indeed put the truck into Drive and began to follow.

Cooper used the time to regain his control. It wasn't always easy being a shifter in his line of work, but he'd spent years learning how to contain his wolf when he needed to.

They followed the SUV down the main streets of Clear Creek, heading north. Cooper wasn't surprised when the first stop was to a run-down apartment complex where the Bradleys dropped off Kade. While Jordan and Lexis lived in a nice house in the central part of town, Kade didn't get the same treatment. He was only a foot soldier. Cooper still believed he would be the key to bringing down the Bradleys.

"Should we go talk to him?" Josiah questioned.

"No, stay with Jordan. I'll call Grant and have him watch Kade's place."

"That'll work," Josiah agreed.

Cooper made the phone call, relieved that the young officer was available and not out on another assignment. While Cooper was busy making arrangements, Josiah kept up the surveillance. Instead of heading home, the Bradleys continued south in the same neighborhood. "Where are they going?" he murmured.

"There's an old store the Bradleys used to own that is boarded up. It's only two blocks from here," Josiah told him.

"I remember," Cooper replied. "It used to be an old bar."

"It closed down about two years ago. I've had one of the street informants watching the place," Josiah said.

"Why didn't you tell me?" Cooper asked.

"Nothing to report yet," Josiah responded.

Cooper shook his head. "You still should have told me."

His partner chuckled. "We've always used our own contacts. Why is this any different?"

He couldn't really answer that. The entire case hit him as weird, and he knew he was missing something big. He hoped now that he had his act together, he would be able to figure out what was bothering him so much. Sure, he hated to see his shifter brethren dying, but something in the back of his mind was trying to break to the surface.

Josiah was right. The SUV pulled to the side of the building. Josiah parked on the other side of the street, a couple of spaces down from the building.

"If they haven't been using this place, why are they here now?" Cooper asked.

"The reason I started watching this place is because while the Bradleys never entered, they have been keeping an eye on the place. Some of my informants saw them hanging around and thought I should know. I grew suspicious," Josiah informed him.

"You've been busy," Cooper said. He didn't know how he'd missed what Josiah had been up to. "You going to tell me what's really going on?"

Josiah sighed while he shifted uncomfortably in his seat. "You remember the first victim? The eighteen year old?"

"Ricky something..." Cooper supplied.

"Ricky Norris. We interviewed his entire family, hoping one of them could tell us who he'd been hanging around with."

Cooper had an idea of what Josiah was going to say. "His sister — a pretty little thing... There was a spark between the two of you."

Josiah nodded. "Cammi. She came to see me a few weeks after that. We went out for coffee and talked for hours."

"She asked you to find out who was responsible for her brother's death," Cooper guessed.

"No," Josiah said quickly. "We talked about Ricky and still do. But she never asked me to do anything. I decided to use some favors I have out on the street to put pressure on finding who is responsible. We have to close this case. It's killing Cammi and the rest of her family. They won't be able to put him to rest until this is over."

Cooper turned to study his partner. "Just tell me if you did anything that you shouldn't have. We'll fix it, but I need to know." He didn't think Josiah would do anything illegal, but Cooper also knew what love could do to a person.

"No, never," Josiah told him.

Cooper breathed in deeply. He brought his partner's scent through his nose. Josiah was telling him the truth. He sagged with relief. "I'm here for you."

Josiah smiled. "Thanks. I know I should have told you, but you were still mourning your relationship with Julie. I didn't want to hurt you any further."

"Jo!" He gripped his partner's shoulder. "I will always have your back. No matter what."

"And I'll have yours." Josiah met his gaze, his sincerity shining through his eyes.

After a few minutes, Cooper released Josiah's shoulder and chuckled. "We really are turning into big old softies."

"Ah, I'm going to blame the power of love," Josiah said.

Cooper nodded before turning back to watch the building and their suspects. "So tell me about your girl," he demanded playfully.

"She's great." Josiah's voice softened. "She's an artist and she is so talented. She's smart and funny, close to her family. I really like her."

He had to smile. It seemed like his partner had found the perfect match for him. Cooper had already done a basic search in the police files of the family. It was standard when they were investigating a death, so he knew Cammi didn't have a criminal record. "You're okay with the shifter side of her?" he had to ask.

While Josiah accepted his shifter side as his partner, it was a whole different situation when the person you were falling in love with had unique abilities that made them so very different. He knew better than anyone. Not that he didn't think that Julie hadn't meant every word she'd said, but Cooper knew they still had a lot to work on.

"I am." Josiah surprised him. "I knew about her before, so maybe that's why I never even considered not getting involved with her because she can transform. All I know is Cammi Norris is the woman for me. I know it's fast, but I can't help the way I feel."

"The connection is stronger than it would normally be because of her abilities. Not only does she care for you, but her wolf has to have accepted you also," Cooper told him.

"So you're saying what? We were meant to be? I thought shifters didn't really have a fated mate and all that. Isn't that one of the myths that was broken when you all came public?"

"No, it's nothing like that. You can still break up. Julie and I are proof of that. I'm just trying to reassure you that even though it might seem fast, your feelings for Cammi should be taken seriously. If both the human and the wolf parts of her want you, you'll both feel the connection deeply," Cooper explained.

"Which is why it really hurt when Julie left," Josiah commented.

"Yes, as a man, it hurt me but as a wolf, I felt rejected. I would have moved on, maybe even fallen in love again, but I will always have feelings for her. I gave her my heart, and that's important," Cooper said.

"Okay." Josiah nodded. "I can accept that."

Cooper was relieved. His partner was a good guy and deserved happiness. Cooper's attention was drawn to an expensive black car driving passed the old bar and slowing. "Check this out."

The BMW pulled alongside the structure next to the Bradleys' SUV. Cooper leaned forward. He knew that car. "Is that…"

A tall man with black hair stepped from the driver side.

"Holy shit!" Josiah grabbed for the camera on the back seat. "That's Mayor Jensen."

The Clear Creek Mayor was the biggest opponent of the shifters getting equal rights. Jensen believed that since the shifters were not completely human, they shouldn't be treated as such. Even though several legal bills against the shifters had failed in Congress, there were still some vocal politicians that wanted the shifters treated like second-class citizens. Cooper didn't know why he'd be meeting with the Bradleys, but he was certain it wasn't for any good reason.

"We need to get the records from Lexis' release," Cooper commented. "We need to see if he had any help getting the charges dropped. Maybe Mike will be able to help. He's probably got someone he could tap for the intel."

Josiah was snapping picture after picture. "I think we found the Bradleys' money man."

"Yeah," Cooper agreed. He couldn't believe this. The mayor being involved with a drug trafficker who Cooper suspected of poisoning the shifters would be even too far-fetched for him to believe, if he wasn't seeing it with his own eyes.

"We're going to nail these assholes," Josiah said gleefully.

"Yes, we are. We have to take this to the captain. We should be able to get a warrant now," Cooper replied. He reached for his cell phone when Josiah grabbed his arm.

"I think we need to talk to the captain in person. The mayor has a lot of powerful friends. Probably has spies watching us and the captain if he knows we're close to busting the Bradleys. We don't want to tip off the wrong person," Josiah said.

"You're right. I don't really want to leave either. We need to watch for any more activity," Cooper said.

"How about this. We'll call Fisher and Turner. We need to let them know we have information for the homicide part of the investigation anyway. Then we'll split up. Turner can take your place and you and Fisher can head back to the station and start the paperwork on the warrant and get Cap updated," Josiah suggested.

"That'll work for me," Cooper agreed.

"Here." Josiah handed him the camera. "Keep an eye out. I'll get hold of Fisher."

Cooper watched the building closely. The two vehicles were parked in an alley, but there was a back lot that should be empty. If he shifted, he'd be able to get closer and maybe overhear something. He glanced at his partner when Josiah had finished his call.

"What?" Josiah asked.

"I want to shift," Cooper told him.

Josiah ran his gaze from the building back to Cooper. He grinned. "It'll take Fisher and Turner about twenty minutes before they get here. Go ahead."

He quickly opened his door and slipped from the front seat to the back. He started to undress as Josiah took over surviving the building. "You owe me lunch after this," Cooper said.

"You got it. I'll pick up the usual and bring it to the station." Josiah always took care of Cooper after a shift. He knew how much energy it took for him to transform back and forth so quickly.

Cooper finished pulling his clothes off before he closed his eyes and concentrated. All he had to do was form a picture in his head and give himself over to the change. It was quick and painless, and in just a few minutes he was furry. He leaned forward and licked his partner's face.

"Yuck!" Josiah pushed him away. "You do that every time."

He did, but since Josiah never stopped him, even though he had to know it was coming, Cooper didn't think his partner really minded. He pawed at the door, letting Josiah know he was ready. Josiah climbed out of the front seat and opened the back door for him. He jumped down and stretched. He hated transforming in a vehicle but in his line of work, he often found himself shifting in strange places. With his run the night before, his wolf was focused and eager to work.

Cooper butted his head against Josiah's hand then took off. He moved with speed to avoid anyone getting a good look at him. He raced across the street before flattening his side against the bar. He concentrated on bringing in the scents and sounds around him. He could hear the low murmur of voices coming through the worn wood that covered the broken window but couldn't make out the words.

As quietly as possible he crept forward, staying in the shadows that the building provided. He made his way to the side where the two vehicles were. Nose to the ground, he breathed deeply. Yes, there were only three fresh scents. Lexis and Jordan Bradley, along with the mayor's. He continued past the closed door where the three men had entered, along the wall to the back of the building. The lot was overgrown with weeds that tickled his nose but he couldn't let that bother him. The stink of piss, vomit and stale beer was strong and he had to ignore the horrible scents. Back here, the windows were also boarded up but they were falling apart. Rot or weather had cracked several of them. Cooper darted under the worst of the damage to stand directly under the small opening that a broken board provided.

"We need more product," Lexis Bradley spoke.

Cooper's ears perked up.

"I'll get you more money, but you need to be careful. Right now the overdoses are being investigated by only a couple of officers. If we have too many deaths, the police force will assign a task force and that won't be good for any of us," Mayor Jensen replied.

"We'll take care of these so-called investigators," Jordan spat. "I know just how to handle them."

Mayor Jensen laughed. "Those detectives will eat you alive, young man. I've got some officers that owe me some favors. I'll have them keep an eye on the case. You two just make sure you're not caught. If you are, I'll make sure you don't make it to trial, if you catch my drift."

"Don't threaten us!" Lexis shouted. "I'll being you and your entire empire down. You want to get rid of the shifters? Fine, I couldn't care less, but we do this *my* way."

"Don't make me laugh," Jensen responded. "You're playing with the big boys now. You follow *my* orders. I can find any small time dealer to do this. I brought you in. Don't forget that."

It sounded like the mayor was walking farther away as he spoke. Cooper pressed himself closer to the side of the bar. He didn't hear any more speaking, so he waited. A few minutes later, the sound of a car starting didn't surprise him. He crept toward the opposite side of the building. Hopefully Fisher and Turner would get there soon. The mayor wouldn't be hard to find, but Cooper didn't want to lose the Bradley cousins.

After what he'd overheard, they needed to make their move soon. He had to get that warrant. He ran back toward his partner to share what he'd learned.

Chapter Five

It was a busy night for calls. Julie collapsed against the back of her seat inside the ambulance after they'd dropped off the fourth patient to the hospital. Two people with heart-attack symptoms, one with a badly cut hand and one small child with a horrible cough had kept the rig going. She was thankful that none of the calls had been fatal but she was dragging and needed a break. The morning with Cooper had been wonderful, but she was feeling the lack of sleep.

"Want to stop for coffee?" she asked her partner.

He grinned at her. "Didn't sleep well?"

She hadn't told Shawn about going to Cooper's house but by his smug expression, he'd figured it out. "What makes you ask that?"

He chuckled. "I ran into Josiah at the café this afternoon before my shift. He mentioned your car being at Cooper's when he picked up his partner this morning."

Living in Clear Creek was like being in a soap opera sometimes. There was no privacy. Especially within the civil servant area. "Oh, so how about that coffee?" she tried to steer the conversation away from her and Cooper. Not that she minded telling Shawn, but she did like to tease her partner.

Shawn paused in putting the vehicle in gear. "That's all I get?"

She smiled. "Was there something else you wanted?" she teased.

"You suck," he complained. She let him drive toward their favorite small coffee shop before giving in.

"I apologized to Cooper," she said. "It went better than I could have ever hoped for."

"So the two of you are back together?" Shawn grinned. "That's awesome."

"Yeah," she agreed. "I'm really lucky."

"He's lucky too. You're a great woman and you two belong together," Shawn told her.

Julie was beginning to believe the truth in that statement. Cooper had been everything she'd ever hoped for. She looked at her friends, like Shawn, with his wife and kids, and was jealous. She wished for that. She wanted to make her home with one man and start raising kids. She needed her brother to come visit and be Uncle Garrett to his nieces and nephews. She could already picture a boy with Cooper's dark hair or a little girl with her hazel eyes. No matter what they looked like, she would love them unconditionally. And Cooper? He would make a fantastic father. He'd... *Wait. If Cooper can shift into a wolf, does that mean our kids would too?* She hadn't even considered that.

As panic built, she had to take a deep breath. Sure, they weren't at the having kids stage yet, but Julie sure hoped they'd get there one day. Maybe Cooper didn't even want children. She tried to think back on any conversations that might have come up but she couldn't remember him ever talking about his future plans. She knew they had plenty of time to discuss things and she'd only gotten him back. She wouldn't let Cooper slip away again. He'd probably think she was crazy even bringing up the subject after she'd scoffed at moving in just that morning. She needed to relax. She had to have faith that she and Cooper would be able to work anything out. They belonged together. Loving a man who could transform really did bring a lot of unique issues to her dating life. A new worry formed. Would she be able to handle the difficulties Cooper's abilities attracted?

She wanted to support him in every way. She knew his life and the decision to become public had to be hard on him. There were rumors that not all the shifters were open about what they were because they feared for their safety. She'd let Cooper down by not being his partner when he'd had to decide. Would she ever be able to make up for her actions and how leaving him had only added to what was going on in his life? Cooper might have been better off if she'd never returned. *God*, the thought made her heart ache. Maybe she'd been selfish in returning home. But Cooper had welcomed her with open arms. She'd make it up to him.

"What's wrong?" Shawn asked. "You turned pale all of a sudden."

She shook her head, unsure how to answer. Shawn didn't know much more about shifters than she did. Plus, he might take her questions the wrong way. He was happy she and Cooper were together, which made her grateful. She knew Shawn, though. He'd tell her not to worry about it. She and Cooper would work it out. And they would, but she really didn't want to make any more mistakes. She could figure out what she needed to know. Some research would help. She'd already done a bunch when the shifters had come out.

She'd collected news articles that that had disproved a lot of old myths, like the full moon shifting, but if she was going to be a true partner to Cooper, she needed to know more.

"Julie?"

She jerked her head to the side to look at Shawn. His hand was on the door knob and the engine was off. They were in the parking lot of the coffee shop. She shook herself from her stupor as she popped her door open.

"You sure you're okay?" Shawn asked.

"Yeah, just thinking," she said. "Let's get some caffeine." She followed Shawn inside and got in line behind him.

She glanced around the crowded shop while wondering how many patrons were human and how many shifter? Wolves weren't the only shifters out there, although she'd never met any others, at least to her knowledge. The local news station in the corner of the store was giving her an idea. The most popular reporter on the local channel had interviewed several of the shifters around Clear Creek. Julie had watched the broadcast online while she'd lived with her brother, and that reporter was her old college roommate. Julie knew the right person to ask her questions. Shelby would have researched everything she could find about shifters before her filming.

Julie pulled out her phone and found Shelby's contact. She sent a quick text about meeting up later. She'd called Shelby to let her know that she was returning to town and they'd promised to get together soon. As busy as her friend was, Julie knew if she didn't tie Shelby down with a time and date, Shelby's mind would be on her next assignment. Not that Julie blamed her. Shelby was dedicated and a hardworking woman—sometimes too dedicated. She had been the same in college. It was usually Julie's influence that had brought any kind of fun to Shelby's life.

The line moved quickly. When it was her turn, she ordered her iced white mocha along with Shawn's green tea and paid for both. She handed over the money as her phone chimed with a message. Julie waved off the change from the barista and stepped to the side. She smiled when she saw Shelby's response. They could meet for an early lunch the next day before Julie's shift. She sent back an affirmative before she slid her cell back in her pocket.

"Texting your boyfriend," Shawn teased.

"Shut up." She couldn't help but to smile though. And why shouldn't she send a quick hi to Cooper, so she did. A minute later her phone alerted again. She glanced down.

Miss you

Her name was called for the drinks so she put her phone away and walked up to the counter. She handed Shawn his beverage and they headed out. When they reached the ambulance, she paused outside the door and took a long drink, just enjoying the bitterness of the espresso and the sweetness of the syrup.

She reached for the door handle as the radio on her shoulder buzzed and the dispatcher's voice sounded. She groaned but hurried to get into her seat so they could get to their call.

"Another overdose," Shawn grunted. "It's getting bad out there."

Julie knew that there'd been an increase in calls related to drugs but she was surprised by Shawn's disgust. "What's going on?" she asked.

"Some shit has hit the streets and it's deadly to the shifters. Cops are trying to find out who is responsible, but we keep getting more and more calls," Shawn told her.

"I'd bet anything that's Cooper's case," she said.

"I think it is," Shawn confirmed. "I haven't heard anything lately but Josiah seemed to be in a good mood earlier."

Thinking back on Cooper's text message, she wondered if Cooper and Josiah were getting close to finding the people responsible. That would be great. She would have to plan some sort of celebration for him.

They raced down the streets, getting closer to the address given to them. Julie braced her arm against the window as Shawn turned a corner too fast. "Slow down," she demanded.

"I'm not losing another patient to this fucking drug," Shawn said, while pressing harder on the gas pedal.

Julie closed her eyes so she didn't have to see them crash.

"Relax," Shawn said with a chuckle. "We're almost there."

Julie sure hoped so. She didn't have much in her stomach and she really hoped she could keep down what she had eaten earlier. She pried open her eyes as Shawn finally slowed the rig down. A group of people were standing in a circle off to the side of the street. She reached between the seats for her bag so she could reach their patient quickly. As Shawn stopped the ambulance, she yanked the door handle and jumped down.

"Step aside," she shouted over the loud crowd as she pushed her way through.

A young man was lying on the ground with two women at his side. The closest looked similar to the male, so she guessed it was his sister. "What's going on?" Julie asked her.

"I don't know," she screeched. "My friend and I were in the store while my brother waited outside. I saw him talking to two guys but then Leslie called my name and I looked away. We finished getting some snacks and when we were heading to check out, I heard someone yell and my brother was on the ground. I dropped my stuff and ran out here, but he was already passed out."

Julie exchanged a look with Shawn as he joined her. *Why was this called in as an overdose if he wasn't doing drugs?*

"We need to get his body temperature down. That's one of the tips the ER doctor gave me," Shawn said as he placed cold packs around their patient.

"I saw him take some pills," someone called out.

Julie glanced up at an older man who stood only a few feet away. "He got them from those two." He pointed, and Julie followed his hand across to two boys the victim's age.

The young men backed up before they turned and sprinted off. Julie didn't have time to worry about them. She could give the cops a description later.

"I'm going to get the gurney and call this in," Shawn said, hopping to his feet.

Julie nodded, busy getting supplies out from her bag. She would prep her patient while Shawn was gone. They'd need to do an IV and get some fluids in him. As she worked, she glanced at the sister. "What's his name?"

"Corey," the girl replied.

"We're going to take care of you, Corey," she said, bending closer to the boy. He couldn't have been older than twenty. He must have trusted the two punks that he'd gotten the pills from. She heard police sirens coming nearer and hoped they'd catch the drug dealers.

"Here we go," Shawn called out.

They worked together to get Corey loaded up. Shawn started to push the gurney, and Julie looked back at her patient's sister. "We're taking him to Medical Center. Get your family and you can meet him there."

The younger girl nodded before she ran off. Julie felt horrible for her. There was a chance that Corey wouldn't make it from what Shawn had said about the other cases. Julie would do everything she could to save him, though.

She ran to catch up to her partner. As she turned the corner, she almost collided with Cooper.

"Hey." He caught her by the shoulders. "You okay?"

"Yeah fine." She was happy to see him but she needed to help Corey.

"You'll want to talk to one of the witnesses. He pointed out the two that gave our boy the drugs," she told him.

"Shawn gave us the description. We have patrol officers looking for them. We'll wrap up here and try to get to the hospital before you leave."

She nodded before sliding past him and into the rig. She went right to Corey's side and got to work. Julie didn't even look up when the doors closed. Shawn would get them where they were going and Cooper would find the dealers. She had to believe that. It was so sad to see men and women, young and old, giving up their lives to this horrible craving for drugs. She didn't blame them, but she wished she could help somehow before they ended up in her ambulance.

Maybe she could find somewhere to volunteer when she wasn't working. She'd discuss it with Cooper.

She peered down at Corey. She closed her eyes and said a little prayer that the kid would make it.

* * * *

Exhausted, Julie pushed through the doors that separated the emergency entrance from the waiting room. Corey was still being treated, but his chance of a full recovery was good. They'd managed to lower his temperature and get fluids in him quickly enough that the drug hadn't been fully digested. The doctors had given him something to counteract the poison. Shawn had gone ahead to clear out the rig and get them ready for their next call. God, she just wanted to go home and get off her feet. It sucked to work twelve hour shifts but she only had to work three or four days a week, and she enjoyed that. Knowing that Cooper would be there when she got off gave her something to look forward to as well.

She spotted Cooper standing against the wall close to the doors and her heart started to beat faster. She slowed down, just taking in his lean body as he spoke into his phone. He looked up and saw her watching. He quickly ended his call before strolling toward her. Julie stopped walking and waited.

"You look tired," he said when he reached her.

"I am." She glanced at her watch. "And I still have a long night ahead of me."

"We found Shawn working restocking and cleaning the ambulance when we arrived and he said the same thing. We all figured a quick break for some food might help. Josiah and Shawn ran to the cafeteria to grab you guys some dinner, so I thought I'd wait on you," Cooper said.

She wanted her hands on him, just for a moment. "Come on." She grabbed hold of him and pulled him outside. The ambulance was in the back bay where they had direct access to the emergency room doors. No one else was allowed to park there, so they would have some privacy. She led him to the back of the rig and opened the door. She pushed him down onto the bench before stepping between his legs. He looked up at her with an amused smile.

"Want something?" he teased.

"No," she said seriously. "Need. I need you." She lowered her lips to his. The spark between them was as evident as it always had been. He opened for her, and Julie slipped her tongue into his mouth. He'd been chewing on mints and the freshness of his taste danced over her taste buds. She moaned, letting him swallow the sound.

Cooper gripped her waist, bringing her closer. She knew she couldn't climb into his lap, even though that was what she really wanted. Not only was she working but they were also out in the open. It wouldn't be good if they got caught. Plus, there was no telling when Josiah and Shawn would return. So she slowly eased off kissing him. She didn't do more than lift her head, though, keeping her body close to his.

"Thank you," she told him.

Cooper chuckled. "I'm pretty sure I should be thanking you. I'm not sure I can, since you melted my brain."

Julie laid her forehead against his. "I was walking out, thinking about how much I was looking forward to going home to you, and there you were."

"I'm glad I could offer you something, even when I'm not near," he said.

"You always have," she assured him. "I was so stupid to leave."

"Hey." He gripped her chin. "We both made mistakes. I should have told you sooner. If I hadn't shifted for the first time during a dangerous situation, your reaction would probably have been less severe. But we're going to work past that. I'll teach you everything there is to know about what I am. I'll share every part of my wolf with you."

She was relieved to hear his promise. It went hand in hand with her thoughts earlier. If they were going to make it, she needed to know everything there was that made Cooper special. Being in his arms felt so right. It didn't matter if their future children were human or shifters. She loved Cooper. "I feel better," she shared.

"Good." Cooper nodded. "Shawn said that Corey will probably survive. He's the first victim that has that chance. I'm proud of you both."

She beamed with pride. "We were lucky. He had just taken them when we got there. Is it your case?"

"Yes, we had a breakthrough today. I'm really hoping that we'll be able round up the people responsible tonight. We're waiting on the call."

"You know who's distributing it?" she asked, excited.

"We do," he confirmed.

"That's wonderful!" She hugged him.

He patted her back. "Now, if we can just get the rest of this shit off the streets, we can keep more people from dying."

"I hope you do."

"We've got a head start. One of my officers found the two boys from earlier. We arrested them," Cooper informed her.

"You caught them?"

"The older gentleman is coming to the station to ID them, but I'm certain we got the right guys. We'll lean on them and find out where they got their stash. They still had some on them," Cooper said.

"We'll celebrate once this is over. I've already thought about it. I think it would be nice to get everyone back together again. You can barbecue," she told him.

"Good idea," he agreed. "It'll be nice to see all our friends once again. Maybe your brother will be able to make it."

That reminded her that she needed to check with Garrett and see when he would be coming down. "I'm having lunch with Shelby tomorrow. I'll mention it to her. I don't think she's ever attended one of our parties."

"Hey!" Shawn called out.

Julie turned to see her partner walking beside Josiah, each of them carrying two Styrofoam containers. "Looks like our dinner is here," she said to Cooper.

"One more kiss," he requested, tugging her back to him.

She consented easily, wrapping her arms around his neck. They kept the kiss soft, since they now had an audience.

"Okay, break it up," Josiah demanded with humor.

Julie straightened and glared at him. Josiah held up his hands, his grin wide. "We brought food," he said.

"I called dispatch and put us on break," Shawn told her, as he passed over one of the boxes.

"Thanks." She accepted her food before she climbed into the back of the rig and sat next to Cooper. Josiah and Shawn joined them and within minutes, they were all stuffing their faces. The hospital had surprisingly good food, and she and Shawn routinely ate their dinners there after a transport.

As she enjoyed her lasagna, she glanced over at the others. Her partner and Josiah had become friends when she'd first started to date Cooper. Because of the hours they worked and the high-stress levels, their relationships were crucial to them not burning out. She'd missed her friends almost as much as she'd missed Cooper.

Josiah glanced up and winked at her. She smiled back. Yeah, they would all get together after the cases ended. Cooper finished first and started collecting trash. Julie closed the lid on hers and handed it over to him. Josiah and Shawn also killed off the rest of theirs. Cooper juggled all the containers as he hopped down from the back of the ambulance to stroll to the dumpsters located off to the side.

"Need to finish straightening up and then we need to go," Shawn said.

She nodded in agreement. She'd love to spend the rest of the night in Cooper's company but she still had hours left on her shift. The four of them had grabbed a quick meal several times before, so Josiah and Cooper knew how to help clean up to make sure the rig was sterile and ready.

Shawn began to wipe down the back while Julie quickly straightened up. She pulled the inventory log down and made notations of what they'd used for Corey while Josiah helped Shawn with the last of the cleaning.

Headlights shined over her and she looked up toward the entrance of the ambulance bays. A black SUV idled facing them.

"Get down!" Josiah shouted and dove for her. He caught her around the waist and they both fell to the hard floor.

Three loud pops echoed around her and she covered her head, not knowing where they were coming from. Fear paralyzed her and she couldn't move. *Those were gun shots!* The squeal of tires seems to echo around the small area before she was shaken.

"Julie." Josiah leaned in to her field of vision. "Are you okay?"

She nodded. "I think so. Cooper? Shawn?"

"Stay here and I'll check on them," he ordered.

The weight on top of her disappeared and she rolled over to peer out of the rig. Her training kicked in and she jumped to her feet when she spotted Cooper on the ground. Shawn stood at the same time as she did. He appeared disheveled but no worse for wear.

"Go check on Cooper," he told her.

Julie didn't waste any time arguing. She leaped from the ambulance as Josiah knelt beside Cooper. She was so damn happy to see Cooper moving his head and arms before he pushed his upper body off the ground. She sprinted to her lover just as Cooper sat up.

"Are you all right?" she shouted.

People were starting to come out of the ER doors. Doctors, nurses and patrons venturing out, now that the excitement was over.

"I'm fine," Cooper said as she reached him.

Julie crashed into him, throwing her arms around his neck. "You sure?"

"Yes, baby." He held her tight. "They missed."

Tears pooled in her eyes and she tried to hold them in. Her throat burned and her stomach was in knots. "Someone shot at you." She couldn't believe it. She knew that his job was dangerous, but Cooper hadn't been out on a call. He'd been having dinner with her.

"It's okay." Cooper petted her back.

Julie drew away a little to study his face. He was dirty and she wiped off his cheek.

"Anyone hurt out here?"

She turned to see who was approaching. She recognized Dr. Rodriquez, who'd taken over Corey's care when she'd dropped him off. "No, we're fine," she said.

"I've called the cops," Dr. Rodriquez told them.

Josiah stood and held out his badge. "We are the police, but we need some more officers. We'll need to secure this area so we can collect evidence, so thanks. If you can get everyone back inside, that would be great."

In the distance, sirens grew in volume.

"Oh, Cooper." She hugged him again. "I was so scared."

"I'm sorry you got mixed up in this. I would never put you in danger on purpose."

"This isn't your fault," she assured him. "This was some random—" She stopped. "You know who took a shot at you." It wasn't a question.

"Let's get you two up." Josiah came back to their sides, Shawn with him.

"Wait!" She held up her hand. "Do you know who that was?"

Cooper looked past her to his partner.

"Our suspects. I recognized them too," Josiah answered.

Her head spun and she gripped the front of Cooper's shirt. This was unbelievable. "But…" She didn't even know what to say.

The first cruiser pulled up as Julie felt like everything was moving too fast around her. Shawn hauled her to her feet and kept an arm around her waist as the cops moved them from their rig. They stood cuddled together as the police started their procedures. It wasn't until Cooper's captain stood in front of her that she realized how much time had passed.

There was now yellow tape blocking access to the ambulance bay. She couldn't see either Cooper or Josiah.

"Cooper?" she asked.

"He's answering questions. Why don't you come with me? Let's find you somewhere to sit. Your partner went to call your boss," Captain Martinez said.

She'd met Cooper's supervisor several times at fundraisers and functions when they'd been dating. He'd always been kind to her and she felt reassured seeing him on scene.

"I'm a trained EMT. I should be handling this better," she whispered.

"You're doing fine. Most people wouldn't handle something like this well," he reassured her.

She decided to believe him. She was cold and just wanted to find that seat he'd promised. "Okay," she agreed. She thought he'd asked her a question, but she wasn't sure.

He led her toward one of the department's SUVs. She'd ask him to turn on the heater, and try to collect her thoughts.

Chapter Six

Cooper watched his captain lead Julie away from the scene. She was pale and shaking, and he really wanted to comfort her, but he had questions to answer.

"You're sure it was Jordan Bradley?" Fisher asked him.

"Positive," he confirmed. He couldn't believe that the young punk had dared to try to kill him. He was even more pissed that Jordan had put Julie and Shawn at risk. He and Josiah were trained to deal with bad people, but the EMTs only wanted to help. They didn't deserve to be caught in the middle of his investigation.

"No sign of the SUV or Jordan," Turner said, as he joined them. "The call went out to every officer with their information. We'll catch them."

"Jordan should have listened to the mayor—or at least practiced better. I'm going to rip his arms off when I get my hands on him," Cooper declared.

"You were lucky," Fisher said. "From what Josiah said, if you hadn't dropped when you did, the first bullet would have hit you."

"Not luck," Cooper corrected. He glanced over at his partner. "Josiah saved us."

"I heard he protected your woman also," Turner said.

Cooper nodded. "He did." Cooper owed Josiah for that. Not only had seen the gun hanging outside the window and called out a warning, but he'd also shielded her with his own body.

"Then don't do something stupid. You owe it to him not to go off half-cocked," Turner said.

Cooper glared at his fellow detective. He knew Turner was right, but he was pissed off. He took a deep breath to calm himself. His wolf was close to the surface, the need to protect and defend strong inside him. He knew it was because Julie had been put in danger but that didn't mean he felt any less angry.

"We got him!" Josiah yelled as he jogged toward them. "The asshole went back to the bar that we are still watching. Lexis pulled up and took the gun. We caught both of them red-handed."

"Thank God!" Cooper rose and looked around for Julie. She was sitting in the back seat of one of the vehicles, drinking a bottle of water. She smiled at something that his captain said, and finally he relaxed. His shoulders slumped with relief and his heart slowed. Even his wolf seemed to fade back.

"The warrant just came through for the Bradleys' place and bar, Kade's apartment and the mayor's office and home. We need to coordinate our searches," Josiah said.

"We're done here," Fisher stated. "I'll have some of the uniforms finish up with witnesses and the crime techs finish their collecting. Let's head back to the station and get this done. I want them all in jail before the night is over."

"I'll let the cap know we're headed in," Cooper offered.

Fisher grinned at him. "Sure, man, let your girl know it'd be best if she went home for the rest of the night." He slapped Cooper on the back. "Have one of the boys drive her, so you know she gets there safely.

Cooper ignored the teasing and walked quickly over to Julie and his boss. "Hey, Cap, we're heading back to the station. The warrant came through," he said.

"Good." Captain Martinez nodded. "I'll follow you in." He turned to Julie. "You take care and I'll see you soon."

She smiled at him before turning her attention to Cooper. "You'll catch these guys?" she asked when they were alone.

Cooper stepped closer to press against her side. He leaned into the SUV so he could touch her. "Already did," he told her.

"Yeah?"

"With the gun in hand," Cooper said. "Now we're going after the big dog. We're going to hit him tonight before he learns about this arrest."

"So it'll be over?" she asked.

He nodded. "There might still be some shit on the street. We'll try to get the names of the dealers that have some. We have the two from earlier that we'll still work at getting intel from, but hopefully that's the last batch. I know the Bradleys, though. We have to wrap everything up air tight or they'll slither through."

"Don't let them!" She gripped the front of his shirt. "You put those bastards behind bars and keep them there."

"I will do my best," he promised. "Why don't you head home? I'll have an officer take you. The ambulance should be released soon but you don't need to stay for that."

"Yes, I want a shower, cold beer and soft bed."

"I have all of those things at my house," he whispered, as he lowered his head closer to hers.

"Then it's a good thing that's where I plan on going."

The happiness that burst inside him at hearing those words made him lightheaded. He'd been concerned that the events of the night might be too much for her. This was the second time that they'd been together and he'd put her in a dangerous situation. The night he'd first shifted and now. He wouldn't blame her if she needed time to think.

"Hey." She cupped his face. "I'm not going anywhere. I came back for you and I am sticking around. You can't get rid of me after one screwed up night."

He kissed her. Dropped his lips on hers and pressed hard. He demanded that she open for him, nipping her bottom lip, and thrusting his tongue inside. He couldn't mark her like he craved, but he wouldn't deny either of them this small connection.

Julie moaned as she slid her arms around his neck. He pulled back slowly.

"I wish you could come home with me," she told him.

"Me too," he responded. "But I'll be there as soon as I can. We'll have your barbecue this weekend, and the next time we both have a few days off, we'll lock all the doors and spend the entire time in bed."

She laughed, just like he'd intended. "You have yourself a deal."

Cooper gave her one last quick kiss before he backed off and waved one of the uniforms over. "I need you to take both the EMTs home. Make sure they get there safely."

"Yes, sir." The young officer hurried over. "Are you ready, ma'am?"

"Where's Shawn?" she asked, glancing around for her partner.

"I'll find him. Just go with him," Cooper ordered.

Julie walked away, and Cooper spotted Shawn heading toward the ambulance. Shawn looked exhausted and ready to collapse at any minute. Cooper knew how it could feel once the adrenaline from a shooting wore out. It wasn't fun and often left people sick after they slowed down. Shawn should go home to his family. He jogged over to send the man on his way. Shawn glanced up as he approached.

"I have a ride for you and Julie. I'll get your rig back for you," Cooper said.

"That'd be great. I talked to our supervisor. We're off the rest of the night, so they have another ambulance already covering for us."

Cooper gripped his shoulder and turned him toward Julie and the officer. "No problem. Now go. You and Julie can start planning the cook-out for this weekend."

"Cool. I'll bring the beer and juice boxes," Shawn told him.

Cooper patted his shoulder and released him. Julie hurried toward her partner to drag him to one of the patrol cars.

With the two of them on their way, it was time for Cooper to find his own partner and get to work. He was not going to miss seeing the expression on the mayor's face when the warrant was served. Cooper knew the man was a bigot, but to actually target shifters to die? That was something out of a Hollywood movie, not typical behavior for Clear Creek.

He was going to take the mayor down, along with anyone else who was involved. He'd make sure that his streets were safe once again then he'd go home and celebrate with the woman he loved.

* * * *

"You sure you don't want me to stay until Cooper gets home?" Shawn asked, catching her hand as she exited the patrol car.

"Go home to your wife and kids. I'll be fine. I promise." She pulled away before closing the door.

Shawn waved and she returned the gesture.

Julie turned and started up the sidewalk. It was weird to think that just that morning she'd taken these same steps, but she'd been scared to death that Cooper would turn her away. It hadn't even been twenty-four hours, but it seemed like a week — or maybe a month — had passed. So much had happened. What if she hadn't been back? Cooper could have been killed or seriously injured and she'd had never shown him her love.

With her knees shaking, she sat on the top step of the deck. Even though it was dark, she always loved being out there. Little by little, she and Cooper had started to make his house into their home. She knew that so why she'd even thought to put off moving in with him she didn't know. She'd tell him as soon as he got back. No more wasting time that they could be spending together.

She needed to call Garrett and tell him what had happened tonight and her decision with Cooper. Julie hoped that her brother would still visit, so she could work on him moving there. When she'd left, he'd looked so sad. Garrett had lots of friends but she was family and that had to be reason to at least consider moving. She knew the fire station had openings, so he could easily transfer. He hadn't been truly happy in

Kermit since his last relationship had ended, and that was over three years ago. Lily hadn't been the right girl for him, but Garrett had loved her. It hadn't come as a surprise when Julie had learned Lily had been cheating on Garrett for months. He'd never really gotten over her. Julie knew he could be happy in Clear Creek. She pulled out her phone to start to work her magic.

"Hello?"

"Hey, bro, how are you?" she greeted.

"I'm good. I didn't expect to hear from you so soon. Did you work things out with Cooper?" he asked.

"Yes," she laughed. "I guess I should say you were right and I had nothing to worry about."

"I thought he was smart. Of course he wanted you back," Garrett said.

"He wants to meet you," she told him. "We're having a barbecue this weekend to celebrate the end of a big case for him, and I wanted to see if you could drive down?"

Garrett was unusually quiet for several moments.

"Garrett? You okay?" she questioned.

"I would love to come. Would you mind if I brought a couple buddies?" he asked.

"Of course not! How is Tom doing?"

"Better, he woke up and shifted. He has to be off work for a while, but he should recover fine. I'm actually heading to the hospital to pick him and Steve up. Tom is being released. Well, he demanded it against his doctor's orders, but they can't keep him there if he wants to leave."

"That's great and I would love to have them come too. Actually it works out good with my next bit of news."

"Cooper proposed?" Garrett guessed.

"No!" she shouted. "Are you crazy?"

"What?" he asked before laughing. "Don't sound so shocked. You both love each other and it will happen eventually."

"He didn't ask me to marry him. He asked me to move in," she said, ignoring the thrill that went through her at even talking about marriage.

"And you said yes?"

"Well not initially, but I'm going to. So my house will be empty and it has plenty of room for you, Tom and Steve. It's actually not in a bad location either. It's only six blocks from the central firehouse. You know, if you wanted to stay longer." She held her breath waiting for Garrett's response to that.

"Stay for how long?" his voice deepened.

"Forever?" she answered.

"You want me to move to Clear Creek?"

"Yes," she said. "I really do. You're miserable in Kermit. We're not too far away from visiting Mom and Dad, but it could be a fresh start. I miss you already and I've only been back a week."

"I miss you too. I hated you leaving, again, but I understand why you had to. I'll talk to Tom and Steve about this weekend and think on the other."

"Is everything else going okay there?" she questioned. There was something off about her brother's tone but she just couldn't figure it out.

"Some shit is going down at work. Some of the guys are giving Steve a hard time about being a shifter, now that Tom's not there. It pisses me off. Both Tom and Steve have busted their asses to help out every member of the team. I didn't even realize that there was a problem. I was talking to Steve earlier because I saw him get into it with Frankie. I don't know what to do," Garrett explained.

Julie wished she knew what to tell him to help. "What did Steve have to say?"

"He told me to forget it. He's used to being treated differently. It's not right, though," Garrett said.

"Stick by their side. Show them that they have at least one friend that has their back," she suggested.

"I will," he assured her.

"And bring them with you. They can meet Cooper and some of the wolves here."

"I think that might be just what they need. Kermit has such a small population of shifters. Maybe seeing Cooper and some of his friends will help."

"I'll bring it up to Cooper," she told him.

"Thanks, so I'll check the schedule and see when we can all come. Tom is still off due to his injury and I'm free, but I'll check with Steve."

"Okay, I love you, bro. Be careful," she said.

"You too."

Julie hung up the call, knowing she should have told her brother about earlier but it had sounded like he had enough on his plate. She wanted to get inside anyway. She was in desperate need of a shower. She braced her hand on the ground to stand when she saw a car pull up to Cooper's house. She tensed as the headlights washed over her. Was this someone else coming after Cooper? She gripped her cell in her hand ready to call for help if it was trouble.

She recognized the vehicle as soon as the lights were turned off. She smiled and rose to her feet. Shelby climbed out of the car. Julie rushed forward to hug her dear friend.

"Hey! I thought we were meeting for lunch tomorrow," she said as she released Shelby.

"My producer called me to cover a scene of an officer-involved shooting and I ran into Josiah and Cooper.

Cooper tells me that you were there too. Are you okay?"

"I'm fine." She waved away Shelby's concern, not wanting to cause her to worry.

"Why are you sitting out here then?"

"I was just enjoying the night. I called my brother and was about to go inside. Want a drink?" she offered.

"Yes," Shelby agreed. "It's been a long day."

"Come on." Julie headed toward the house.

"When the call came in over the radio, he didn't have anyone else available. There's a big party at the mayor's fundraiser event and I was free. I agreed to cover it and now I'm glad I did. You weren't even going to call me, were you?" she asked.

Julie wouldn't have. It would have never crossed her mind. Plus, she was planning on having lunch with Shelby the next day. "I was just really tired and wanted to get home." She pulled out her keys and unlocked the door. Cooper hadn't changed the locks while she'd been gone. It was a good thing he hadn't because she hadn't even thought about it when he'd left the house earlier.

She pushed open the front door and flipped on the light switch. "Let's go to the kitchen," she suggested.

Shelby followed behind her as she turned on the rest of the lights. When they got to the kitchen, Julie opened the fridge. "We've got beer or wine," she offered.

"I'll take a beer," Shelby replied.

Julie pulled out two bottles. "It's good to see you." She grabbed the bottle opener off the hook beside the fridge and popped off both lids. "Thanks for coming to visit me while I was in Kermit. You're the only person I saw from here."

"You needed to see a friendly face. I always suspected you'd come back. I just didn't think it would take so long," Shelby said.

"It wouldn't have had my dad not had the cancer scare. I'm glad I was there for my family, but I'm even happier being back."

"And obviously things worked out between you and Cooper." She waved her hand around the kitchen.

"Yes, I knew I overreacted and was scared, but I couldn't get past what I saw. It helped after the shifters became public. I could talk to my family about Cooper, the real reason I left, and they supported both of us. They'd always loved Cooper."

"You have questions? That's why you wanted to meet tomorrow. Do you want to go ahead and ask them?" Shelby offered. "Although I still want lunch tomorrow. I'm putting off my yoga class for you."

Julie laughed. Shelby hated yoga. Something about not being able to focus and keep her mind from racing. She didn't understand it but for some reason, Shelby was determined to master the craft.

"I guess I just wanted to see if you had any books or websites you could recommend. I don't even know where to start."

"I'll send you some links. I've probably got more than anyone else that I know about. As soon as I found out shifting was really possible, I went a bit overboard. I just find it so fascinating," Shelby said. "Is there anything in particular that you're worried about?"

"Cooper asked me to move in," Julie replied. "That got me thinking about starting a family and all the next steps. I don't know any more about shifters than what the news has said, and there are conflicting reports there."

"Yes, the shifters are the biggest hot button in all of the media. While most polls show that humans accept shifters and are happy to have them out in the open, it seems like the biggest opponents always happen to be the loudest. I've been tracking all the forced registration bills that have been introduced and it surprises me every time. But living here in Clear Creek? Cooper is already known as one of the good guys. He's respected on the police force and you have a strong Pack behind him. I've met with the Alpha and he is a very nice man."

"Alpha," she repeated. She'd not gotten there yet.

"Relax." Shelby pushed Julie's beer toward her. "Take a drink."

Julie followed Shelby's advice. The cold brew was refreshing and gave her time to get her thoughts in order.

"Just take things one step at a time. Cooper is a patient man—obviously, after waiting for you this long. He'll help you through learning everything you need to," Shelby assured her.

"I know," Julie agreed. "But after tonight? Watching someone take a shot at him… I want to be able to protect him. I need to be more informed so I can make sure no one tries to hurt him again."

"He's a cop. That's part of his job, but I understand. I'll get you the links tonight. If you have any questions, you can ask me."

"I promise to talk to Cooper about anything serious, but I just want to know more," Julie said. She drank more of her beer, finally feeling more relaxed.

"Loving Cooper will only make you stronger. From everything I've seen, the Pack is just one extended family. I wouldn't be surprised if someone there wouldn't also be willing to speak with you," Shelby said.

"I get nervous when I think about meeting them," Julie confessed.

"You're going to have to accept the shifters. Otherwise, it won't work between you and Cooper," Shelby told her.

"It's not that." Julie waved her hand. "I'm scared they won't think I'm good enough. I love him but if his Pack doesn't accept me, I don't know what will happen."

"They'll accept you. You were meant for Cooper. Even I can see that and I don't have any special abilities. I can see you and Cooper being together for a long time."

"Thanks." Julie smiled. She sure hoped so. "Let me ask you one question, though."

"Shoot," Shelby replied.

"When we have children… Will they be shifters?" she questioned.

"Does it matter?" Shelby responded quickly.

Julie nodded. "Yes, but not for the reason you probably think. I would love them either way. But will I be able to keep them safe if they are? Would it be better if Cooper was with another shifter?"

Shelby grasped her hand. "That's where you're lucky. You have awesome friends and family and will have an entire Pack that will have your back. Any children of yours would be treasured and looked after."

Julie took a deep breath. She hoped Cooper's people were as accepting as her friend.

"To answer your question, I'm not really sure. The wolf shifters haven't discussed that with me. They are very protective about their kids. That is going to be a question for Cooper," Shelby said.

Julie laughed. "If it doesn't scare him away."

"I think you and Cooper are pretty much on the same page when it comes to family. I wouldn't worry about it too much."

Shelby's phone rang before Julie could reply. She backed off to give her friend the opportunity to answer the call. Just the little time she'd spent talking to Shelby had helped her feel better. Julie knew she'd done the right thing confiding in her.

"Hello?" Shelby spoke into her cell.

Julie could only hear her part of the conversation but she didn't miss the excitement in Shelby's eyes.

"Thanks! I'll be there!" Julie jumped off her stool before she hung up.

"What's going on?" Julie asked.

"That was one of my contacts from the police department. They just informed me that the mayor is about to be taken into custody — right in the middle of his very important fundraiser," Shelby answered.

"What? Why?"

"I didn't get that, but I will once I get there. I don't have time to change but, oh well. I have to go." Shelby hugged her quickly.

Julie thought Shelby looked just as put together as she always did. Her expensive tan suit complemented her dark skin beautifully. She'd never seen Shelby look anything but perfect. "Go. You look fine."

"There is no way I would miss this," Shelby said, as she headed toward the door.

Now that Shelby mentioned it, Julie found it strange that the star reporter hadn't been at the event already. "Why weren't you there tonight?"

Shelby grimaced. "I refuse to cover anything with the mayor. He is the most bigoted, hateful man I've ever met."

"The mayor?" Julie questioned.

"You missed a lot being gone these last few months," Shelby said as she pulled open the door. "The mayor is a horrible man and if he's being taken down tonight, I want to be there."

"Go!" Julie waved her on. "Good luck."

Shelby grinned. "*He's* going to need the luck." She jogged down the steps, and Julie had to shake her head. She wondered about the mayor and what he was being busted for. She'd take a quick shower then turn on the local channel. It might be fun to watch.

* * * *

Cooper stood next to Josiah, Fisher and Turner in front of his captain. Other officers were fanned out behind them as they gathered on the front steps of the mayor's mansion.

"We will serve Mayor Jensen the arrest warrant then proceed on with the search of his office. Follow all procedures and do your jobs well," Captain Martinez said.

Cooper rubbed his hands together in anticipation. He couldn't wait to see Jensen's face when he was finally taken down.

"Let's go," Captain Martinez ordered.

Fisher and Turner fell in line behind the captain and he and Josiah after them. It was only right that the four of them were the ones who took down the mayor for drug trafficking. They'd worked hard on this case and it was time for someone to pay.

The security guard at the door didn't try to stop them from entering the crowded event. Cooper glanced around, trying to spot his target.

"Fisher, Turner, go right," Captain Martinez said. "Burns, Grainger, left. Let's find him and get this taken care of quickly."

"Yes, sir," Cooper acknowledged.

He broke off with Josiah, passing partygoers, who looked surprised to see them. They didn't fit in with the expensive tuxes and gowns in their jeans and T-shirts. Cooper patted the weapon at his side, reassuring himself that he was prepared if anyone gave him trouble.

He spotted the mayor standing in the center of a large room laughing and clinking glasses with one of the city council members. He nudged Josiah toward Jensen.

"Got him," Josiah murmured.

Cooper crossed the room with long strides until he was in front of the mayor. "Mayor Jensen," he called.

The mayor turned toward him. Cooper was amused to see his fake smile slip into a sneer. "What are you doing here?" Jensen asked. "I know I didn't invite any of your kind."

Oh yeah, the mayor knew who he was. "Mayor Jensen," Cooper said loudly and clearly. "You are under arrest for drug trafficking."

"What?" Jensen shouted.

Cooper reached back and grabbed the handcuffs from his belt. He strolled forward and clamped a hand down on the mayor's shoulder.

"What is the meaning of this?" Jensen yelled.

"Mayor Jensen," Captain Martinez appeared in front of them. "This is a warrant for your arrest."

"You can't do this!" Jensen hollered. He looked around, and Cooper followed suit, preparing for trouble.

It didn't seem like the mayor had many supporters now. The people that the mayor had just been talking to were quickly putting distance between themselves and Jensen.

Josiah took the warrant from the captain and held it up to Jensen. As his partner started to read Jensen his Miranda rights, Cooper finished securing him. The final snick of the cuffs and Cooper felt lighter than he had in months.

"Do you understand your rights?" Josiah asked Jensen.

Since Cooper couldn't understand much of what the mayor screamed, he just pushed the man forward to escort him from the party. He took Jensen's right arm, allowing Josiah to take the left.

Captain Martinez led the way, which wasn't too difficult since people were rushing to clear a path. At the front door, Cooper spotted a news cameraman and reporter. He recognized Shelby from when he'd met her previously. It appeared that the mayor was going to get his fifteen minutes of fame and more. Cooper was proud to be involved.

Even as Shelby shouted questions at Jensen, the mayor continued to cuss and threaten the officers. Cooper grinned, making sure to pass right in front of the camera.

It was good to be a cop and stand up for what was right.

Chapter Seven

Cooper grinned as he walked into the kitchen and spotted Julie bent over, pulling containers out of the bottom cabinet. He wasn't sure what she was looking for or even if she'd find anything in the mess of plastic, but he sure enjoyed the view. He crept forward silently until he was right behind her.

She screamed when he grabbed her around the waist and yanked her back.

"Look what I found," he whispered into her ear. He trailed his fingers down her neck and inside her tank top.

"What are you doing?" Julie asked, as she pressed back into him.

The pressure on his cock was just what he wanted.

"If I have to explain it to you, I must be doing something wrong," he teased. He cupped her breast before he rubbed his thumb over her hard nipple.

"We have guests that will be here soon," she clearly tried to sound stern but failed, since she was still pushing her ass against his erection. His wolf itched as he fought to the surface intent of claiming Julie again.

"We have plenty of time," he assured her. He spun her around before lifting her to sit on the counter. Julie laughed, reaching for him as he quickly moved in between her legs before he lowered his mouth to hers. She kissed him with passion and enthusiasm. He would never tire of her taste or the feel of her under him. They were just starting their life together. Today was the first step, bringing their loved friends and family closer — to make sure that the inner circle around them was strong.

"I really don't think we should do this," she gave a token protest. "Someone could arrive early."

He hummed in response as he slowly lifted her top over her head. She raised her arms to help. He knew she didn't really mind taking a break from getting the party ready. "Not one of our friends are the early bird type."

"Still..." She reached for his T-shirt. "We should hurry."

"Yes," he agreed. They twisted, tugged and removed each article until they were both naked. It wasn't easy with her still seated on the marble countertop, but they made do.

He pushed her to lie back before he gripped her hips and pulled her to the edge of the counter. Cooper laid his palms on her inner thighs and began to spread her legs. He dipped a finger into her moist pussy. She bucked silently, demanding more.

Cooper chuckled. "Maybe you're right. We might not have time," he taunted.

She growled — a sound very much like a wolf, even though she was human — before she raised herself up and grabbed his shoulder. "Don't make me hurt you," she warned.

"Never," he promised. He added a second digit, relishing every soft sound that came from Julie's mouth.

"Please," she begged.

He peered down at her, taking in the way she had thrown her head back and clenched eyes closed. "Look at me," he demanded.

She opened her eyes, and he could see that passion clouded her vision. He grasped his erection until he was poised at her entrance.

"Cooper," she pleaded.

He pressed forward. Julie sighed as he filled her. Cooper kept his gaze on hers. Inside, his wolf calmed to let his human side enjoy being with her. He pumped his hips with long, deliberate strides. Julie scratched her nails into the counter, and he had a fleeting wonder whether or not she'd leave marks behind.

"More... Please, more," she chanted, lifting her hips trying to get him deeper and faster. "More."

He could never have resisted her pleas. He slammed himself in hard. Julie cried out with pleasure. He drew back then plunged again, over and over until sweat trickled down his neck and Julie's voice echoed through the kitchen, bouncing off the walls. Cooper groaned as her inner muscles tightened around his cock and he yelled as he came. Julie shuddered as she went over the edge herself.

* * * *

"Everything is ready," Cooper said as he joined her on the back deck. "I told you we would have plenty of time."

Even if they hadn't been able to finish setting up, it would have been worth it. She ran her hand over his ass then squeezed. "We'll have even more after everyone leaves," she taunted.

"Maybe then we can also discuss you moving in?" he asked.

There hadn't been much time to talk about their relationship with Cooper working with the district attorney in putting the mayor away for good. Julie turned in Cooper's arms, wrapping hers around his neck. "I think we can probably even talk my brother into helping." Garrett, Tom and Steve had driven in the night before and were staying at her house.

"I like him," Cooper said.

She hadn't been worried about her brother and lover getting along. They were good, honest and kind. They had a lot in common and Julie knew they would be great friends. "I'm glad."

"Now." He gripped her hips. "How much time do we have?"

"Not enough for whatever you're thinking about doing," Josiah said behind her.

Julie spun around. Josiah stood at the sliding glass door leading from the house with a case of beer. A very pretty redhead was at his side, holding what looked like a pie.

"Perfect timing, as usual," Julie teased. She tried to get loose from Cooper but he only tightened his hold.

"It's good to see you again, Cammi," Cooper greeted the woman.

"Hi, and you must be Julie. I brought one of my mom's pecan pies. She makes the best I've ever tasted."

"Thank her for us." Julie smiled. "And make yourself at home." She turned to Cooper. "Are you going to let me go?"

"No," he replied.

She elbowed him, and he chuckled. He did release her, though. She rose to her tiptoes and kissed him quickly before walking over to Cammi. Cooper had already told her that Josiah would be bringing the woman he'd started to date. Julie was happy to see Josiah settling down. She hoped the two of them made each other happy. "Let me show you around," she told Cammi. "You"—she pointed at Josiah—"help your partner light the grill. And don't catch anything on fire!"

"Well if you do, at least you'll have trained professionals," Garrett called as he joined them. They all laughed.

"Good to see you again," Julie said to Tom and Steve. "Let me introduce you to Josiah and Cammi. Josiah is Cooper's partner."

Garrett slung an arm around her shoulder. "So you have to put up with Coop all day?" he asked Josiah.

Josiah grinned. "Yep."

"I bet you know all his secrets," Garrett said. "We should talk."

"No." Cooper pushed Josiah to the side. "You can help me with the grill, Mr. Fireman," he joked.

Julie took Cammi through the house on a quick tour so she'd know where the restroom and kitchen was in case she needed anything. They'd just returned to the deck to get a drink when Shawn popped his head through the open doorway. "The fun has arrived!"

Julie waved her partner out. "Where are the kids?"

"Here!" Two small boys ran out yelling and hugged her. Shawn's wife was a nurse at the hospital and had to work, but Julie was glad the rest of the family could come.

Introductions were made quickly and loudly and the boys hollered and sprinted to Cooper.

Julie loved watching him with the boys. He was a natural nurturer and it showed how much he cared by the way he bent down and talked to them.

"Help me with the coolers?" she asked Shawn.

He nodded, and they headed back inside. It took several trips but once they were done they both grabbed a cold bottle. She glanced around at the backyard full of friends and family. The weather was perfect. Cooper stood at the grill talking with Garrett and Steve. Shawn's kids were running around kicking a soccer ball while Josiah and his new girlfriend cheered them on from the lounge chairs. Julie was so happy, watching the people she loved most in the world.

"Nice party," Shelby said, as she joined Julie at the large picnic table.

"It is. I'm glad you could make it. You don't usually," Julie replied.

"My boss was so impressed with my report on the mayor's arrest and the follow up pieces on his corruption that I have a week off."

"That's great," Julie told her. It had only been a couple of days but Julie could already see how the take down of the mayor had relaxed Cooper. He'd told her the entire story about the drugs, pay offs and threats that Jensen would be convicted of. The Bradley cousins had tried to make a deal, but the district attorney wasn't buying it. No one needed the Bradleys to talk. They had enough evidence on Jensen to make sure they all went away for a long time.

"So I'm going to take a few days to catch up on some reading and just relax before I go visit my parents," Shelby said.

Julie leaned over and grabbed a beer from the cooler at the end of the table. She passed it to Shelby as she spotted Mike coming through the gate. She waved at him and he returned the gesture as he headed over to Cooper.

"And who is that fine specimen of a man?" Shelby practically purred.

Julie rolled her eyes. "That's Cooper's old college roommate, Mike Riley."

"The criminal lawyer?" Shelby asked, with something close to disgust in her tone.

Julie turned to her friend surprised. "Yes, why?"

"I've done some reports on clients of his. He's good at what he does," Shelby stated. "Even when they should be in jail."

Since she didn't know much about law, Julie couldn't really say whether or not what Mike did was wrong. She did know that Mike was a great guy and she couldn't see him defending anyone for something horrible. She'd have to ask Cooper.

"Anyway" — Shelby made it a point to turn her back to where Mike stood — "did the files that I sent help?"

Shelby's reaction to Mike was very suspicious. Julie would have to see about getting them together to watch the fireworks. She couldn't think of a more perfect match for her friend. Something was off with Shelby's attitude toward him. *This might get really interesting.* She wanted to see her friend happy. Shelby didn't date a lot, always blaming her busy schedule, and from what Cooper had told her about Mike, they had that in common.

"Julie." Shelby waved her hand in front of Julie's face. "The files?"

True to her word, Shelby had forwarded everything she had on shifters. The night before, Julie had been reading through some of it when Cooper had got home. He'd taken the laptop from her and set it on the coffee table before drawing her into his arms. He'd wanted to talk to her if she had any questions. He claimed the news still didn't have everything right and he'd rather she knew for sure. Julie had to admit that what Cooper had said made a lot of sense. She'd promised him she'd always go to him first. "Yes, but Cooper and I decided to talk about my concerns first."

Shelby grinned. "I thought he would."

"Burgers are ready!" Cooper yelled.

Julie and Shelby strolled over to the grill. She kept her eyes on her man as she walked toward him. He looked damn hot in his faded jeans and tank top. She loved it when he showed off his muscular arms. He grinned at her as she approached.

"Having fun?" he asked.

Julie nodded. "We need to do this more often."

"Maybe next time we can invite my Alpha?"

Julie paused in reaching for a plate. She hadn't even thought of that. "We should. I want to get to know your Pack."

"I want that too. They're really good people. I'd like you to meet Alpha Jeremy and his family first," Cooper told her.

Julie could see how much his request meant to Cooper. "I wish you'd have said something sooner."

"I thought it would be better just to have our friends this weekend. But when we're both off next, I think it's time you got to know my family. That's what my Pack is, and I want you to look at them like that."

"I will," she assured him. She had faith that Cooper's Pack would mean as much to her as they did to him. All she needed to do was to learn how to open herself to the new world that Cooper was opening up to her. She'd learned an important lesson, to give her trust to Cooper. She'd never make a mistake like she had done when she'd run. She'd balance her human beliefs with what she needed to do to support Cooper. No matter what they had to deal with in the future, she knew that having him at her side made her a very lucky woman.

PACK INVESTIGATOR

Dedication

For family, those of blood, and those by choice.

Chapter One

The rumble of the fire-truck engine that surrounded Garrett Sullivan was so familiar to him that in his exhausted yet hyper state Garrett felt at peace. There had been no injuries from the fire that the crew was returning from. He'd never worked with such a flawless team.

They pulled into the bay of the central fire station in Clear Creek and he grinned. He wanted a nice hot shower and it wasn't his turn to clean up the gear or to replace supplies in the trucks. He could head straight to the locker room.

After he jumped down from the truck, he strolled through the open garage, taking in the differences between his current station and his old one. Garrett was glad he'd made the move three months ago. Even better, his two best friends, Tom and Steve, had transferred with him, although their reasons had been quite different from his.

He nodded as he passed a couple of the guys before he pushed open the swinging door and entered the locker room. Even the rundown facilities there didn't bother him. Garrett had wanted a fresh start, to leave the city of his birth for the first time, forge ahead in his career and hopefully find love.

Garrett pulled his sweat-soaked T-shirt over his head and dropped it onto the old tiled floor. He glanced up as Tom walked in. Garrett lifted his chin to his best friend. Tom looked better than he had in months. Tom and Steve had wanted to connect with the local wolf shifter Pack and Garrett had been able to help them achieve that goal. In Kermit they'd been lone wolves as there hadn't been enough shifters to form an effective Pack there. They'd tried but with no Alpha or Beta, all the shifters had fought for dominance. Garrett was human, but luckily he had an in with one of the local shifters in Clear Creek. His sister's shifter boyfriend, Cooper, had been happy to help get Tom and Steve connected with the local Pack.

"I've never seen a fire spread so quickly," Tom stated as he walked in.

"I heard the captain talking to the fire investigator. Lieutenant Haas told the cap that this was the third suspicious fire like this in the city in the past two weeks. The other fires were in the northern part of the city. He's certain they have an arsonist," Garrett said.

As soon as he'd seen the investigator and his captain with their heads close together, Garrett had known something was up. He'd crept closer even though he'd known he shouldn't have been eavesdropping. It wasn't like his captain wouldn't tell him the truth if Garrett asked. He just wanted to hear it from the investigator's mouth.

If he'd remained in Kermit, he'd probably have his certification to move into the investigating part of fighting fires. He knew that he'd made enemies by associating with the shifters and he was sure no opening would have been offered to him had he stayed. So instead of finishing he'd transferred as a firefighter. But even in Kermit, he'd heard how Lieutenant Haas was the best investigator in the state. Garrett hadn't officially met the man but he'd kept an eye out for him.

When he'd spotted him speaking with the captain, Garrett hadn't been able to resist. He might not have been part of the community for long but he was already invested in every soul that lived in Clear Creek. "They haven't found a connection yet but they are sure it's the work of the same person," Garrett finished telling Tom.

"That's weird," Tom replied. "But I've heard good things about Lieutenant Haas and his team. I'm sure if anyone can find the person responsible it is them. I'll be glad not to have to fight a fire like that again, though."

"Julie promised it was never boring here in Clear Creek," Garrett said. He unsnapped the watch from his wrist and set it inside his locker.

"She's right there," Tom agreed.

Tom started to undress so Garrett went back to preparing for his own shower. He still had another five hours left of his shift and he hoped there wasn't another call. His portion of the city ran from the creek to the outskirts to the center of town. Mostly they handled small fires due to residents burning trash, out-of-control kitchen flames or traffic situations where they needed to get people out of their smashed vehicles with heavy equipment. Tonight had been the first fully engulfed home he'd fought as part of Clear Creek Fire Department.

Adrenaline still coursed through his body and he needed to work some of it out before he could get to sleep. He could have gone straight to the gym like some of the other guys but he didn't want to be around everyone. He wasn't going to get laid while on shift so he needed to figure out how to relax. First he was going to start with a hot shower, then settle on the couch with the latest thriller he'd picked up at the local bookstore. Once he finished his shift tonight he had the next two days off and planned to find someone to spend the time with him in his bed. He just needed to make it a few more hours. He dropped his pants then picked up his fallen garments. He dumped the rest of his stuff in his locker before he picked up his shower bag. He passed by the entrance to the showers, snatching a towel off the shelf as he strolled to the last cubicle.

The Clear Creek station showers were made up of single stalls so at least he had some privacy. He hung his towel on the hook outside the curtain and his bag on the inside before he yanked the curtain closed. He turned on the hot water knob, knowing that the water would start out warm and heat from there. He'd learned early on that there was no cold water available. Some mix-up with plumbing, but he'd rather have hot than cold anyway.

Standing under the stream, he grabbed the soap from his bag and lathered his hands. His cock was hard from the excitement of the night, a result of too much adrenaline and testosterone. He gripped his erection at the base and slid his hand down and back up. He pumped himself several times, tension in his entire body. The feel of his own hand was a poor substitute for being buried inside a warm, tight pussy, but he had to make do. He increased his speed, knowing that he wouldn't have much time for privacy. Tom would be entering the showers at any minute and Garrett didn't want to be overheard when he came. He tugged harder, tightening his grip until he was thrusting his hips along. He shoved his free fist into his mouth to muffle his shout as he climaxed.

Spent, he rested his back against the stall and took deep breaths. Once he'd recovered somewhat he quickly finished washing up. He heard the water turn on in one of the stalls down the lane before Tom started to hum. Garrett grinned as he shut off his own water. He grabbed the towel from the hook and dried himself then wrapped it around his waist. He stepped out of the stall and jolted when the alarm started to go off again.

"Shit!" Tom yelled.

Garrett rushed to his locker and pulled on a clean uniform. His fingers flew in the familiar rhythm of closing the buttons of his uniform shirt as his mind cleared to the task ahead. He didn't think about what he was doing until he was in full gear and sitting in the back of the engine rig. Steve was on his right and Tom on his left.

Once they arrived on scene they all jumped out and began to work. The captain shouted orders but they weren't necessary. The crew knew their jobs and they performed well. He and Tom had the task of clearing of the structure. Tom led the way, as he normally did, using his shifter abilities as much as the smoke allowed. It didn't matter whether the firefighter was human or shifter, smoke made it difficult to see. Garrett stayed at his back so he could keep an eye on his partner while Tom concentrated on sniffing out any occupants who might still be inside.

Tom stopped walking before he lifted his fist. Garrett gripped his shoulder to show he was with Tom every step of the way. After a few seconds, he pointed to the right. Garrett slapped his hand down twice and moved to the first door. The front of the house wasn't engulfed in flames yet, so once Garrett was sure he wasn't opening the door to where the fire existed, he pushed it open. There wasn't too much smoke in here and with his mask he could see pretty clearly. He paused in the center of the room and slowly scanned the surroundings. He heard it then. A soft whimper in the direction of the closet. Garrett rushed forward and threw open the door. A small bundle was at the bottom. Garrett crouched down and gently peeled away the blue blanket. He peered down at the trembling child with a tear-streaked face. He held out his arms and the boy jumped into them. He stood then turned and strolled out of the room, intent on getting the boy to safety.

Tom was braced in front of the entry, waving him forward. The fire was spreading fast so he huddled his upper body around the precious package in his arms and ran. He headed straight out of the front entrance into the fresh air.

Someone tried to take the child from his arms but the boy cried out and clung to Garrett harder. Garrett shook his head to warn the others off. He'd take the boy to the ambulance.

Steve appeared in front of him and pointed toward the street. Garrett saw the flashing lights of the police and emergency vehicles lined up. His gear was heavy, his helmet had started to fog up, but he was not going to let go of the kid until he saw the EMTs. Steve led the way and he followed through the busy firefighters and police personal.

From the open back of the ambulance, a figure jumped down and jogged toward him. He grinned — he could entrust the terrified child to his sister. Julie reached for him and the paleness on her face revealed her fear for the boy.

"Are you okay?" she asked.

He nodded before he lifted his arms to hand the boy over.

"No!" the kid screamed as he tightened his arms around Garrett's neck.

"It's okay," Julie told the frightened child. "This is my brother. He'll take you over to my rig for us."

The boy stopped yelling and settled down. Garrett shook his head but staggered forward. He was getting tired and he really needed to get his helmet off. Julie's partner, Shawn, smiled at him when they reached the rig. Julie jumped up into the back and reached once again for the boy. Garrett nodded toward the gurney, telling her he'd set the child there. He climbed up before he carefully set the boy down on the bed. He ripped off his mask and took a deep breath of fresh air. The oxygen tank had helped him when he was in the house, but there was nothing like that first fresh breath. He looked at the boy, who was watching him with wide eyes. Garrett sat next to him.

"Hi, little man. My name's Garrett," he introduced himself. "What's yours?"

"Nick Bolton," the small child answered.

"It's good to meet you, Nick," Garrett said. "This is my sister, Julie. She needs to check you out to make sure you're okay."

The boy nodded before he started to cough. Julie moved forward, placing an oxygen mask around his nose and mouth. She spoke quietly to Nick as she worked. Garrett glanced over his shoulder and saw that his unit appeared to have the fire under control and it was almost out. He sighed in relief. Shawn passed him a bottle of water before he was subjected to a quick but thorough examination of his own. He wasn't surprised. His sister and her partner took just as good care of the firefighters as they did any victims.

He spotted Tom jogging toward him and stood. Nick shot his hand out and grabbed his wrist faster than Garrett would have thought possible for such a young child.

"I'm not going anywhere," he assured the kid. "I'll be right here but I need to talk to my friend."

Nick eyed him for several seconds before he nodded and released Garrett. Tom was there as Garrett hopped down out of the rig. They stepped a few feet away, where they wouldn't be overheard but Nick would still be able to see him.

"No one else in the house," Tom informed him.

"Someone left that kid alone?" Garrett asked, pissed off that anyone could be so irresponsible. There was no way a child that age could stay by himself in a house.

"It looks like some kind of altercation took place in the master bedroom. The fire was started in the kitchen. The cap called in Lieutenant Haas. He's going to want to talk to the boy," Tom said.

Garrett glanced back over at Nick. He was following Julie's instructions but Nick's gaze never left Garrett. "I'll talk to him," Garrett offered.

"One more thing." Tom gripped his shoulder.

Garrett didn't like Tom's serious tone. He braced himself for bad news.

"The boy's a shifter. Steve smelled it on him right away."

"Okay," Garrett said slowly, confused. Tom should know that Garrett had no problem with shifters. He'd been friends with Tom and Steve a while now and his sister was living with a shifter.

"He's scared, traumatized, and his dad's missing. You have to keep him calm. At his age he hasn't shifted yet, but these events could cause him to lose control. If he shifts this early he won't know how to change back to human form."

Garrett sucked in a sharp breath. He was still learning about shifters and hadn't considered how the ability would affect a child.

"He seems to have taken to you already. You know shifters get emotionally involved easily, especially when they're young. He's going to need you to help him control his urges. His wolf will want to protect the boy and take over. You can't let that happen."

"Okay." Garrett wasn't sure how he would accomplish the task, but he would make sure Nick remained calm and in human form.

"The cap ordered you to stay with the boy. Child services will meet you at the hospital. That's where I assume you're headed?"

Garrett knew his sister's routine and could tell she was preparing Nick for transport. "Yes."

"I'll check up on you in a little bit. One of us will bring you some clothes," Tom said.

He was grateful to have such good friends. He stripped off his outer gear until he only remained in a T-shirt and his utility pants. Tom bundled up Garrett's uniform before he strolled away. Garrett was hot and sweaty but he needed to check on Nick more than cool down.

"Hey," he said as he climbed back inside the rig. "You doing okay?"

"Where's my dad?" Nick pulled down his mask and asked. "I heard that man say no one was else was inside."

Damn shifter hearing. "We don't know," Garrett admitted.

Nick struggled to sit up. Julie pressed her hand down on his shoulder while Garrett grabbed both of Nick's hands. "It's okay, buddy. We're looking for him."

"I want to help!" Nick cried.

"First we have to take you to the hospital and have you checked out by the doctors," Garrett said.

"I want my dad!" Nick wailed.

"I know." Garrett brushed back the dark hair that had fallen into Nick's eyes. "I know you do. But your dad would want us to take care of you first, wouldn't he?"

Tears had started to pool in Nick's eyes. He sniffed but nodded.

"Then let us do that. I'll stay with you," he promised. "See all the police officers?" He pointed out into the yard of the house.

"Yeah," Nick mumbled.

"They are going to look for your dad. That's their job," he said.

"You swear?" Nick asked. "They'll find my dad?"

Julie cleared her throat, catching his attention. She shook her head at him. He knew he shouldn't make promises that he couldn't keep. He glanced back at Nick. "I swear that they'll do everything they can."

Nick seemed satisfied and leaned back, settling in. Garrett let out a breath of relief.

Julie placed the mask back over Nick's face before she turned and grabbed a water bottle from a small fridge. She handed it to Garrett and he didn't waste any time gulping the refreshing liquid down.

"We need to go," she said. "You coming along?"

Nick tensed but Garrett patted his arm and soothed him. "Yep."

"Okay," she said. "Let's go, Shawn," she called out to her partner.

Shawn came running up before he slammed the doors closed. Julie went back to her clipboard, writing something down, so Garrett just held Nick's hand and relaxed. It was going to be a really long night.

* * * *

Lillian Harper hurried down the hospital corridor toward her charge. It was almost one in the morning but when she'd been called about a shifter child being rescued from a fire, she'd taken the case. All the other social workers were human so as the only wolf shifter, Lily took most of the shifter cases that arose in the department.

This case was an emergency placement since the child's father Randy Bolton had been reported missing. Lily's concern was the boy but she still prayed that the kid's father was okay. The fourth floor of the Medical Center Hospital was one of the quieter areas. It was reserved for post-surgery patients but Lily had asked for her charge to be taken up there. That way he wouldn't get frightened with all the sounds and the crowd of the emergency room. Twelve years working with the Clear Creek child services afforded her some favors.

She'd already placed a call to her Alpha to get information on the Bolton family. Her hours didn't allow her to make many of the Pack meetings so she wasn't certain whether or not she'd met Nick or his dad, Randy.

Alpha Jeremy spoke very highly of Randy and Nick and was willing to take Nick in if need be. He was also planning to make a call to Randy's partner in the law firm where he worked. Apparently the partner was a shifter and close to Nick as well. Lily was glad she'd called her Alpha. If the boy needed immediate placement, Jeremy would do for the time being. She couldn't place him there long since the Alpha had to go out of town in a few days to meet with the Alpha Council and his trip couldn't be postponed. At least she'd be able to place Nick somewhere safe while they looked for the boy's dad and she made more permanent arrangements. If the cops didn't find Randy then Nick would need long-term care. She preferred to keep the shifter children with others like them, because they could teach the children tricks on how to deal with the wolf if it decided to try to transform. Children didn't have the easiest time dealing with the change during traumatic events.

She knew wonderful human foster parents that would make a good match if she needed to place Nick for longer than a couple of days. For now Nick needed someone he trusted and was comfortable with. She waved at the head nurse as she passed by the desk. She'd called earlier, finding out that Nick was in room twelve. It was one of the largest on the floor.

As she got closer to Nick's room, she could hear the soft murmur of voices coming from inside. She'd been told that the firefighter who'd rescued Nick was staying with him until she could get there. Apparently Nick had attached himself to his hero and didn't want the fireman to leave him.

Lily knocked gently on the door frame before she entered the room. Nick was lying in the big hospital bed and next to him was a large man in a CCFD T-shirt. He glanced up as she stepped in and her breath caught at his handsome face. He had to be one of the hottest men she'd ever seen. His dark brown hair was disheveled and he had dark circles under his eyes, but when he spotted her his smile transformed his entire face and made him look years younger. He had a somewhat wholesome boyish look to him that she liked. He stood up, groaning a little. He had to have been at least six feet two.

"You must be Lillian," he said. "We were told to expect you."

She accepted his handshake and jolted as their palms connected. He jerked a little himself but his smile never left his face. "Call me Lily, and you are?"

"Garrett Sullivan," he responded.

"Nice to meet you." She had to let go of his hand even though it was the last thing she wanted to do. She turned toward the boy in the bed. "And you must be Nick." She walked over to the left side, allowing Garrett to remain on the right. "I'm very sorry this happened to you," she said honestly.

"Did you find my dad yet?" he asked.

Her heart ached that she couldn't tell him good news. "Not yet, sweetie," she said.

"Oh." Nick's bottom lip trembled and he reached for Garrett's hand.

"They're working very hard, though. They called the Alpha and he even put some of the Pack out to search for him," she told him.

"Hear that?" Garrett patted Nick's hand. "You've got the cops and the Pack on your side, that's good news."

Nick nodded. "But Dad wouldn't want me to be here all by myself. If he knew where I was he'd come, so where is he?"

He was a smart kid for the age of five. Lily just wasn't sure how to explain things to him. Garrett glanced at her and their gazes met. She offered him a small smile, hoping he understood that she didn't know how to answer Nick. "Well, that's why everyone is looking. They want to get your dad here to you," she said.

"Okay," Nick replied.

"As a matter of fact, the policemen want to come and talk to you, to see if you could help them. I need to check with your doctor but if he says it's okay, would you be willing to talk to the police?"

"I want to help," Nick stated clearly.

"I'll stay with you and if you want to stop or you get scared or tired you just tell me," Lily said.

"I want Garrett to stay too," Nick demanded.

The poor boy was hanging onto his hero with everything he had. It would be best to break the connection sooner rather than later. Nick was becoming too attached to this human stranger.

"I think it would be best if Mr. Sullivan went ahead and got back to his job. It's important that he rests so he can help the next family he comes across," she explained.

Nick started to shake, and she knew she'd said the wrong thing. *Crap!* She needed to keep him calm.

"I'm sure he'll be back to visit you," she tried.

It didn't work, Nick started to cry and climb out of bed.

"Hey, little man." Garrett swept him up in his arms, somehow managing to avoid the IV line in his hand. "Relax, I'm not going anywhere. Miss Lily just didn't know that. Didn't I say I'd stay with you tonight?"

"Ye…yeah," Nick spoke as he continued to cry. "But what if there's another fire and you're not there? I don't want you to leave, though."

Garrett glared at her for a second before he sat on the bed and held Nick to his chest. "I'm not on shift anymore. It's already ended. There's plenty of guys at the station that will be there in case of another fire. I promise it'll be okay that I stay with you. My boss already said so."

Nick sniffled before he wiped his nose with his hand.

Lily grabbed some napkins and wiped his face then hands. "I'm sorry I upset you," she said. "If Mr. — uh, I mean Garrett, wants to stay with you he can." She didn't know how she was going to explain it to her office but she'd find a way. It was obvious that Garrett planned on sticking around.

"You're not mad?" Nick asked peering up at her.

"At you?" she asked, shocked. "Of course not! I think you're being very brave but you feel comfortable with Garrett and that's okay."

Nick sighed before he laid his head on Garrett's chest. The picture the two of them made was heartwarming. The huge fireman holding the tiny scared boy in his arms, offering him comfort. It was a moment she'd have loved to photograph.

"Excuse me."

Lily spun around and saw Dr. Hernandez at the door. "Hey, Doc," she greeted. She'd gotten to know the older doctor well over the years.

"Miss Harper." Dr. Hernandez smiled at her. "I'm happy to see you with our little patient here."

Nick didn't lift his head from Garrett's chest but he did wave at the doctor. "He gave me a candy bar," Nick told her.

"Well," Lily laughed. "If it was doctor-ordered I'd say that you must have been a really good boy."

"Yes he has," Dr. Hernandez agreed. "Do you have a moment?" He gestured toward the hall.

Lily patted Nick's arm. "I'm going to talk to the doctor. I'll be right back."

"You'll see if I can help the police?" Nick sounded eager.

"You bet," she answered.

She followed the doc out but didn't close the door. "How is he?"

"He's very well. He had some slight smoke inhalation but between fluids, oxygen and his shifter abilities he's almost back to normal."

Lily relaxed a little. "That's great. The cops want to talk to him but I told them I'd have to check with you first."

"I'll leave that decision up to you," Hernandez said. "Physically he's fine. I don't know what toll this took on him emotionally or mentally so watch out for signs of stress. You know what to look for."

She nodded. The child's welfare was always her first priority. "Thanks."

"I want to keep him overnight but as long as he gets some sleep he should be released in the morning," Hernandez said.

Lily offered her hand. "Sounds good." She would have to decide what to do with him, but for the night he was safe in the hospital.

"I'll talk to you later," Hernandez said before he walked farther down the hall.

She turned back toward the room and almost bumped into Garrett. He stood blocking the entrance. While she wanted to go to him and place her hand on his big solid chest and rub him down, marking him with her scent, Lily had enough control to resist. But barely.

"Now what?" he asked. When he wasn't glaring at her she could get lost in his eyes. The disapproval earlier had actually made her hands start to sweat and her stomach tighten. There was just something about him that called to the wolf inside.

Lily shook her head. This was ridiculous. She had a job to do!

"I'll let the officers know they can interview him. He needs to get some sleep and then we'll see what happens next," she said. She didn't mean to sound so sharp but Garrett was affecting her way too much.

His eyes narrowed but he didn't say anything. He just spun on his heel and headed back to Nick's side. She had to stop herself from bowing her head and running after him. She closed her palms tightly, making fists. The bite of her nails into her flesh helped clear the fog from her brain. Lily shuddered. Garrett might be a human but he had dominance radiating off him. It was a turn-on for her but she couldn't fantasize about what she would like him to do to her. Not until Nick was safe and she was home alone.

She rolled her shoulders back and strolled into the room, preparing to take care of Nick and ignore her attraction to Garrett. It didn't help when she spotted him sitting on Nick's bed, stroking the boy's hair as they spoke softly.

Nick looked up and smiled at her. "Garrett said he'd get some games for us to play, are you going to stay?"

Lily nodded. She could play a few games before she got back to working on Nick's case. "Of course," she said with false cheer. The boy needed normalcy, and Lily was a big girl. She wasn't a slave to her hormones. She wasn't sixteen again, for heaven's sake. Garrett was only a man, yes an extremely attractive man, but Lily was in control, she tried to assure herself.

Chapter Two

Garrett lifted his head from the back of the chair he'd fallen asleep in and yawned. Bleary eyed, he peered at his surroundings. Nick was curled into a ball at the top of the bed. Lily was in a chair and had it up against the side of the bed with her arms crossed on the mattress, pillowing her head. The night before, or more accurately the early morning, had found them watching cartoons and playing several games that one of the nurses had brought up to them.

The activities had helped keep Nick's mind off his dad and the events from earlier. They'd played until Nick had nodded off. Nick hadn't even woken when the two officers from missing persons had shown up. Lily had sent them away, asking them to come back later this morning.

He hated to admit it, under the circumstances that had brought the three of them together, but he'd enjoyed sitting around with Lily and Nick. He'd felt just a little guilty laughing as he'd teased Nick about how Nick kept winning. The boy's dad was missing, possibly dead in the worst case scenario, and he'd had a better night then he could remember in a very long time.

Garrett stretched his arms over his head and bit back a groan as his back popped. He didn't regret spending the night in Nick's hospital room but his body was letting him know that he wasn't as young as he used to be. Hell, he was pushing forty and he was much too old to sleep in a chair.

He rose to his feet but made sure that he remained quiet so he didn't wake Nick or Lily. He wanted them to get as much rest as they could. There was a busy day ahead for both of them. He didn't know what Lily had planned for Nick but he was going to insist he had a say in things. He went into the attached bathroom first to take a piss, then he washed his face and rinsed out his mouth. He had his bag from earlier but he needed coffee before he really cleaned up good. He exited the bathroom and saw Lieutenant Haas hovering at the door. The lieutenant spotted him and gestured back toward the hall. Garrett nodded before he followed Haas out of the room.

"I'm not surprised to see you still here," Haas said as a way of greeting. "We haven't met officially but I've seen you around. I heard all about the boy and how he's connected with you. I was hoping I could use that to help get him to talk to me."

"I'm happy to help," Garrett told him. "Can you tell me anything about your investigation?"

"I can actually." Haas motioned to the elevator. "Do you have time for a cup of coffee? There is a small café downstairs instead of the main cafeteria. I've had the pleasure of picking up a cup or two in the past."

"That'd be fantastic," he replied.

Haas led the way to the elevator and they took it down to the ground level, then walked over to the entrance of Café Cantata. The scents flowing out made Garrett's mouth water and his stomach rumble. He needed sustenance. He couldn't even remember the last time he'd eaten—a late lunch, he thought, before the two fires had kept him out all night.

"Why don't you grab a table? I'll get our order. Large coffee sound good?" Lieutenant Haas asked.

"Yes please." He headed to the back of the café where they would have some quiet and could talk. He peered out of the window, was surprised to see the sun shining and it appearing to be a beautiful day. It was crazy how being inside the hospital made time seem to stand still. While those on the outside went about their days the few inside the cold, sterile building were praying to get out.

Garrett shook himself out of his weird thoughts as Haas headed toward him with a tray. There were two large cups of coffee, a couple of muffins, a breakfast sandwich and a container of creamer on it.

"I wasn't sure how you took it," Haas stated as he set the tray down. "I also suspected that you'd need some food."

"Appreciate it." Garrett reached for the cup first as he needed the caffeine fix. He took several sips, even as it burned his tongue and the roof of his mouth. He finally set it down so he could add a spoonful of sugar and a dash of cream.

Haas chuckled. "Here, eat the sandwich too." He pushed the food toward Garrett.

"Thanks." He dug in and they spent a few minutes in silence as Garrett polished off his entire coffee and the sandwich plus one of the muffins.

"Refill?"

He looked up to the young lady who held up a pot.

"House blend, right?" she asked.

Garrett nodded. He didn't know or care. He just wanted more of whatever wonderful brew they'd created. Now that he'd gotten some sustenance he could think more clearly. He fixed up his second cup before he sat back while the waitress poured more coffee for Haas also. "You said you could tell me something about the case?"

Lieutenant Haas stirred his own coffee before he took his spoon out and set it aside. "I looked into you. You almost completed all the schooling to become an investigator. You put in the time, had top grades before dropping it all to move here. Why?"

This wasn't where he'd thought the conversation would be headed but he didn't have any issues sharing his past. It shouldn't be hard for Haas to figure out his story. He shrugged. "My sister came to stay with me for a while. She had some things to figure out. We became close again and when she moved back here she invited me to visit. I did, and decided I wanted to start over here. It's a good town and my sister and her partner are here."

"It seems like a strange time to start over, when you were just about finished with your training," Haas commented.

Leaving Kermit hadn't been an easy decision, especially when he'd almost accomplished one of his goals. But he knew after he'd become friends with Tom and Steve, as well as the other shifters, that he'd never move up in the ranks of the KFD. There was still too much hatred and fear between the human authorities and the shifters. He'd chosen the shifters' side and that hadn't been the right move for his career in Kermit.

He was still struggling with the feelings of failure for not standing up for shifter rights. Instead he had talked his two best friends into moving to Clear Creek with him. They'd passed on the trouble to someone else. He had to live with that decision—to know that he was selfish enough that he'd picked his own survival over what he believed in. "I wasn't going anywhere there," Garrett said honestly. "Here I can become someone I'm proud of."

Haas smiled. "I'm glad to hear you say that."

"Why's that?" Garrett questioned.

"My partner just retired. Bad timing for it, since this is the first serial arsonist case this city has ever seen," Haas responded.

"Serial arsonist?" Garrett asked. "So it's confirmed? All these fires are connected."

Haas nodded. "It gets worse."

"What?"

"All the buildings belonged to shifters," Haas told him quietly.

"You're shitting me." Garrett had to work to keep his voice down.

Haas leaned forward. "Residential, commercial, all of them were owned by shifters. That is the only connection that I can find."

"Unbelievable." Garrett's stomach dropped and he wished he hadn't eaten all that food.

"From what I've learned about you from your co-workers and captain, you'll have no problem working hard for shifters," Haas said.

"Of course not, my friends as well as my sister's boyfriend are shifters," Garrett said.

"That's why I want you," Haas stated.

"For what?" Garrett had a suspicion but he didn't see how it could work. "I'm not an investigator."

"Your captain has approved you to work as my assistant for the time being," Haas told him. "Provided you wouldn't mind, of course."

Garrett had to tamp down his excitement. Having this opportunity was something he'd only dreamed of, especially with his training not being complete. But he had his hands full and he wasn't sure what was going to happen to Nick. Plus this chance came at the expense of who he'd left behind in Kermit. "I'd like to but..."

"I'll work with anything you currently have going on. I know you're watching over the boy you rescued and I understand."

Relief washed over him. "That's very kind of you. Can I ask, why me?" Garrett knew other firefighters who would jump at the experience Haas was offering.

"I'm a shifter," Haas said.

Garrett waited for more information. When Haas didn't continue, Garrett nodded. "I didn't know that but pardon my asking, what does that have to do with anything?"

Haas grinned. "Your answer was what I expected from you. Cooper Grainger contacted me to help with how the fire departments in Kermit are run. While we work on this case I'd like to get more details from you. I knew you wouldn't have a problem working closely with me because my shifter status."

He was surprised to hear that Cooper had asked Haas for help. When Garrett had first brought it up, Cooper hadn't been sure how to help but had promised to try. Still, Garrett had imagined that Cooper would use his police connections.

"Do you normally work with the officials in Kermit?" Garrett questioned.

"No," Haas replied. "But I have made a lot of contacts in the years I've done this job. I think Cooper is hoping I can use those and my own experiences to see where the biggest problems are."

Garrett was starting to understand. "I really would be open to working this case with you. I'd like to help the shifters still in Kermit as well," he admitted.

"I know," Haas said. "So what do you say about partnering up?"

"I don't have my certification," Garrett reminded him.

"Right now that doesn't matter. With these arson cases, the new mayor has given me leave to pretty much use any resources I come across. He wants this case solved quickly. With all the fallout from the old mayor getting arrested, he doesn't want any more negative publicity than we've had in the last three months," Haas told him.

Garrett hadn't been around when the previous mayor had been arrested for drug trafficking and targeting the shifters. He knew quite a bit about the case because Cooper had been one of the detectives involved in the takedown. "I understand."

"We can call this a trial run for a partnership and see how we work together," Haas suggested. "If we find we make a good team, we'll work out a schedule to get your education and testing completed."

The opportunity was almost too good to believe. It was definitely way too good to pass up. "When do we start?" he asked.

"Let's begin with last night's fire," Haas suggested. "Did you know Nick prior to last night?"

"No, it just happened to have been my turn to search for survivors inside the structure. He just clamped onto me and didn't want me to leave his side," Garrett replied.

"That may be the best thing that boy could have done," Haas said.

"What do you mean?" Garrett asked.

"I assume that the social worker spoke to you last night?"

He nodded as he watched Haas' features. There was something that was bothering him and it worried Garrett.

"I've worked with Lillian before and Nick is in good hands, but I'm not sure how safe he is going to be right now with his dad missing and us not knowing why," Haas stated. "I've spoken to both the Alpha and Randy's business partner this morning. Alpha Jeremy had a security breach last night and Mr. Bolton's law firm was broken into."

Garrett sat back as he sucked in a breath. The case was about so much more than the fire. For the criminals to hit two shifter places that close together, wow, they were looking for something. Or someone. "Are they looking for Nick?"

"No," Haas said quickly. "I don't believe so. The struggle at the house and the break-ins suggest that Randy was taken for a reason. The neighbor that called in the fire also reported seeing Randy taken from the house. We know for sure that his hands were tied and he was barely walking on his own. Like he has something they want. I fear that if whoever took Randy doesn't get what they want, they might come after the boy."

His chest tightened and it was hard for Garrett to breathe. He clenched his hands into fists before forcing his body to take in a long, deep breath. Just the thought of someone hurting Nick made him want to kill them.

Haas remained silent but his gaze was steady with Garrett's.

"The connection between the two of you is unbelievable," Haas noted, his voice full of awe.

"I don't know what it is about him but all my instincts are screaming at me to protect him," Garrett whispered. "I need to make sure that he'll be surrounded by enough security when he leaves here that we don't have to worry about him getting kidnapped. That has to be our first priority." He knew he wasn't in a position to make demands but Nick had to be safe. "I know that Lily is working with the cops but I have to be involved."

"I agree," Haas replied. "I don't think Lily knows about the two instances. When I spoke to our Alpha he stated that Nick was supposed to go over there but he was going to talk to her about other arrangements. He plans to have the Pack spread out over the town so they're visible to anyone who is paying attention to the Pack. He doesn't want to put the kid in harm's way any more than we do."

Garrett opened his mouth to say he'd take him but Haas held up his hand. "I know you're going to offer but I don't think that will work either."

"Why not?" Garrett couldn't keep the hurt from his tone.

"We'll be working a ton of hours and you'll be gone most of the time. He'll need someone to stay with him until this is solved," Haas explained.

Okay so he knew, *knew*, Haas was right but he still wanted the boy close to him.

"Maybe with a cop and an EMT?" he suggested. Julie would probably want to kill him at first but he knew she wouldn't be able to turn away a boy in need. Plus Nick was a part of Cooper's Pack, so Garrett was certain he could get the cop on his side.

"Cooper and your sister? That's" — Haas sat back — "a really good idea. I haven't met your sister yet but Cooper is a great cop."

When he didn't say anything else, Garrett raised an eyebrow. "But?"

"No, no buts." Haas waved his hand as he spoke. "I've spent all morning trying to come up with a solution and you did it for me."

Pride filled Garrett's soul and he couldn't help but smile. It felt good to be appreciated.

"Now we just have to convince Lily," Haas said. "She's by the book and what we're talking about isn't regulation. She'd have to bend some of the rules."

"I saw how much she cares about Nick," Garrett told him. And he had. Lily wasn't what he'd expected when he'd pictured a woman working in social services. For some reason he'd anticipated an older lady who looked like his grandma. He didn't know why he'd thought that but when Lily had walked in with her long blonde hair, clear blue eyes, and cute, pert nose, he'd been shocked. She appeared to be around the same age as he was, but that wasn't what had thrown him for a loop. Lily was stunning.

"She does care," Haas agreed. "We just have to find a way to convince her."

Garrett drained his cup before he held it up to the waitress for a refill. "I'm going to need more coffee."

Haas laughed. "We'll come back to that. What do you know about the other fires?"

* * * *

Lily woke to a small whimper close to her ear. She opened her eyes and saw Nick thrashing but still asleep. She pushed back her chair, moved closer to the small boy and ran her hand over his hair. "Shh," she soothed.

Nick settled before he blinked his eyes open. "Garrett?"

It was sweet that the boy's first thought was of Garrett. "He'll be back, hon."

"He left?" Nick popped up.

"No," she assured him. "Look, his bag is still in the corner there," she told him, pointing to where Garrett had been sleeping. "I bet he just went to get coffee." She couldn't see Garrett taking off without a goodbye to the kid.

"Not just coffee," Garrett announced as he walked in. "I got a chocolate milk here too. I wonder who I'll give it to."

"Me!" Nick cried as he waved his hands.

"Well, I guess you can have it," Garrett teased.

Lily was surprised when he passed her a large to-go cup as he made his way to the bed. "Yum," she murmured as the aroma of the fresh coffee drifted up to her.

"House blend," Garrett said before he winked at her. And damn if her knees didn't go weak.

She didn't care what it was as long as it was brewed strong.

Nick giggled as Garrett reached down and tickled him. Lily found herself smiling as she watched them.

"Okay, little man," Garrett said to Nick. "You drink this and I'll turn on some cartoons for you. I need to speak with Lily for a minute."

"Sure," Nick agreed easily.

Lily sipped on her beverage as Garrett got Nick sitting up in bed with his drink and *Scooby Doo* on the television mounted on the wall. Once Nick was busy, Garrett motioned her into the hall.

Since he had brought her an amazingly good coffee, she rose without question.

"We'll just be in the hall," he called to Nick before following her out and closing the door behind them.

"What's going on?" she questioned as she leaned against the wall.

"I need to talk to you about where you're going to take Nick once he's released," Garrett told her.

Lily had been waiting for this conversation. "I've already spoken to the Alpha of the Pack. He'll take Nick in until we find his dad."

Garrett was shaking his head before she'd even finished her sentence. "That's not going to work."

"And why not?" she asked skeptically. Garrett seemed like a nice guy and he was hot as fuck but he wasn't going to tell her how to do her job.

"Listen," he said as he held up his hands. "I just spoke to Lieutenant Haas. The Alpha compound had a breach last night."

"Oh my god." Lily had to tighten her hand on her cup to keep from dropping it. "Was anyone hurt?"

"No, the guards responded quickly and no one got in. But it might not be safe for Nick. Someone is targeting shifters," Garrett said.

Lily glanced back toward the door that Nick was safe behind. This did complicate matters. She couldn't put Nick in any more danger. It was her job to keep him safe. "Okay, I have other homes I can place him in. Human families that shouldn't be targets."

"They won't be able to protect him. What if whoever took his dad comes back for Nick? That might be what the attempted break-in was about. Plus Randy's business was broken in to," Garrett argued. "He needs to be with shifters but not somewhere that anyone would look for him."

Lily agreed but her choices were limited.

"So here's what we'll do. I put a call into my sister and asked if she and Cooper could take Nick for a few days. They're working different shifts right now so someone will always be with him. Plus we have a couple of buddies, shifters, that will hang out when Julie is alone with Nick," Garrett told her.

Lily wasn't entirely sure how she'd lost the upper hand of the conversation with Garrett but she was determined to let him know that she wouldn't be bullied into doing what he wanted. No, her job was to care for and protect Nick.

"I understand how you feel but it is against department policy to place Nick with someone who is not trained for this type of situation," she told him.

"You were going to place him with his Alpha," Garrett replied.

"Yes, and depending on what Jeremy says about the break-in I still might. He's met all our requirements and is qualified to foster children temporarily. If he's not able to take Nick now, I have other homes that are fully capable of seeing to Nick's needs," she said with confidence. "I can get patrol cops to watch the area."

When he groaned, she had to work to suppress the shudder her body had in reaction to him. Damn, that sound echoed down her spine.

"I understand you care about the boy but so do I," she assured him.

"He needs protection, more than just cops sitting in front of the house. Especially since this guy likes to burn homes to the ground," Garrett argued. "This is a special case. You have to be able to do something."

Lily sighed. They were just going around in circles.

"Let him stay with Cooper and Julie. Cooper's a police officer and he can ensure his safety. Julie is a trained EMT so his health will be looked after. This is the best idea if you really think about it," Garrett repeated his earlier argument.

"It's not just up to me. I have superiors that I have to answer to," she said. She was weakening and knew it.

Garrett's dark eyes softened. He reached out and grasped her elbow. The heat of his palm burned into her flesh. She had to work to control how his touch affected her.

"Try, just please see what you can do."

She was going to give in and it had nothing to do with his damn puppy dog eyes, she tried to tell herself. "I have to call my superior and Jeremy. See what they think."

He grinned. "That's all I ask."

Chapter Three

Garrett glanced up from where he'd spread out his papers and laptop on the kitchen table when the back door to his sister's house opened. Julie was currently at the stove making dinner while he was reading over the files that Haas had brought him.

Cooper entered the kitchen, letting in a cold gust of wind. The warmth of the kitchen against the chill of the fall night had Garrett shivering just a little.

"Shut the door!" Julie called out. "You're letting the cold in."

"Mike, hurry up," Cooper yelled.

Mike Riley came rushing in and closed the door. "Hey." Mike nodded to him. "Good to see you."

Garrett stood and held up his hand. Cooper, of course, had gone straight to Julie to get his welcoming kiss.

"You too," Garrett said to Mike. He'd first met Mike when his sister had thrown a barbecue for hers and Cooper's friends and family to get to know each other. Mike was one of Cooper's best friends from their college days. Garrett had become fast friends with the lawyer.

"Next time we should leave out arson, break-ins and kidnapping and just grab a beer," Mike said.

Garrett lifted an eyebrow in question.

"Randy Bolton is my law partner," Mike explained.

"The break-in?" Garrett asked.

"I don't know what they were looking for but I doubt they found anything. They trashed the place but I didn't find anything missing."

That is weird. Garrett needed to find out how all the shifters were connected. Lieutenant Haas was already starting that line of research and Garrett had a feeling that would be where they found their answers. That didn't mean that he couldn't ask Mike a few questions, even if he wasn't officially assigned to the case until the next day.

Garrett pulled out a chair from the table and motioned for Mike to do the same. Cooper joined them as Julie finished off making dinner. She pulled down plates from the cabinets and he knew they didn't have much time to talk before Nick would come in.

"What's next?" Garrett questioned because if he knew Cooper and Mike they would have a plan.

"Our Alpha is heading out in the morning to California to talk to the Council and ask if they can give us any help. While he's gone we'll continue to look for Randy and protect Nick," Cooper answered.

"It was a good idea bringing Nick here," Mike added.

"It's all I could think of to keep him safe," Garrett admitted. "I feel like it's my responsibility. I don't know why, but I'm going to do it."

"Follow your instincts," Cooper told him.

Garrett knew that shifters believed strongly in fate and instinct. He was glad he had someone to talk to.

While Nick was out of the room, he wanted to mention Nick's social worker too. Lily hadn't been far from his thoughts since they'd separated earlier. She was planning to stop by later to drop off some clothes and stuff for Nick. She'd said it was normal procedure but Garrett had a feeling that this wasn't just an everyday case for her either. The connection between Lily and Nick was as strong as the one he had with the kid.

"You concentrate on finding out who is responsible for these arsons and we'll look for Randy," Cooper told him.

"I'll help with Nick as much as I can," Mike offered. "We're pretty tight—he even calls me uncle, so hopefully he won't feel too out of place."

"That'd be great," Garrett agreed.

"Uncle Mike?" Nick's sleepy voice carried from the doorway.

They all turned toward the small child.

"Hey there, kiddo." Mike stood up from the table with open arms.

Nick rushed forward and launched himself at the lawyer. Mike picked him up and hugged him tight. Garrett watched the two of them and felt a warmth flow through him. Nick had a good support group if the worst happened and he lost his dad.

"Did you find my dad?" Nick asked once Mike had set him down.

"Not yet, buddy," Mike answered. He crouched in front of Nick. "But we won't stop looking."

When Nick nodded slowly before he turned toward Garrett, he knew the kid needed him. He pushed back his chair, intending to stand, but before he had a chance Nick was climbing onto his lap. Garrett slid his arm around the boy's back and held him close.

"Are you about ready to eat?" Julie came up to them and ran her hand over Nick's shaggy brown hair.

Nick shrugged before he buried his face in Garrett's chest. Garrett could feel Nick's body shaking but the waterworks hadn't started yet.

"Hey!" Garrett said to Nick. "Julie made homemade macaroni and cheese. It's our mom's recipe and it rocks."

Nick pulled back a little and peered up at him. "I guess I can eat."

"That's my boy," Garrett praised.

Nick laughed, which is what Garrett wanted.

"Cooper, help me set the table so we can all eat," Julie said after she smiled at them.

"Let's get you washed up," Garrett said, rising with the child still in his arms.

He strolled out of the kitchen, carrying Nick to the hall bathroom. There he set Nick back down before Garrett gripped Nick's shoulder and bent. "It's going to be okay," Garrett assured him.

"What if no one can find my dad? What if he's in heaven with my mommy?" Nick questioned with real fear.

"No," Garrett said while he rubbed Nick's arms. "You can't think like that. Your dad is out there and you have everyone in this town on your side. If anyone can find your dad it's the Pack."

"You'll stay with me until my dad comes back?" Nick asked next.

"As much as I can," he promised. "I have to go to work and try to find who started the fire in your house and some other places. But when I'm not there I will be here."

"Do you live here? You said this is your sister's house."

Wow, this kid is full of questions. Hard questions that Garrett wasn't certain he had answers to or should even be responding to. He really needed to talk to Lily.

"No, I don't live here. I have a place closer to town that I share with two roommates. We're all firefighters so it helps having them there with me to work on the yard and keep up with house," Garrett explained. He didn't know why he was telling Nick so much information when he'd asked a simple question. He just wanted Nick to know that Garrett wasn't going anywhere.

"Can I see your house?"

Garrett laughed. "Sure, as soon as I know you're safe."

"Okay, can we eat now?"

"Let's wash our hands," Garrett suggested. He hoisted Nick up and helped him before following suit. Once done, they walked out of the bathroom and down the hall side by side.

They must have been gone longer than Garrett had thought, since the table had been cleared of his work and set with a steaming bowl of food right in center. They also had an additional guest.

Lily stood at the table laughing at something Julie was saying. It appeared his sister's friendly personality had already drawn Lily in. He enjoyed seeing the women together. Julie was so important to him that whoever he was interested in had to get along with her. And he was more than interested in Lily. She looked beautiful in a long cream sweater with her blonde hair shining and hanging past her shoulders. His fingers actually twitched with the urge to find out if the strands were as soft and silky as they looked. She glanced up as they walked in and her blue eyes met his, causing his steps to falter. As he tripped he had to reach out and grasp Nick's shoulder. The kid looked back at him, grinning. Embarrassed, all he could do was hope that he wasn't blushing. Luckily the others in the room weren't paying him any attention.

"Hi." He smiled as he greeted her.

"Sorry to disturb your dinner," she said as she strolled forward. She crouched down in front of Nick. "I brought some stuff for you."

"Did you get my stuffed wolf? I left him on the bed," Nick asked softly.

"I'll have to check with the fire investigator to see if I can get into the house," Lily said. "I'm not sure how bad the fire damage is."

"You'll try though?" Nick pressed.

"Absolutely," she said. "But for tonight, maybe you'll hang onto this guy?" She walked back toward the doorway where a few bags were piled up. She bent down, and Garrett really wasn't trying to watch the way the soft black pants stretched and showcased her ass, but damn.

As she rummaged through the bags, Garrett reached down and had to adjust his cock, which had hardened seeing her on her knees. Fuck, he barely knew the woman and all he could think about was pushing her down, yanking away any barrier between them and mounting her.

He blinked. Where in the hell had that thought come from? Crap, he really didn't need these thoughts when he was in his sister's crowded kitchen.

"Ah ha!" Lily announced as she pulled something from one of the plastic bags. She turned and offered Nick a rather large, soft-looking stuffed wolf.

"Wow!" Nick rushed forward and took the animal from her.

"I know it can be scary sleeping in a strange place. So I thought this little guy could help you. You can name him and keep him with you," she said.

Nick hugged the stuffed wolf tightly. "Thank you."

"You're very welcome," she said as she ruffled his hair. She looked up at Garrett. "He should have enough clothes for a few days, there's also a new toothbrush and some other things I thought he might like. If you need anything, just let me know and I can bring it over. I'll be over tomorrow to check on him."

She started to step back but Garrett wasn't ready to let her go yet. "Why don't you stay for dinner?" he asked.

"Oh, I don't want to intrude." She waved off his invitation.

"We'd like you to stay." Garrett rested his hand on Nick's shoulder.

The boy bobbed his head in agreement.

"There really is plenty and we can talk a little more," Julie added. She was glancing between Garrett and Lily, and the sparkle in her eyes Garrett knew well. His sister was aware of the attraction between the two of them.

Lily appeared unsure so Garrett nudged Nick forward. The boy went right over and grabbed Lily's hand, pulling her toward the table. "Julie made mac and cheese that her mama used to make for her. It's supposed to be really good."

"Well, how could I say no to that?" Lily asked with a smile.

"Let's eat!" Cooper cried.

Everyone moved around the table until they were seated. Garrett found himself at one end with Cooper across from him. To his right sat Lily and Mike and on the left side of the table Nick and Julie were already passing the dishes around. He was pleased with Lily and Nick being on either side of him as well as Julie leaning over to help Nick load up his plate.

It had been such a long time since he'd sat down for a full family meal that he found himself just watching everyone else at first. Cooper and Mike were talking about something to do with the Pack, Julie handed Lily the platter of fresh bread, while Nick was already digging into the mac and cheese, making smacking noises.

He smiled. He'd missed the last several holidays at his parents', even with Julie being in town at the time. He'd been on the schedule at the fire department. It was just another reminder of the unfairness of how the Kermit captain had treated him and anyone who was a shifter or supported them. The holidays were approaching fast and he knew he'd be welcomed back here with his sister and their new family. Maybe their parents would even be able to make the drive down. Garrett hoped so.

He wondered where Nick would be. Could they find his dad and reunite Nick and Randy before Thanksgiving? Garrett would make damn sure, wherever the boy was, that Nick had the best time possible.

"So what are you going to name your new friend?" Lily asked Nick as she picked up her fork.

Nick glanced over at him. Garrett tilted his head to show he was interested in the answer as well.

"Garrett," Nick said quietly.

Garrett's heart filled with so much love and pride he was actually speechless.

"That's great." Julie hugged Nick.

Garrett managed to nod. This small boy was showing him how much he was missing in his own life. He hadn't thought about settling down yet, although he would love to find someone to share his life with. He glanced at Lily and saw her eyes on him.

When he caught her gaze, she reached out and covered his hand with hers, giving him a squeeze. He closed his fingers over hers and didn't want to let go.

"I think it's wonderful," Lily agreed.

Nick looked at Garrett. "That way I don't forget you when my dad comes back."

"Ah, kid." He released Lily to grasp Nick's hand. "Even when you're home with your dad I won't be going anywhere. We're buds, right?" When Nick mentioned his dad and Garrett saw the hope in his eyes, it was hard not to just gather the small child up and hide him from the world. Garrett prayed that they would find Randy and that Nick would indeed be going back home with his dad.

"Of course." Nick nodded quickly.

"There you go!" Garrett patted his hand before he began to fill his plate. "Now let's eat so we can watch a movie before bed. I'll even let you pick what we watch."

Nick started to bounce in his seat as he began to tell Lily about Cooper and Julie's movie collection.

* * * *

Dinner had been fantastic and Lily had really enjoyed seeing Nick being so accepted and cared for. She'd also liked watching Garrett interact with his family and friends. It felt comfortable and, while Garrett and Julie weren't shifters, the entire evening had had the sense of Pack.

It had been a whirlwind twenty-four hours but as she hugged Nick goodbye and made plans with Julie to meet up the next day, Lily was proud of the job she was doing.

She'd grown up in the foster-care system. Of course that was before the shifters were public, so it had been a lot different for her then than it was now. She hadn't known what the changes her body had been going through meant. If it hadn't been for a teacher in her middle school that had picked up the signs, there was no telling what would have happened to her.

Instead, Mrs. April Summers had watched out for her and when Lily had been ready to shift, she'd gotten in touch with Jeremy's father, Craig, who had been the Alpha of the Pack at the time. Craig had taken her under his wing and made sure she was ready.

It had been hard to hide her shifting ability from her foster family but Lily knew she had been lucky. She could have easily been moved to a larger city that used group homes instead of the family placements that took place in Clear Creek. Craig had even offered to have her moved to a shifter family but Lily had loved the Houstons, who'd taken her in. Plus she'd had two other foster children in the home that she'd been close with. There'd been lots of family dinners, much like what she'd just experienced that night.

"Let me walk you out," Garrett offered, coming up behind her.

Lily hadn't missed the way he'd kept his eyes on her all night. Garrett wasn't very subtle in the way he'd been checking her out. Not that she minded. It was good to know that he felt the same attraction as she did.

She waved one last time before walking out of the front door that Garrett held open for her. The evening had cooled down even more, making her glad she'd worn her most comfortable sweater.

Unlike in most movies and some books, shifters didn't actually have the ability to heal all wounds. They weren't werewolves or whatever mystical creature the media like to portray them as. They were humans who had a slight alteration to their DNA that allowed them to be able to shift. Her parents had died instantly from the crash. She'd been spending the night with a friend as her parents had gone out to dinner to celebrate their anniversary.

Garrett closing the door behind her pulled her from her thoughts and she turned toward him.

"Thanks for asking me to stay for dinner. I enjoyed it," she told him.

"I'm glad you stayed," he replied as he cupped her elbow while they walked down the steps.

"Nick seems to be settling in well," she noted.

"Hmm," he hummed in agreement.

He seemed distracted, so Lily glanced around the property as she attempted to ignore the heat from Garrett's hand on hers. Cooper and Julie had a beautiful house just on the edge of town. The woods around the property were gorgeous, and Lily could only imagine how much enjoyment Cooper felt running in his own back yard, literally. She lived in town, close to her office, and only ran in Pack territory.

The sidewalk was lit by small solar lights, leading them to the drive where she'd parked her car. Lily dug her keys out of her purse and hit the fob to unlock her vehicle. While the actual driveway was dark, there was enough of a moon to allow her to see somewhat around her. In the city there would have been streetlights but so far out they were all alone, especially with the trees that blocked them from the front of the house.

Garrett reached the door first but instead of opening it he turned back around and leaned against it. "Can I ask you a question?"

"Yes." The picture Garrett made, with his muscular arms crossed over his chest and his long legs braced apart, was enough to almost make her drop to her knees right there in the middle of the drive.

He pushed off her car and leaned close. "You feel this too?" he whispered.

Lily wasn't going to play games. She knew exactly what Garrett meant and didn't pretend otherwise. "Yes, it's a new feeling for me but I felt it the second we met."

Garrett nodded. "I didn't think it was a shifter thing but I wanted to make sure."

Lily laughed nervously. "No, I can assure you that this is new for me."

"Thank God!" Garrett said before he pushed himself off the car. He stepped directly in front of her and wrapped his fingers around her waist.

She looked up into his eyes and saw the same need that she knew shone from her eyes back at him. He lowered his mouth slowly, as if giving her time to tell him no or pull away, but Lily had no intention of denying him.

Lily lifted onto her tiptoes and closed the distance. The first touch was soft but as their lips pressed together, Garrett took another step forward and removed the space between them. Lily grasped his shoulders as he licked at her bottom lip. She opened for him, allowing him to sweep his tongue inside her mouth.

She moaned. The bold rich flavor of the coffee from earlier mixed with Garrett's unique taste made her just a tad lightheaded with need. She tightened her hold on him just before he lifted her off her feet and swung her around.

Her back touched the cold metal of her car but she didn't care about the chill as Garrett blocked her in with his big, strong body. She let her head fall back as Garrett moved his lips down her neck. The shudders that ran through her body were caused by the need.

Garrett slid one hand over her ass before he lifted the back of her knee so that she could wrap her leg around his waist. He then hauled her up until she could feel his hard cock against her jean-covered pussy.

God, she wished they were alone and naked. She should really stop him before they got carried away but she couldn't make the words come out of her mouth. Instead, needy moans and whimpers escaped.

"You taste just as good as I suspected," Garrett murmured against her skin.

"Uh," she managed.

He pulled back to peer down at her. "Kiss me again."

She did. This time Garrett buried his hands in her hair and gripped her hard. The slight sting upped her arousal and she growled before nipping his lip. He drew back, grinning before he dove in and slammed his mouth on hers. She humped against him, the front of her jeans pressing against her clit perfectly. Her panties were wet with desire.

"Please," she begged softly as she ripped her mouth away. She didn't know what exactly she was asking for, just something. He was driving her mad.

Garrett cursed then slid his hand under her sweater to the waistband of her pants. His fingers grazed her stomach then, oh yes, he was playing with her clit.

She hiked her leg higher, giving him better access to rub where she really wanted him. He dipped a finger inside her and she sobbed out in relief. He plunged his digit in and out before he added another. Lily was overwhelmed by the arousal but did manage to fumble with his button and zipper so she could fit her hand inside his jeans. It was awkward as she was still riding his fingers while trying to jack him at the same time. It didn't matter though. She was so close.

His legs shook as the tingling in her clit signaled her approaching release. She leaned forward and closed her mouth down on the fabric of Garrett's shirt as she came. He rubbed his thumb over her clit until she sagged against him. She still grasped his erection and he was hard as steel.

Lily lifted her head and was glad for the darkness that surrounded them. Garrett lowered his mouth and this time the kiss was soft and gentle. She started to move her hand again, sliding her palm over him, and swallowed his moan.

She wondered just how many sounds she could pull from him. She planned to find that out later. Lily broke the kiss and nudged him back so she could lower her leg. He'd gripped her so tightly that she wondered if she would have bruises later. If so, she would wear them with pride.

Once there was enough distance between them, she dropped down to her knees. The cold concrete jolted her but she was determined to get his hard cock in her mouth. She tugged on the waistband of his jeans until his erection sprang out. Holding the base with her right hand, she licked at his mushroomed head. The saltiness of his pre-cum was unique and all Garrett.

Garrett slid his fingers through her hair to grip her head. Lily stopped teasing his cockhead and lowered her mouth down on him. She pulled back, sucking hard, and Garrett groaned loudly. She repeated the move faster and with more suction until he was thrusting into her mouth and she knew he was on the very edge.

As his hips faltered, she reached up and rolled his balls with her free hand.

He cried out just before he pulled away and covered her hand with his. Together they jerked his cock until he spilled onto the concrete beside her. Lily watched him the entire time.

Once spent, he fell to his knees beside her and gathered her into his arms. Lily rested her cheek against his chest.

"I want to take you home and lay you in my bed but I promised Nick I would stay here," he said.

"I understand."

Garrett placed his hand under her chin and raised her face. "This isn't a one off. I want to see more of you."

She grinned. "I guarantee it."

Chapter Four

Garrett sipped his second cup of coffee as he once again reviewed the case notes. Haas was on the way to pick him up and he wanted to be completely ready. His body still hummed from the night before, and with the house quiet around him it took everything in him to concentrate and not think back to how sexy Lily had been, lost in passion.

His cock had been half hard all morning and that was after he'd jacked off in the shower earlier. He'd hated to watch Lily go but until they found Randy Bolton and whoever was responsible for the arsons, he didn't know how much time they'd have to spend together.

The reasons for solving this case fast were starting to pile up. The advance in his career, getting to spend more time with Lily and most important was reuniting Nick with his father.

He'd peeked in on Nick before he'd come downstairs and the boy had been curled up in the middle of the bed with his new wolf cradled in his arms. It was adorable.

"You're up early," Cooper said as he entered the kitchen.

Garrett grinned. "Haas is on his way. We wanted to get an early start. Coffee's fresh."

Cooper stopped in the middle of the kitchen and took a deep breath. "Oh God! I don't know when the last time there was coffee that I didn't have to make first thing in the morning."

"Julie has never been a morning person, even before she took the night shift," Garrett said.

"That's why she took it," Cooper agreed. "I don't mind. Most of my work takes place at night. That's when most of the deals are made and when trouble hits the streets. I've been working days for a couple of weeks now and I'm getting pretty sick of not seeing her enough. I can't wait until White and Johnson get back from vacation."

As a narcotics detectives in a city that had a lot of tourists who came to party, Cooper and his partner, Josiah, were busy. He could see how Cooper and Julie made their relationship work. They both had devoted their lives to helping others and had still managed to find love and each other.

Garrett knew he'd be lucky if he ever found what they had, but he had hopes. The previous evening with Lily was one of the best he could remember.

Cooper filled his mug before walking over to sit at the table across from him. "You know that you moving here means the world to her," Cooper said.

Garrett closed the folder he'd been reading and took in Cooper. It was obvious in the way that Cooper was watching him that he had something to say to Garrett.

"I think it's worked out for the best," Garrett agreed.

"She was worried about you after she came back here. We've discussed how the Kermit Fire Department treated you but I don't think you told Julie everything."

"No," Garrett agreed. "She had enough going on trying to win you back."

Cooper shook his head. "She didn't have to do more than return. My heart always belonged to her."

Garrett believed him. When Julie had found out about Cooper's ability to shift she'd freaked out. It had been before the shifters had announced their presence and she hadn't known what to think. The time she'd spent in Kermit with him had strengthened Garrett and his sister's bond, but Garrett hadn't been certain Cooper would be able to forgive her for taking off.

Cooper had and Garrett was grateful that his sister now had her true love.

"She might not have come back if you hadn't pushed her," Cooper told him.

"She was miserable," Garrett replied honestly.

"What I'm trying to say is that I have you to thank for giving her the nudge she needed. You're family," Cooper said.

"Thanks." Garrett wasn't sure what else he could say.

"Sure," Cooper said. "So if there's anything you're not sure about or have questions on you can come to me."

Garrett picked up his mug and leaned back in his chair. There was so much happening in his life. What was Cooper hinting at? "Okay."

Cooper grinned. "You know shifters have increased senses don't you?"

"Yes." Garrett frowned. "And..."

"You were gone a while last night walking Lily out. When you returned I could smell her on you," Cooper said.

He could feel the embarrassment heat his cheeks as he blushed. After he'd returned to the house the night before he had gone straight to the bathroom to clean up.

Obviously his efforts hadn't fooled everyone. "Well...I..."

Cooper laughed. "It's okay, man. I know exactly how you feel."

Garrett held up his hands. He so didn't want to know anything about Cooper and Julie's sex life.

"All I'm saying is that I've been there. You have a connection with Lily. If there's anything you want to talk about, I'm here for you."

Garrett set his mug down. "I really appreciate it. I don't know why what I feel for Lily is so strong. I just want to get to know her better. There's something about her," he admitted. "But I have to find out who is responsible for these fires. I want to get Nick back home."

"We're heading out again this morning to track down any leads. Julie has a few days off so she'll stay with Nick, and Tom is heading over after his shift," Cooper said. "You just concentrate on your job. Everything else will work out. I don't see Lily going anywhere."

That was exactly what Garrett needed to hear. A horn honked out front so Garrett stood and gathered up his laptop and the files. He slipped them into his backpack before he picked up his cup. He strolled to the sink, as he thought about his and Cooper's conversation. After he rinsed out his mug he turned to Cooper. "Thanks," he said.

Cooper waved him off. "We'll call if we get anything."

Garrett grabbed his gear and walked out. Once out of the front door, he jogged to the idling SUV. Haas nodded at him after he'd opened the passenger door. "You ready for this?"

"Yes, I've read through the cases several times. I think we should start with the law office," he suggested.

"Break-ins aren't really in our jurisdiction," Haas pointed out.

"It's all connected," Garrett said. He knew in his gut that the key to finding the person or persons responsible was through Randy and Mike's office. There was a reason that Randy had been taken. No other fires had been set with residents on the premises.

"Okay, spell it out for me," Haas told him.

"What do an abandoned building, a closed hardware store and two family houses have in common? That's the approach I'm taking," Garrett said.

"All the properties were owned by shifters," Haas replied.

"I did a search on the owners. Randy represented the owners of the hardware store in a case when they were sued by an employee that claimed to have been hurt while on duty. The courts sided with the owners that the employee had actually been injured while off on his own time. Mike told me last night that he is currently on the counsel for the owners of the building where a company out of California is trying to buy the land. That property was damaged by arson then we have Randy's house," Garrett said.

"That's good. So the fire that the law firm haven't been connected to is the other house fire," Haas stated.

"I didn't find anything in the public records so maybe we should ask Mike about them," Garrett suggested.

"I agree," Haas replied.

Garrett glanced out of the window as Haas drove them closer to town. He felt really good about his input and he was pleased that Haas was listening to him. The main street leading into downtown Clear Creek wasn't busy this early in the morning. Garrett knew that later the restaurants would be packed and the tourists would be going from shop to shop picking up their souvenirs and trinkets.

The tourists brought in a lot of money for the town, using the forests and nature preserves as hiking trails and relaxing in the beautiful scenery. Until Garrett had moved there he'd never visited the city and now he regretted it. Clear Creek was a wonderful little oasis, but what made it so great were the residents. They were a strong community that relied on one another and Garrett wanted to do his best for them. He vowed that no more residents would live in fear of the arsonist that was haunting them.

As they passed the local bakery, three men in suits sat at an outside table enjoying the morning and laughing together. One of them could be the guy they were after. It could be anyone. They needed to figure out that last piece to connect all the fires and hopefully that would lead them to where Randy was.

"Should we call ahead?" Garrett asked as Haas turned onto the street where Mike's law office was. He was only two blocks from downtown so they would be pulling up within minutes.

"Mike's always in early," Haas told him. "Man works more than I do."

"That's right," Garrett said. "You know Mike from the Pack?"

"Yes," Haas agreed. "We hang out a little on the weekends when we can, too."

"I was able to ask him a few questions at dinner. I saw him last night but I didn't want to bring up too much in case Nick walked in," Garrett said.

"That's smart. That boy's been through enough," Haas said.

Mike's BMW was already parked when they pulled into the small lot in front of the building. Another vehicle was next to Mike's but Garrett didn't recognize who it belonged to. Garrett grabbed his backpack and swung it over his shoulder as he exited the SUV.

The office was lit up but there was no one at the reception desk.

"Hey, Mike!" Haas called out.

When there was no answer, Haas shrugged and Garrett followed him past the empty desk into the hall. There were three doors closed but Garrett could hear voices coming from behind one. As they got closer, the fact that Mike was in the middle of an argument was obvious. So was the detail that it was a woman's voice bickering back.

"I can't help you," Mike said loudly before Haas knocked on the door.

There was a moment of silence, some shuffling, before it was cracked ajar and Mike stuck his head out. "Oh. Hi, guys."

Garrett couldn't see past Mike but now his curiosity was killing him.

"Sorry to intrude so early but we were hoping to catch you before you got started for the day," Haas explained.

"Yeah, sure." Mike glanced over his shoulder before opening the door.

Garrett was shocked to see Shelby Holt, the local reporter, standing next to Mike's desk. Garrett had met the gorgeous lady several times, as she was one of Julie's best friends. The reason he was surprised to see her in Mike's office was that it was common knowledge that the two of them couldn't stand one another. So it didn't make sense that the two of them were meeting early in the morning in private. Especially when it appeared that they hadn't just been arguing. Mike's tie was crooked and while Shelby was dressed gracefully, there were wrinkles in her skirt. Garrett didn't know what to think but he was aware whatever was going on was none of his business.

"Hey, Shelby," Garrett greeted.

"Gentleman," she replied back with a nod.

Mike turned to Shelby. "Maybe we can continue this discussion later?"

Shelby ran her gaze over Garrett, then Haas and finally Mike. "Sure."

No one said anything as she picked up her purse and on those needle heels strolled out of the room. Even though Garrett wasn't interested in her and didn't find her nearly as attractive as Lily, he couldn't take his eyes off her as she exited. There was just something about Shelby that screamed class.

"Sorry to interrupt," Haas said to Mike, which pulled Garrett's attention back to the men.

"It's okay," Mike said while straightening his tie and frowning. "Our conversation wasn't going anywhere."

Garrett wanted to offer his ear but refrained. Maybe he'd call Mike later, since Mike looked like he needed a friend.

"We wanted to discuss the break-in and your firm's connection to the arson fires," Haas stated.

"Connection?" Mike asked and motioned for them to sit.

Garrett waited until Haas took the left chair before dropping down into the right. They faced the desk as Mike slid into his own chair.

Haas nodded at Garrett.

Garrett scooted up in his chair as he pulled his backpack onto his lap. He took out the case file and opened it. "Your firm represented the Wilson Hardware firm in a lawsuit against Ralph Money."

"Randy handled that case but he spoke to me about it. The owner, Carl Wilson, had an employee that he wrote up for missing some shifts. Carl was about to fire him, he suspected him of using drugs, and Mr. Money kept screwing up orders. Instead Ralph claimed an injury and tried to sue but we proved he'd actually gotten it on a camping trip with some friends. We obtained some paperwork from when Ralph first had the injury treated."

"Did you have any contact with Mr. Money after the trial?" Haas questioned.

"He yelled some profanities and made some rude remarks afterwards but no, we never heard from him again that I know of," Mike said.

"What can you tell us about the sale of the property you're currently handling? The Hampton place out north," Haas asked.

"I can't give you too much information since it's still in negotiations. All I can really say is that a company out of California wants the land pretty damn bad. The owners hadn't even thought about selling and are taking their time on deciding. The company believes they just want more money but that's not it," Mike explained.

"What is the problem?" Garrett questioned.

"The owners? You'll have their information in your records from the fire, I'm sure," Mike said.

"Rodney and Greg Hampton," Haas supplied.

"Greg is all for selling while Rodney wants to keep the property. It's been difficult to negotiate the offer."

"Anything feel kinky about the offer?" Haas asked.

"No, I've done enough of these that it's pretty routine," Mike responded.

"How about the Franks family?" Haas questioned.

"Franks?" Mike repeated.

"Victor or Lucy Franks?" Garrett said.

"Those names don't sound familiar at all," Mike said.

Garrett shuffled through a few pages before he saw another name. "Alex Franks?"

Mike started to shake his head before his eyes widened. "Wait! I know that name!" He picked up papers and shuffled through them then threw them back down. "Damn it! Where have I heard that name before?" Mike jumped up and raced from the room.

Garrett exchanged a confused look with Haas before they rose and ran after him. The door across from his office was open. Garrett reached the door first and gasped at the sight of the disaster. Filing cabinets were turned over, papers littered the floor and pictures hung at weird angles. Mike was mumbling to himself as he searched the desk.

"Is this from the break-in?" Haas asked.

Mike glanced up for a split second. "Yes, we cleaned the reception area and my office first. We were going to work on Randy's office today." He pounded his fist on the desk. "I think I recognize the name but I'm not sure. I need some time to sort through this mess."

"Sure, we appreciate any help you can give," Haas replied.

"Give me a few hours and I'll give you a call. This afternoon I'm on one of the search party teams but I'll find why that name rings a bell," he promised.

"Thanks, man," Garrett said sincerely.

"Sure." Mike waved them off. "Now get out of here. I'll call you."

Haas gripped Garrett's shoulder so he turned and followed the investigator down the hall and out of the door.

"The law firm is the connection," Garrett said after he was back in Haas' SUV.

"Let's head to the Bolton house before I take you into my office," Haas suggested.

He nodded in agreement. "He might have taken some files home. That might be why whoever started the fire did so."

"I agree," Haas said.

He grabbed his backpack and pulled out a small notebook. Garrett wanted to get his thoughts down. They now knew that the connection was Randy, Mike and the law firm. That was more than they'd had the day before. He also wanted to go back and search through the files for everything on the names that Mike had given them. He was especially interested in the young man who'd tried to sue the owners of the hardware store. The threats he'd made could have led to going after the lawyers. The question was how they would connect with the other fires.

As Garrett scribbled down the avenues he wanted to proceed, Haas drove them toward the Bolton house. By the time they pulled up in front of the half-burnt structure, Garrett was done and replacing his notebook. He climbed out of the vehicle before swinging his backpack over his shoulder.

Garrett paused halfway up the walk to the house. It was funny how when he went back to a house that had been on fire it always struck him how different the place looked when there wasn't smoke or flames billowing out. Or without the firefighters, cops and other authorities that were always out during a fire.

What he'd worried would be a complete loss now sat tall with minimal damage.

"The kitchen and living room are the worst," Haas told him. "They'll be able to fix them up."

Garrett nodded. At least Nick wasn't going to lose his home. Well, if they found his dad. No one had told Nick how bad it could be. Randy might already be dead. Garrett hoped not. He wanted to reunite Nick with his dad, but sometimes the evil in the world won. "Let's find something."

He followed Haas up to the porch. It wouldn't be until they got inside the house that they really had to be cautious in case the structure was unstable.

Haas unlocked and pushed open the door, allowing Garrett to enter first. He pulled his flashlight from the front pocket of his bag and turned it on. There wouldn't be any electricity until the structure was inspected to ensure there weren't electrical issues that could cause another fire.

The interior of the house was damp from the water that had been sprayed. The scent of the soot filled the area and made his eyes water. He glanced over his shoulder but noted that Haas didn't seem to be having any problems. That surprised him, since he knew that shifters had better senses than humans.

"Let's see if he has an office here," Haas suggested.

Garrett nodded. It was a good bet that Randy did, being a lawyer. They passed the room that he'd found Nick in, the next was what appeared to be the master bedroom.

The cops were right. It was clear that a struggle had taken place. Items were littered on the floor, a lamp had been knocked over and even a picture had fallen.

"They took him from here," Garrett guessed.

"Looks like it," Haas agreed.

Garrett continued on past the bathroom to the only other entrance. The place was wrecked, just as Randy's office had been. Someone had been looking hard for something and since they'd taken Randy, they probably hadn't found it yet.

"What do they want?" he asked out loud.

"Whatever it is, we need to find it," Haas said.

"I'll take the right side of the room," Garrett offered.

"Okay."

Garrett set his backpack down on the desk and crouched beside it. There wasn't much water damage in here but it was a mess. He started to shuffle through the papers and found several legal documents and hand-written notes. He quickly scanned them before stacking them out of the way. He moved on to the next pile and saw that Haas was doing the same thing over on his side of the room. He left the broken pieces of furniture alone and stepped over them, going to the filing cabinet at the corner on his side.

He pulled open the top drawer but it was empty. The second and third were as well, so he guessed that was where all the papers on the floor had come from.

The bottom drawer's handle was bent, and when he tried to open it, it stuck. He yanked harder but it still wouldn't budge. He peered over his shoulder at Haas. "Help me with this?"

Haas dropped the pages in his hand onto the desk before making his way over. "Grab a hold of the cabinet so it doesn't tip," Haas said.

Garrett braced the cabinet against the wall as Haas bent and tried to pull it open. Haas gave a few more tugs before he shook his head. "It's not budging. Someone obviously tried before us. I really want in there."

"Hang on," Garrett said before rushing over to his bag. He pulled out the knife he had hidden in an inner zipper pocket. It was as long as he could legally carry and should work. He flicked it open before handing it to Haas. "Let's see if we can pry it open."

Haas shoved the blade into the opening and at the same time used what Garrett could only describe as shifter strength, and a loud pop sounded. The drawer came falling out as the knife dropped.

"Damn," Garrett said, impressed.

"I hope I don't have to pay for that." He pointed down at the drawer that was hanging off its hinges.

"I think if we find Randy he'll forgive us breaking his filing cabinet," Garrett told him.

Haas snorted. "Good point."

Garrett dropped to his knees and peered inside the now open drawer. All that was inside was a gray metal lockbox. "There's not a bomb in it?" he asked, only half joking.

Haas shoved his shoulder. "Just pick it up."

He did so before he cautiously shook it. It didn't sound like anything too heavy was inside.

"I think it's just papers," Haas said as he leaned forward.

"Great, more paperwork to go through," Garrett bitched. The small latch had a padlock. He raised an eyebrow at his partner.

With a heavy sigh, Haas picked the knife back up and in only a couple of seconds had the lock open. Garrett lifted the lid. Inside was one manila file folder. He picked it up and opened it as he sat back onto his butt. It was a legal document and the names jumped out at Garrett.

He glanced over his shoulder, Haas reading from behind him. "I guess we know where to start," Garrett said.

"I need to call the Alpha," Haas told him.

Garrett's cell started to ring. He dug the device out of his pocket and saw Mike's name on the caller ID. "I bet he found what we did."

Haas grinned. "Let's get things moving. We'll get that boy reunited with his dad soon."

Chapter Five

Lily moved the bag of breakfast sandwiches to her other hand as she tried to balance the drink carrier of lattes so she could knock on the front door. She also had her laptop bag with her papers inside. She could hear Nick yell before the big wooden door was opened.

Nick stood grinning at her. "Did you bring me a sausage and cheese biscuit like I asked?"

She laughed. "You bet." Lily was glad she'd called ahead and asked Julie if it'd be okay if she brought breakfast for her visit. The smile on Nick's face was worth the wait in the busy café.

"Come on!" Nick grabbed the bag out of her hand and raced away.

Lily shook her head at his energy so early in the morning. She'd slept great the night before and could only credit Garrett for that. She'd been exhausted by the time she'd made it back to her apartment, had barely been able to undress and pull down the covers. With the unpredictable hours that her job required it was hard for her to maintain a relationship. If she met a man that wasn't in some kind of public service career she found that they quickly got tired of her having to leave in the middle of a date or the night. The only serious relationship she'd had had ended over a year ago. She'd dated a police officer who was also a member of the Pack. Evan had understood the obligations she'd had as he also had the same. Lily didn't know when it had happened but somewhere in the time they'd been seeing each other their relationship had turned more to friendship instead of them being lovers. They'd tried a little longer to bring the passion back but it had been a fruitless effort. They remained the best of friends but that was it.

She had hope that Garrett wouldn't be threatened by her work like some of the others. He didn't seem like the type that'd stray because she wasn't around. Add in the fact that he was putting his case before the start of anything with her, as he should, spoke of like-mindedness.

That hadn't stopped her from pulling out her favorite vibrator that morning and fantasizing that it was him pleasuring her instead of her toy. She'd climaxed hard with his name on her lips. Now she couldn't wait to see him again. She knew that he wouldn't be at his sister's this morning but she could still pick up traces of his scent in the air.

Julie came around the corner and smiled. "You better hurry or Nick's likely to eat all the food."

"He was pretty excited," she agreed. She held up the carrier with the three to-go cups. "I bought the adults lattes."

"Awesome!" Julie took the drinks and turned back toward the kitchen.

Lily hurried to follow behind. Nick was pulling out the wrapped packages and setting them in the middle of the table. Tom stood over his shoulder helping as

Nick talked non-stop. "My dad takes me to the café every Sunday to get these sandwiches," Nick said as he climbed onto his knees to be higher in the chair.

Lily was even happier that she was able to bring something to Nick that meant so much. She hoped that Garrett, Cooper and the others were closer to finding Randy. The last few days had been hard on the boy but that was nothing compared to what Nick would go through if Randy wasn't found.

The Pack was searching the city up and down but last she'd heard there'd been no sign of where Randy could have been taken. She'd placed a call to the Alpha on her way over and even he had sounded more worried than he had before.

"Well, I hope to see you both there soon," Tom told Nick. "I've only been there a couple of times but every meal I've eaten has been fantastic."

"My dad says we go once a week 'cause it's a tradition," Nick shared.

"Tradition?" Julie corrected gently.

"Yeah! That!"

Lily laughed. "That is important," she agreed.

Nick started to put his food toward his mouth but paused. "I'm gonna see my dad again, right?"

"We're doing everything we can," Lily assured the boy.

"Okay," he said then stuffed his sandwich into his mouth.

The smile on her face didn't seem to want to go away. Lily opened her own breakfast and began to eat. "So what do you have planned for today?" she asked after swallowing her last bite.

"Tom's going to show me how to breathe," Nick answered.

Lily glanced up at the other shifter.

"Relaxing techniques," Tom clarified.

"That's a good idea," she said and meant it. With everything that Nick was going through, the last thing they needed was for the boy to shift. The trauma of not knowing how to control the animal or transform back to human could devastate the boy.

Most shifters changed for the first time when they hit puberty. Of course, a small percentage transformed earlier or later than that. But as young as Nick was, he hadn't started the training provided by the Pack to make sure he was ready. He still had a few years so Tom's help would come in handy. Especially if the worst happened and Randy wasn't found soon and wouldn't be coming home to Nick.

"Then Julie said she'd play some board games with me. She has them all!"

Julie laughed. "Maybe not all but we do have a lot. We host a lot of barbecues with the Pack."

"Maybe I can come next time," Nick said.

"You'll be the very first invited," Julie told him.

"Thanks!" Nick bounced in his chair. "You wanna play?" he asked turning toward Lily.

"I'd love to but I have to go to work," she replied. She made a pouty face. "If I don't, my boss will show up here looking for me."

"They can play too," Nick offered.

"That's very sweet," Lily ran her hand over Nick's hair. He was such a kind boy. She wanted to meet Randy and tell him what a fine job he was doing raising Nick.

Tom's cell rang, drawing their attention. He pulled the phone from his back pocket to glance at the screen. "I've got to take this," he told them before he stood and exited the kitchen.

"Is there anything that you need, now that you've had time to go through the bags I brought last night?" she asked, getting to the purpose of her visit.

Nick shook his head while Julie smiled at her.

"I think we have everything we need. I washed the clothes you brought earlier so he'll have plenty of clean ones. I always wash new items since there is no telling where the store kept them. He loves his stuffed wolf," Julie said.

"When I got scared last night I hugged him like Garrett told me and I felt better," Nick said.

"That's good." Lily patted his hand. "That's why I brought him to you."

"I think my dad will like him too," Nick said.

Tom entered the room, and Lily could easily pick up the scent of excitement. "Hey, buddy, why don't you wash up and meet me in the living room."

"'Kay," Nick said as he climbed down from his chair.

"What is it?" Lily asked after Nick was gone.

"That was Garrett. They think they've found the guys. They're getting ready to go after them," Tom said.

Lily jumped up. "Really?"

"That's great." Julie was next to her.

Tom strolled closer. "Hopefully Randy will be there. They found an abandoned property that would be perfect for hiding someone," Tom said quietly.

Lily glanced back toward the doorway that Nick had gone through. "Let's pray."

Tom nodded. "I'll stay here and make sure no one comes after the boy. They'll call as soon as they know for sure."

"Can you stay?" Julie asked her.

"Of course," Lily replied. "We'll want to see how Randy is doing but our first priority is to reunite Nick with his dad." She would have to call into the office but she had no doubt that her boss would want her with Nick while the cops did their job.

"I'm going to try to keep Nick and myself distracted. I'm going to go ahead and work with him. We don't know what condition Randy will be in," Tom said.

"Yeah," Lily agreed. No matter what, Nick would need to see his father to know that he'd really been found.

"I'll make some more coffee," Julie offered.

"Thanks," Tom said before he went to join Nick.

Lily walked back to the table and sat. "I hope this is really it."

"Garrett wouldn't give us false hope. They must have something solid if he's calling Tom," Julie stated.

Just hearing Garrett's name had Lily's body flushing with heat. Julie laughed, making her glance up.

"I used to react the same way when anyone mentioned Cooper. Should I ask what your intentions are toward my brother?" Julie teased.

"Depends," Lily joked back. "Are you asking about the next forty-eight hours or long-term?" Because she knew how she wanted to celebrate with Garrett. Her plan would involve the closest flat surface and her and Garrett naked. She probably shouldn't mention that to Julie.

"Forget I asked," Julie grinned while waving her hand in the air.

* * * *

Garrett watched as more Pack members showed up at Haas' office to help with the search that they were heading up. Cooper and his partner, Josiah, had been the first to arrive, followed closely by the Alpha, Beta and several guards. It was lucky that the Clear Creek police and fire departments had so many shifters in their employment. But he wasn't certain that would've mattered anyway. He had a feeling that the Pack would have shown up either way. Garrett spotted Steve entering the office and rose to check in with his friend.

"Tom's going to stay at your sister's house to make sure she and the kid are safe. The social worker is over there too. Hopefully by the time we get through with this that boy will have his dad to go home with," Steve told him.

He had to hope. Garrett didn't know how most of the cases like this turned out but he wanted Nick to go home even if Garrett would miss him. He hadn't been lying when he'd told Nick that Garrett would be around. Now that he'd spent time with the boy he had an interest in ensuring that Nick remained happy and healthy. He was going to do his best for the child. Since they were Pack and Garrett was allowed to mingle and attend Pack functions due to his sister, he wouldn't lose track of Nick.

"I don't want to get his hopes up but I really think we'll find Randy on this property," Garrett confessed. "It just makes the most sense."

"So we're not dealing with shifters? And this threat isn't to shifters, just to Randy specifically?" Tom asked.

"From all the intel we gathered, Randy has been the target the entire time. Ralph Money went up against him in court. He'd been injured and tried to sue his employer. He'd been hurt on a camping trip with some friends. Randy interviewed those guys and that's when he first met Rodney Hampton and Alex Franks."

"How'd they go from a lawsuit to arson and kidnapping?" Steve questioned.

"We're guessing they set the fire to keep the company in California from buying up the property. If the property was damaged it wouldn't be worth as much. He didn't want to sell while his brother did," Garrett explained.

"Okay, I can see that," Steve agreed.

"Moving to the next fire we come across Alex's motive to help. Alex is estranged from his family so we assume the house fire was to hurt his parents. His parents found a journal from a long time ago that Alex had written several posts in about wanting to purposely burn down the house. They'd given it to Randy to hold since Randy was handling all their legal papers. Alex's parents thought right away that their son might be responsible. Randy had the journal in case the cops wanted it later. The file we found from Randy's place makes it appear that Randy was collecting evidence against Alex."

"Once you know who all the players are it isn't difficult to connect," Steve said.

"Yeah, they were going to get caught one way or another. They made too many mistakes. Still, I don't think they're the sharpest guys. One name led to another to the next. They all went against Randy at some point. Add in that each one was involved in the place that the fires happened and it just clicks together. Not sure what they thought would happen after they kidnapped Randy," Garrett replied.

"Maybe they were going to blame the fires on Randy?" Steve guessed.

Garrett shook his head. "I don't think so. They would have had to make sure Randy didn't have an alibi for each one. I don't think these guys are that organized."

"Huh." Tom scratched the top of his head. "Money?"

"That's a possibility," Garrett said. "Or maybe they just hated him and wanted to make sure he disappeared. I don't think they planned on the Pack getting involved."

"Then they don't know anything about our Pack," Steve told him. "We wouldn't have given up searching."

"Thank God," Garrett said. "But I don't think they know much about shifters. I can't really explain why I believe that but it's my gut feeling."

"So basically this just comes down to a bunch of punks burning shit down and targeting Randy?" Steve asked.

Garrett's gut cramped. "Yeah."

"That's fucked up," Steve stated.

"I know."

"Sullivan!" Haas called from across the office.

"I'll catch up with you in a bit." Garrett patted his friend's shoulder before jogging over to his partner. "What's up?" he asked as he reached Haas, Cooper and Josiah.

"The CCPD is going to run this operation and we'll stand as back up," Haas said. "You can't carry since you don't have your investigator qualifications yet so I want you to stay with one of the shifters as much as you can. You're standing second entry team so the place will be secure before you move in."

"You think they'll be dangerous?" he questioned.

"Yes, they kidnapped someone. There is no telling what condition Randy is in. Once we get inside, your job is to help the team find him. The shifters with you should be able to pick up on his scent. The ambulance will be close by," Haas answered.

Haas pointed at a map. Once Mike had told them about the property that Alex's uncle had owned and was still abandoned, they'd had a pretty good idea that was where they would be hiding. They'd downloaded the property blueprints from the county clerk. Mike having told them that the buyers wouldn't be back for another three weeks made it almost obvious where Randy could be hidden. The Pack would be able to pick up any sign of him and they could go into the rescue and arrest with an advantage. "Here's where you'll enter," he said. "I'll go in the front doors with CCPD."

Garrett nodded.

"We're ready to go," Cooper called out to them.

Garrett followed his partner, feeling the excitement rush through his blood. His adrenaline was high as he climbed up in the back of the van that would take them to the property. This was even better than fighting fires. There was just something about the investigating part that had always been a draw to him. He liked putting the pieces of the puzzle together and making sure the bad guys couldn't hurt anyone again. He would've gone into police work but he also enjoyed actually fighting the fires — well, saving a family home or a business that the victims had put all their heart and soul into. At five years old, when he'd gotten a bright red fire engine for Christmas, he'd been determined to wear the uniform.

Inside the van with him were four other men. If Garrett understood correctly, they were all shifters. He was the only one that wasn't armed and that pissed him off. On the one hand, if he'd have finished his qualifications he'd be able to go in with the full team taking down the suspects. However, he'd never regret his decision to come to Clear Creek. He'd just have to make sure that he buckled down and finished his training.

"Hey, man, I'm Johnny."

Garrett shook the hand of the tall red-headed man next to him. "Garrett," he replied.

"You're Julie's brother, right?"

"Yep."

Johnny laughed as he bobbed his head up and down. Garrett would place Johnny's age in his early twenties. Johnny had a puppy quality to him but Garrett would never admit that out loud. He didn't want to insult the man even though Garrett found it endearing. "She's made Cooper real happy. We're thrilled they're back together. Welcome to the family."

Johnny appeared so genuine that Garrett had to grin back. That was what he liked about the Pack. They were so welcoming. He hoped, if a relationship developed with Lily, that he'd be just as accepted as her partner. "Thanks," Garrett said sincerely.

"Just stick with me," Johnny said. "We'll have some fun and get Randy back home to his boy."

"Sounds good to me," Garrett agreed. He leaned back, resting against the side of the van.

His partner sat in front of him writing in a small notebook. Haas glanced at him and winked before getting back to it. The van didn't have any windows so Garrett couldn't follow where they were. He pictured the drive to the old property in his mind. It would only take the team ten minutes to get to their position to gather before entering the property. The time seemed to fly by. Garrett shook himself from his thoughts as the vehicle slowed before it came to a stop.

"Stay here," Haas ordered then made his way to the back doors just as they opened.

Haas jumped down. Two men met him at the end of the van and they all leaned in together to talk. Garrett wished he had enhanced hearing like the shifters.

Instead he just rubbed his hands together in anticipation.

"Ready?" Johnny asked as he bumped Garrett's shoulder.

"Yeah, can you hear what they're talking about?" Garrett questioned.

"Haas sent a couple of boys to keep an eye out while we got organized. There's an old house with one man that keeps peeking out the front window. That's where we think Randy is being held. No other suspects have been spotted," Johnny whispered.

"So the place isn't empty, that's good news," Garrett said.

"This is it," Johnny replied. "I just have a feeling."

"I sure hope so," Garrett said. "I want to get the kid back to his dad."

"I'd heard you've gone above and beyond for the boy. Everyone's talking about how you even had him placed with your sister and Cooper. You impressed a lot of the Pack."

"I just wanted him safe," Garrett told him.

"And that's how we knew you were one of us." Johnny slapped his shoulder just as Haas climbed back inside the van. The doors closed behind him and Haas grinned at Garrett.

"It's on," Haas said.

Garrett blew out a breath that he hadn't been aware he'd been holding. It was on indeed. Hopefully Randy could make it another hour or even less. They were only minutes away from his rescue.

The van started moving, and Garrett slammed his hand down on the seat between him and Johnny. The shifter chuckled next to him as they lurched to the side.

"Hang on, boy," Johnny teased.

Garrett huffed but resisted sparring with the man.

"We're pulling in," the driver called back.

"The van will park at the side of the house. I'm with team one and we'll head to the front. Garrett, you're with team two and will hit the back. There will be two more squads covering the sides," Haas explained.

"There won't be any mistakes," Johnny promised.

"No, there won't," Haas repeated.

The sound of the tires grew louder when they moved off the blacktop to the dirt road leading up to the house.

"Countdown," the driver hollered back.

Garrett closed his eyes and started to count backward. When he got to ten he could feel the men around him tense in anticipation. *Five...four...three... two...one.*

The doors flew open, and Garrett joined the others in jumping out of the van with Johnny by his side. They raced around the side of the house to the flimsy back door. Two of the officers yanked the screen wide before one of them put their boot in the side and kicked it, allowing them entry. Garrett wanted to see what was happening but he had to wait until it was safe. Until he could carry a firearm he couldn't risk going into the house before the cops cleared the house and had the suspects under control. He rocked back on his heels. *Come on, come on.*

"Clear," someone yelled from inside the house. Garrett rushed forward with Johnny right there with him.

There was one man in the kitchen, lying on his stomach with his hands cuffed behind his back. Garrett wished he was alone with the creep. The man had taken Nick's dad from him and caused the boy to go through way too much. There was no telling what he'd done to Randy.

"This way." Johnny nudged Garrett's shoulder.

He nodded before he followed the shifter to the right of the kitchen where a padlocked door was. Johnny easily ripped the lock away from the latch. *Damn, what I wouldn't give for shifter strength.*

Garrett stuck his head through the door. A set of stairs led down to a basement. There was a small amount of light at the bottom which must have come from windows somewhere. He held up his hand. *There!* He could hear muffled sounds coming from the dark. "Someone's down here," he whispered to Johnny.

"Follow me," Johnny said. He held his gun in his hands as he stepped forward.

Garrett pulled out his flashlight from the loop in his pants and shone it over the rickety steps as he followed.

He swept the light to the left then right. A lone figure was seated, chained down to a chair.

"Jeez," Johnny muttered.

Garrett ran past Johnny until he was on his knees in front of Randy. The man looked a lot different from his picture but Garrett had to attribute that to his broken nose, black eye and swollen cheek. The kidnappers had worked him over but he appeared to be breathing normally and was awake. "It's okay," he told Randy. "We're going to get you out of here."

"Mmmph," Randy managed.

Garrett removed the tape from over his mouth. He was as careful as he could manage. He pulled slowly but firmly, hoping that Randy's shifting genes would keep Garrett from hurting him bad.

"Thank God," Randy murmured. He started wiggling around. "Get me out of here."

He had to grin at the impatience in the man's tone. "Just give me a second," he said. He glanced over his shoulder at Johnny. "Can you get these chains undone while I cut the rest of the tape off?"

Johnny nodded before he came closer to grip the metal binding Randy and yanked. Garrett used his knife on the duct tape around Randy's feet and hands. The kidnappers had bound Randy thoroughly. Tape, rope around his waist and finally chains had all been used to keep him in place. That would normally be somewhat overkill but with Randy being a shifter they must not have wanted to take any chances.

Once they'd freed Randy, Garrett reached down and helped him onto his feet. Randy's legs shook so Garrett kept his arm around Randy's waist to help him upstairs.

"We've got the EMTs here. Any injuries I can't see?" Garrett asked him.

Randy shook his head. "Nah, they beat on me at the house and when they first got me here but after that they pretty much left me alone."

"Good." Garrett was so damn relieved. The muscles in his neck and back relaxed, and for the first time in days he knew he'd truly be able to reunite Nick with his dad.

They reached the stairs as Randy turned to him. "Sorry, I'm not sure we've met."

Garrett laughed. "Garrett." He tightened his grip a second. "I was the one who rescued Nick from the fire. I'm working with the fire investigator."

Randy's knees went out and Garrett struggled to hold him up. "Rescued?" Randy whispered.

Since Garrett couldn't carry Randy up the stairs by himself he turned Randy and sat him on one of the steps. Tears filled Randy's eyes. "They told me he died in the fire," Randy said. "I wanted to join my boy. I begged them just to finish me off. They just laughed and said not yet."

He crouched in front of Randy and gripped his knee. "Nick's fine, I carried him out myself. He's staying with my sister and a police detective to ensure he remains safe."

"You swear?" Randy grasped the front of his shirt. "Nick's okay?"

"How about we get upstairs and make sure everything is taken care of here? Get permission to reunite you with your boy," Garrett said.

"Please," Randy replied before he hauled himself up. "I'm getting my legs back. They're just a little sore from sitting for so long."

Pride, Garrett mused. Randy wanted to walk out on his own. To show the kidnappers that they hadn't beaten him. He could understand, admire even, the need. Still, Garrett hovered behind Randy as they made their way up into the main house.

The kitchen was full of activity. As the suspects were being led out, Garrett caught sight of one of them just as the kidnapper spotted Randy. The kidnapper yelled and broke free from the uniformed officer who had a hold of his arm. Garrett jumped forward as he pushed Randy behind him and to the side, out of the way. The kidnapper barreled into Garrett. There wasn't much more he could do since his hands were tied, but still, the full body hit slammed Garrett back into a cabinet. His head bounced off the wood and Garrett saw stars just for a minute.

The commotion in the kitchen was loud and when Garrett blinked his eyes open he saw the kidnapper on the ground with Johnny on his back. The man's nose was bleeding onto the white tiled floor.

"You okay?" Haas asked as he approached Garrett.

Garrett shook his head. "Yeah, fine."

Haas patted his shoulder. Garrett just remained where he was as the Clear Creek Police Department cleared the house. Randy leaned against the wall next to him and they stood in silence. Once the place was cleared, Cooper and Josiah strolled over.

"I just got off the phone with Julie," Cooper said. "We haven't told Nick but I think he'd sure be glad to see his dad."

Randy sighed. "I want to see my boy."

Chapter Six

It was hard for Lily, Julie and Tom to remain calm and not tell Nick about his dad being found or the fact that he was on his way. Lily could barely keep herself from watching the front window giving away the surprise. It had only been thirty minutes since Julie had gotten off the phone with her mate, Cooper.

Still, the anticipation had her jiggling her leg. She glanced over at Julie and saw that she too was having trouble concentrating on the game of Candyland that they were playing with Nick and Tom.

A vehicle pulling up in front of the house had all three adults tensing.

"What's wrong?" Nick asked, as he looked from one to another.

She exchanged a look with Julie and received a huge grin and nod. "Come here, Nick," Lily said to the boy.

Nick jumped up and hurried over. "Are you okay? Are you leaving?"

Lily shook her head. "I believe Garrett's back. He has a surprise for you. Why don't you go get the door for him?"

"Another present?" Nick jumped up and down. "What is it?"

She laughed. "Well, go see!"

"Okay!" Nick yelled as he ran for the door.

Lily and Julie followed behind at a slower pace. Through the front window she could see Cooper, Josiah, Garrett and another man she recognized from her file as Randy exiting the black SUV.

The door swung open and Nick screamed, "Daddy!"

Randy dropped to his knees while he threw his arms open. Nick ran forward until he was close enough to leap into his dad's hold. They hugged for a long time. Garrett remained close but Cooper and Josiah walked up to the front door where she, Julie and Tom waited.

"Everything okay?" Tom asked.

"CCPD will take the case from here and we reunited Nick and his dad so I'd say that everything is pretty damn good. I invited Mike over as well and thought we'd barbecue," Cooper said.

"Sounds good to me," Julie commented. She turned toward Lily. "You can stay a little while longer?"

"I need to finish some paperwork so that I can release Nick back to his father. I can do that now and get it out of the way," Lily answered. "That way Nick can go home with him."

"I'll talk with Garrett and Randy about where they'll stay. I don't believe the house is fit for them," Cooper said.

One of the questions she'd have for Randy would be where he and Nick would go. She could happily let Cooper start working on that. She'd hate for any of the paperwork to have to be put on hold. With how close the Pack was, she was sure that someone would step in to help if need be. Shit, she wouldn't be surprised if

Garrett offered his own home since he was so fond of Nick.

As Cooper, Julie, Josiah and Tom spoke quietly, Lily walked off to join Garrett in front of the SUV. She leaned back and crossed her arms over her chest. "You kept your promise to him."

Garrett's smile was radiant. "I did. When I saw him chained to the chair all I could think was that Nick would be with his dad very soon. Made me feel good."

"As you should." She bumped his arm with hers. "So I hear we're invited to a barbecue."

"Yes, I guessed Cooper would do that. That man loves to grill. I think he looks for any excuse."

She laughed. Randy and Nick finally broke apart and the young boy peered over at Garrett.

"You did it!" Nick shouted and launched himself at Garrett.

Garrett caught him but fell back against the vehicle. Lily had placed her hand on his back to try to soften the blow. Nick was squealing and excitedly babbling. Lily couldn't understand what the kid was saying but it was obvious how happy Nick was.

Randy had stood and walked over to them. Lily smiled and held her hand out. "I don't think we've met officially through the Pack. I'm Lily Harper. I was assigned as Nick's social worker."

Randy took her hand in his before he drew her into a hug. "Thank you for taking such good care of my boy."

Lily patted his back then drew away. "I only had a small part in that. Garrett did most of the caring."

"Yes." Randy peered over at Garrett and Nick. "But you let it happen. I know you could have placed him in a foster home but instead you allowed him to stay where he felt safe."

"It's not usual but I had a feeling this was the best place for him," Lily said honestly.

"Is there anything I need to do for me to take custody of him? I won't be separated from him again. At least not for a very, very long time," Randy said.

"There's some paperwork, but I assure you that Nick won't be going anywhere without you," Lily said.

Garrett put Nick back down but kept holding the boy's hand. "Shall we take this inside?" he asked.

"Come on, Dad!" Nick grabbed Randy's hand with his free one before he started forward.

Lily followed behind, and when Garrett peered over his shoulder at her and winked, a slow ball of hot arousal grew in her stomach. She missed a step and almost fell on her face but managed to grab a hold of the railing. She took a few deep breaths to calm herself before she slipped away to the restroom closest to the kitchen. She splashed cold water on her neck and held her hands to make sure she was in control. With a house full of shifters, they'd be able to pick up any change in her scent. What she needed to do was get the paperwork completed and submitted so Randy would have full custody of Nick back. The order from the judge only gave the state temporary custody of him so it would be no problem to transfer the records.

She strolled into the kitchen and right smack into the middle of organized chaos. Cooper and Tom were pulling packages of meat out of the deep freeze as Josiah came up from the basement with two cases of beer. Julie stood at the stove stirring something in a saucepan. Garrett and Randy sat at the table beside Nick. Garrett was peeling potatoes and Randy was holding the stuffed wolf that Lily had purchased.

"Looks like it's going to be a party," she commented.

"It is," Julie said with a wide grin.

"If you don't mind me taking up some space here at the table, I can go ahead and get Nick taken care of," Lily said.

"Please," Julie replied. "Let's get it all over with so we can really celebrate."

She grabbed her bag that she'd set aside earlier and pulled out her laptop before taking a seat. She opened the lid of her computer and powered it on. She glanced over the top as she felt Garrett's gaze on her. She smiled then opened the program to finish the work so she could have a little fun later.

* * * *

It was a good gathering, Garrett mused. Mike had shown up and it had been decided that Randy and Nick would go home with him. Garrett would miss the kid but he knew that it was important that Nick's schedule went back to normal quickly. Or as normal as it could be under the circumstances. Nick needed to be around the people that were familiar to him. The boy would have more changes ahead of him as he and Randy healed. He didn't think Nick would ever forget the fear or the confusion that he'd experienced.

He tightened his hand on the beer bottle he was holding as he stood out on the back porch watching his friends talk and laugh. Tom and Steve were throwing a ball around to Nick. Cooper, Mike and Randy were discussing an upcoming Pack meeting and how they were handling the fallout of the mayor's arrest just months before. Cooper had been responsible for the takedown of the public official who'd been manufacturing drugs that were deadly to shifters. Garrett had moved to town right after so he'd missed the excitement and he was kind of glad about that.

For a town so full of shifters there were a lot of cases for the Clear Creek Police Department. Especially as there was still some fallout from the shifters going public. Clear Creek was also a tourist place and there were a lot of people who acted stupid while in the city when they drank too much. Garrett himself worked more shifts then he had in Kermit. Traffic accidents were common and he saw way too much drinking and driving.

Garrett would have been worried crazy if he'd been around during the investigation into taking the mayor down. Actually, until he'd met Tom and Steve, and Julie had fallen in love with Cooper, Garrett hadn't given much thought about shifters. Now he felt strongly that the shifters deserved the same rights as he and all the humans. It reminded him that Haas had promised to look into the Kermit Fire Department problems. He'd have to follow up about that. He really wanted to make sure the shifters that were left behind had someone looking out for them.

He'd have to go back to fighting fires full time now that the investigation was complete, until he worked out his certifications and determined whether he could for sure work with Haas. He didn't really mind since he did enjoy that aspect of his job. But he was still going to finish getting his qualifications. The last few days of working with Haas and having a taste of the job he could do had him wanting more.

The glass door behind him opened so he turned as Julie and Lily strolled out with more drinks. He drained the rest of his beer and set it down on the closest table. "Here, let me take those," he offered while holding his hand out for the tray. It appeared they'd be moving on from beer to harder liquor.

"Thanks, bro." Julie grinned at him before skipping off to her lover. Lily was still standing in front of him and he really wanted to lean forward and place his lips over hers. To taste her as he had done before, but he knew that if he started something there at his sister's house he'd be regretting it later. He wouldn't be able to stop this time. He wanted Lily under him in a soft bed, craved to taste more than just her lips. His erection was almost painful. Maybe he could talk her into slipping out and they could disappear together. It wouldn't come as a surprise to anyone at the house. Julie and Cooper had been giving him smug smiles all night, and Tom and Steve had been bumping into him all night with their eyes on Lily. Yeah, it was obvious that he wanted her, and luckily he was pretty damn sure that she felt the same way.

God, he didn't know if he'd ever wanted anyone as much.

Lily breathed in deeply, and he knew the moment that she picked up on his lust as her eyes widened before dropping down to his pants. Fuck, his cock twitched as her attention narrowed on him. She licked her lips, and he barely held in a moan.

"Hey, bring those drinks over so we can have a toast before everyone starts to leave," Cooper hollered.

Garrett straightened his shoulders before he leaned closer to her. "One drink," he murmured. "Just one and then let's get the hell out of here."

Her face was flushed. "Please."

With a nod, he turned and walked to where the others had gathered around. He ignored the knowing looks as he set the tray down.

Cooper poured out shots of whiskey as Josiah handed them out.

"What about me?" Nick asked from beside his dad.

"Not for a few more years," Randy told him, but Lily passed over a juice box to Nick.

Nick beamed at her.

"To Randy coming home!" Cooper held up his glass.

"Yeah, Daddy!" Nick shouted.

Randy smiled. "To my friends who took care of my boy and reunited him with me."

Garrett tilted his head and swallowed the liquor down in one shot. The whiskey burned in just the right way.

He set his glass back down just as Lily did the same. They caught gazes and Garrett couldn't resist moving closer so that he brushed his arm against hers. She shifted just a little so that she could press back into him.

"Well." Mike cleared his throat while grinning. "I better get Randy and Nick back to my place."

"Yeah," Randy said. "I could use a hot shower and a bed."

"Can I sleep with you tonight?" Nick asked. "Me and Garrett?"

Randy glanced over at him. "I think he's talking about his wolf," Garrett told Randy.

Everyone laughed, and Randy picked Nick up in his arms. "You bet, buddy."

"Yeah!" Nick cried. He looked over at Garrett. "Are you coming?"

Garrett ruffled the boy's hair. "No, little man, I have to go to my own house. I'll have to get back to fighting fires tomorrow."

"Saving people like me?" Nick asked with all innocence.

Damn, Garrett was going to miss him. "Yep, but I'll see you soon. I told you that I'd be around."

"Okay," Nick agreed.

Randy hugged Nick to him. "I'll check on our house in the morning and as soon as we can move back in and everything is cleaned up we'll have Garrett and all our friends over for our own barbecue."

"You can see my toys!" Nick said.

"Of course," Garrett told him.

"Let's get your stuff together and get going," Randy said.

"We're going to take off too," Tom stated.

Garrett nodded his agreement. As the group said their goodbyes, he stayed close to Lily. The arousal from earlier hadn't faded. It wasn't until they were out front standing alone that nerves hit. Luckily he'd left his vehicle at Julie's.

Lily paused in front of her own ride. "Are you coming over?" she asked.

Relieved, he nodded. "I'd invite you back to my house but Tom and Steve will be there." He shuffled closer. "And the plans I have for you require us to be all alone."

She raised an eyebrow—a perfect arch that was sexy as hell. "Oh yeah?"

He slid up to press her against her vehicle. His cock rubbed against her stomach and that slight pressure was enough to have his knees going weak. He lifted her chin so she could look into his eyes. "That's a promise."

He couldn't resist—didn't have to—and dropped his mouth on top of hers. She moaned and opened for him. He thrust his tongue inside—her flavor was just as intoxicating as he remembered. There was a touch of the whiskey that they'd all had and a little of the beer that had been passed around. But it was her unique taste that had him deepening the kiss as he ran his hands up her sides.

Before he got carried away, he forced himself to gentle the kiss until their lips just rested on one another's. "We have to get out of here."

Her laughter was soft. "Yes, we better. Good thing I live alone. Follow me?"

He nodded then did the hardest thing he could ever remember doing. He drew back from her.

"Okay." Lily straightened her shirt before running her hand through her hair. "Okay, let's go."

Garrett waited until she was inside her car with the engine rumbling before he jogged over to his own ride. He climbed inside and jerked when the radio blared loudly. He chuckled as he turned the volume down. The last time he'd been inside he'd put on some old rock and roll.

Lily was backing out of the drive so Garrett put his vehicle in gear and followed closely. There would be no chance of him losing her. As he drove into town, he tried to think of anything other than what he would be engaging in later. If he didn't calm down he wouldn't last long enough to do half of what he had planned.

In less than ten minutes, excitement rushed through him again when, in front of him, Lily's blinker came on.

The small duplex had two tiny but neat yards side by side with only a narrow strip of concrete between them. A single step led to the front door. The outside looked newly painted in a dark brown shade with white trim. He turned off his vehicle before pushing open the door. Lily stopped halfway up the sidewalk to wait on him.

He walked closer, taking in the way she ran her palms over her jeans. Maybe she was feeling a little bit nervous too. Weirdly, that calmed him a little. When he reached her, Garrett slid his arm around her waist and propelled her forward. "Hope the walls aren't too thin."

"Young man, bartender, lives beside me. He works nights," she told him. "And he's human."

So they had plenty of privacy. That was good to know. Lily used the keys in her hand to unlock the deadbolt. He let her enter first but when she crossed over the threshold he reached for her as he kicked the door closed with his foot.

Lily turned in his arms as he pushed her back against the wall. Garrett's breath whooshed out then she kissed him. He grabbed her wrists and held her close as he plundered her mouth. He quickly moved down her neck to nibble on the flesh there. Her nails dug into his chest but he didn't mind the sharp bite of pain. No, instead it turned him on further. He whirled them around so that this time it was his back pressed to the wood.

He lifted his mouth long enough to whisper, "Either we need to get to your bed or I'm going to take you right here." He kissed her again but this time she held onto his shoulders while guiding him down the hall.

Garrett couldn't stop touching her, and it seemed she had the same thought since they had to take the walk slowly so they didn't trip. When they did get to the bedroom, Lily gave him a hard shove. He fell back but managed to catch himself just in time to open his arms as she leaped at him.

He staggered, barely kept to his feet then turned still, holding her until the edge of the bed hit his knees. She bounced a couple of times after he dropped her down. Lily threw her head back and laughed while Garrett pulled his shirt over his head.

He made sure to be gentle but firm with his hands as he leaned forward and pulled her down the bed before he brushed his lips against her neck. With both hands, he pushed up her blouse to reveal her soft silky skin.

He tasted every inch of her flesh as he removed each garment until she was gloriously naked and panting in need. As he settled on his knees, cushioned on the thick carpet, he lifted her leg to spread her so he could lower his mouth to her sweet wet pussy. He licked one long strip, which caused her to arch. He tightened his hold on her leg then buried his head at her entrance, really getting into pleasuring her. He used his tongue to spear her and Lily couldn't hold back her moan. When he added his fingers, she lifted her hips off the bed just a little. Garrett growled, bringing his left arm over her waist to hold her down. She tasted sweet and he couldn't get enough of her flavor. He ran his tongue through her folds causing her to shudder. He added a finger as he sucked on her clit. Lily cried out while bucking up. It took more force to hold her down than he thought. He liked that fight, how she allowed herself to just let go. He wanted more, he didn't think he'd ever get tired of having her this way.

"I told you that I had a plan," he murmured. "This is just phase one."

"I can't...can't take more," she stuttered. "Pl...lease."

"You'll take this and more," he told her. "Now enjoy." He went back to work until she gripped his head, then she bucked up, almost knocking him back. She climaxed, and he licked up every bit of her juice.

Garrett rose quickly while struggling to unbuckle his belt. His fingers trembled but he managed to undo the buckle and pull it through the hoops of his jeans. Lily scooted up to help with the button and zippers of his pants and he was grateful. Her eyes were wide, sweat had gathered around her hairline, but she obviously still had enough brain power to remove the last of his clothing. He would have to make sure this round took away the rest of her ability to think.

He stood in front of her, naked with his hard cock ready for phase two. "Up on the bed," he ordered. "Grab a hold of the headboard."

She hurried to comply, and Garrett couldn't hide his smile. Lily followed orders so well. There would be a lot more exploring later. But right now he needed, or would explode before he was inside her. He stroked his shaft once but had to remove his hand so he didn't spill before he could feel her clamp around him.

"Do we need protection?" he asked. He might not have been with a shifter before but he knew the rules. They couldn't pass any diseases between each other so the only concern would be pregnancy. If she was on birth control he would be able to come inside her. He shuddered just thinking about how much he wanted to coat her insides with his seed.

"No!" she said in a strong voice. "I want you to fill me. I want to take all of you in me."

"Thank God," he whispered. It was what he wanted too. He kneeled on the bed then scooted forward. She opened her legs then lifted her hand, and with one finger crooked it at him, telling him to come closer. He chuckled, but that changed when she cupped her own breasts in her hand and kneaded. He moaned, gripped her hips to lift them and positioned himself at her entrance. He pushed in, firmly, with a solid thrust.

"Yes," she hissed.

He couldn't have agreed more. Her inner muscles clamped down around him. Lily was warm and tight. He withdrew before rocking back. In and out, harder and faster, until sweat trickled down his back.

He pushed in hard then paused. Lily threw her head back, arched, and yes, she still had a grip of the headboard.

"Tighten your hands." He waited for her to do so.

When Garrett was pleased with her obedience, he held her waist off her bed and started to thrust strongly. The sound of their flesh slapping against one another almost drowned out her cries and his moans.

Good, so damn good. He bit his lip, knowing he was too damn close to release. He wanted to draw this out. He didn't want to stop — ever stop.

"Garrett!" she called as she climaxed.

It was enough to push him over the edge. He closed his eyes and pumped his hips a few more times before he came, hard — harder than he could ever remember.

He slumped forward while at the same time Lily's hand dropped down. Garrett opened his eyes and peered at her. She had a look on her face that could only be described as pure satisfaction. Very gently he leaned forward to press a soft kiss on her lips. "Ready for phase three?" he asked.

She groaned. "I don't know if I'll survive it," she said then grinned. "But bring it on."

Chapter Seven

Lily rolled over and bumped into the body that was so close to her. She rose slightly so she could peer down at Garrett as he remained asleep. He looked younger this morning and she didn't bother to resist the urge to touch him. She pushed back a piece of hair over his forehead. He didn't even move. Of course he was exhausted, she had been too.

A quick glance at the clock showed that it was a little after seven. Normally she was up and out of bed before six every morning. She liked to start her day with a good hard workout but since she'd had what she could only describe as a good hard workout the night before, she'd needed the extra sleep. She scooted off the bed and felt a twinge in her back. A soft chuckle escaped and she covered her mouth. Acrobatic might be a better description for the events earlier.

She stood and stretched her body then glanced back at the bed. Oh, how she wanted to climb back in with him but she needed a shower, coffee and food. She'd have to go into the office. The last few days she'd gotten behind. There was always paperwork to file, custody applications to check on, and kids to make sure they felt safe and happy. After strolling into the bathroom, she closed the door behind her then turned on the shower. She gave it a few minutes before she checked the temperature and climbed in.

There was a reason that she'd gone into social work. The small voices that didn't have enough authority to speak up for themselves were what she strived to work for. As long as she had a job with the state there wouldn't be a child that got lost in the system. Like she had.

There hadn't been anyone to stand for her, beside her. She'd just been a small girl that no one had known what to do with. Lily hadn't known how to explain what was going on with her body. Why she'd felt as if there was something inside just tearing to get free. This had been before the shifters had gone public and no one had even thought being a shifter was possible. Lily had never even imagined it.

She'd been thirteen the first time she'd shifted. The foster home that she'd run from had been too full, with an overworked mom and a dad who didn't care about anything other than the money.

The older kids had run that place. When Lily hadn't messed around sexually with one of the sixteen year olds, he'd punched her and blamed her injury on one of the other kids. Lily had been too scared to speak up. Later he'd come at her and Lily had known she couldn't stay. A knee in the balls had gotten the boy off her and she'd escaped through a window. She'd run in the middle of the night, while the others had been watching a movie.

She could still remember the chill, the sounds of the woods that she'd wandered into, and the terror that someone would come after her. She'd screamed as her body had begun to transform. Two days she'd been stuck in her wolf form. At first all she'd done was curl up and whimper. She hadn't known what was going on or why. Finally she'd allowed herself to relax into her new form and let the wolf take over. She'd hunted for a rabbit, eaten and had found a cold stream. The further away she'd moved from civilization, the safer she'd felt. Her entire life had changed when she'd caught the scent of the Pack. Of course she hadn't known what it was at the time but she'd followed the smell until she'd come across the Alpha in human form.

Lily had been scared but he'd very calmly spoken to her until she'd relaxed. Little by little, he'd gained her trust until he'd told her how to shift back. The minute she was human again, he'd thrown a blanket around her and cuddled her close. She'd never had to return to that house or any other foster home.

She rinsed the conditioner from her hair and turned off the water. The towel was soft against her as she dried off before she wrapped it around her body. She opened the door to the bedroom and steam floated out around her. Surprised to see the bed empty, she glanced around her bedroom but Garrett was nowhere to be found.

Panic hit first. Could he have taken off on her? Left while she'd been in the shower? No, Garrett wasn't like that. She might not know him well but she could read people. She walked over to her closet and pulled out one of her suits—a gray pair of pants and matching jacket. She chose a purple short-sleeve shirt to go with it. She laid them on the bed before going to the dresser and gathering her bra and panties.

Lily dressed quickly, leaving her jacket off and her feet naked, before she ran her hands through her hair.

She would find out where Garrett had disappeared to then finish getting ready.

As soon as she walked out of the room, she picked up the scent of coffee brewing. Mmm, he'd started the pot and had found the good stuff she kept in the freezer.

She stepped into the kitchen and caught her breath. Garrett was whistling as he stood at the stove. He only had on a pair of jeans and they rode low on his hips. Faint finger marks were on his sides and scratches were on his back. It was probably perverse that she found that sexy and felt a thrill at having left him a reminder of her on his body.

He turned and grinned. "Good morning."

How had she gotten so lucky? He had to be one of the best looking men she'd ever seen. He also had a kind heart, smart brain and was one hell of a lover. "Hi," she said.

"I'm making omelets. Since you had ham and cheese in your fridge I figured it would be good to use that."

"Yes," she replied. "Thank you for making breakfast."

"My pleasure. I have to go into the station and check my schedule then meet up with Haas. Seeing as you're dressed for work, I'm guessing you have to go into your office," he said.

"I do," she agreed.

"Well, I was hoping that I could also make you dinner." He turned back to the pan and flipped the eggs before he looked back at her. "If that's okay with you."

It was hard not to smile. Okay, she was and didn't want to hide it. She'd never been good at playing games with men. "I'd like that," she admitted.

"Good." He expertly transferred the eggs onto two plates then picked them up. "Take these and I'll get the coffee."

She was overwhelmed so she did as told and carried their breakfast to the small table situated in the corner of her kitchen. A touch to her lower back had her jumping slightly.

"You okay?"

"I was worried when you weren't still in bed. I thought maybe you'd taken off. I mean...not really, but the thought did flash through my head and then I come down here and you're all sexy and making me food and I..." She trailed off and felt her face flush. She was babbling like an idiot.

"Hey." He turned her around. "I know we haven't had a lot of time to talk. That's probably my fault, as I can't seem to keep my hands off of you, but I wouldn't have come home with you last night if I didn't want something solid with you."

"No?" she asked.

He kissed her. "I want a meal with you tonight, maybe take a walk, and talk. Then, yes, I plan to be back in your bed. But that's not all. We'll start with one meal and then have another then another."

"You seem to have this all worked out," she commented.

Garrett grinned. "I'm a planner."

That caused her to laugh. "I've noticed." She ran her hands down his chest. "I've enjoyed your plans so far." He was right about not being able to keep their hands off each other. She craved him again, already. Her body was still humming from his attentions the night before, but still she wanted more.

"Good," he said. His eyebrow rose when she moved her hands down to his jeans. He'd zipped them but hadn't buttoned them. The sound of her slowly tugging the zipper down was loud in the kitchen. "I have the feeling our breakfast is going to get cold."

"You seem to be fixated on food," she teased. "Maybe I can get to you thinking about something else."

His moan was music to her ears as she reached inside his pants and grasped his cock. He was already hard and she liked the weight of him in her hand. She stroked him a few times until he lifted his hips. She released him before she dropped to her knees in front of him.

Lily tugged down his jeans, his erection at the same level as her mouth. She once again grasped his cock and held him steady, then she licked at the tip. Garrett shuddered. Lily peered up at him, feeling powerful, having him hot and ready. She bent forward and closed her lips around his cock. His pre-cum was salty but not as bitter as she'd tasted before. She liked the flavor of him, musky and strong. Up and down she sucked and nibbled on his shaft then really went to town on him. When he gripped her wet hair and held on tight she hummed around the cock in her mouth.

"Oh god," he murmured. "I'm going to come."

She popped off. "Fuck my mouth."

He groaned as he adjusted his hands. He held her head while he rocked his hips. His cock slid against her tongue. Lily locked her lips tightly around him. With quicker, harder thrusts, Garrett used her mouth just the way she wanted. What was it about him that was so damn perfect? He knew just how she needed him. But she didn't want to think about that. She just wanted to enjoy the feel of him in her mouth.

Lily closed her eyes and tilted her back to give him better access to her throat. She held onto his hips when he slowed, groaned and shot. She swallowed every drop before she leaned back on her heels.

Garrett was already reaching for her. "Hope you don't have your heart set on wearing this suit," he said as he lifted her up and plopped her on the table.

The mugs of coffee, or maybe it was the plates, crashed to the floor, clattering and breaking but she couldn't force herself to care.

"My turn," he said.

* * * *

Garrett knocked on Haas' office door, peering through the small window as he did so. He'd waited until the end of shift so he wouldn't be bothering Haas and he could go straight to Lily's after as planned. Haas was staring at his computer screen but his head popped up at Garrett's intrusion.

"Come in." Haas waved at him.

"Hey, I just wanted to touch base with you," Garrett said as he entered.

"I'm glad you're here," Haas told him. "I was going to give you a call later."

Garrett sat in one of the visitor chairs and stretched out his legs. "I wanted to thank you for the chance to work this case with you."

Haas sat back in his chair with some amusement on his face.

"I'm going to get my qualifications," he said. "This is what I want to do."

"I'm glad to hear that, especially since I got approval to fast track you," Haas stated. "Six weeks. It'll keep you busy but I think you can do it."

Garrett straightened. "What?"

"You heard me fine," Haas said, and he grinned. "I want you as my partner and I'm willing to call in a few favors to see that it gets done. I expect you to work hard. When done you'll prove to me that I chose right."

"I will," Garrett agreed.

"I've spoken to your captain, he's willing to give you some leeway for studying and taking your tests. Keep me updated as you go through the steps," Haas said.

"You've got everything laid out," Garrett commented.

"You could say that," Haas told him. "Now there is something else I want your help with."

He leaned forward. "All right."

Haas turned the monitor screen toward him. "Take a look at these."

The names were very familiar to him, two of his best friends, his roommates.

"That's bullshit," Garrett said. Every mark on the report showed that both Tom's and Steve's evaluations were all low. According to the logs they shouldn't even be on duty.

"Now check these out." Haas clicked his mouse and two more evaluations popped up, this time from the Clear Creek Fire Department. Every mark was high and they were recommended for promotion.

"I agree with these." Garrett pointed.

"I thought you would. I went through every single shifter's file from the KFD. Not one of them received a mark over a one. This is enough that I can start an internal investigation. I'll have to follow procedures but the ball is already rolling on that."

"You're going to take them down?" Garrett rubbed his hands together. Excitement rushed through him.

"We are," Haas said.

This was it. Garrett was getting everything he'd ever wanted. He had his sister close, friends that he cared for like family, the job of his dreams and a woman that he couldn't get enough of.

Yes, he was one lucky man. And he was going to enjoy every minute of it.

Garrett leaned over the desk and shook Haas's hand. As he left the office he felt lighter than he could ever remember. He smiled and waved at people as he made his way back to his vehicle. Now he had a woman to see.

The drive to Lily's didn't take long. He liked her place and hoped he'd be spending more time there. While he was grateful that Julie's house was available for him, it wasn't his own home.

Lily opened the door before he'd even reached it. She was smiling as she waited on him. He hurried up the walk until he was right in front of her. She wore soft gray pants and a white T-shirt. Her hair was wet so he guessed that she had showered after she'd gotten home.

He wrapped his arm around her back and yanked her close, kissing her deeply as she responded with passion. Garrett nibbled on her lower lip before he drew away.

"Unless you want to give your neighbors a show we better get into the house," he told her.

Lily laughed. "I think Mrs. Brazos across the street would enjoy it but I'd rather take this somewhere more private."

Garrett nuzzled her neck then pushed her inside and closed the door. The scent of cooking meat filled the air and his stomach growled.

"Hungry?" she asked with a lifted eyebrow.

He nodded. "Very." He wasn't just talking about food.

"It'll be ready in about a half an hour," she said.

Garrett grinned. "That will give us plenty of time."

"For?" she teased.

"This," he said before he picked her up.

She squealed but wrapped her legs around his waist. Garrett attacked her neck as he carried her into the living room. He dropped her on the couch, following her down. He covered her body with his, already returning his lips to the soft skin of her neck. Lily pushed her hand under his shirt and scoured her nails down his back.

Garrett growled against her flesh.

"Now, I need you now," she said as she pulled at his clothes. "I've been thinking about you all day."

He'd been hard and wanting since he'd left her house that morning so he knew how she felt.

"Get naked," he demanded. He backed off enough as he yanked off his shirt and Lily followed his order. Once they were both naked, Garrett ran his hands up her body. He started at her ankles and rubbed all the way until he cupped her breasts.

Lily moaned and arched into his touch.

He bent and took one of her pebbled nipples into his mouth.

"Yes," she hissed.

Garrett trailed a finger down until he found her pussy. She was already wet. She hadn't been lying when she'd told him that she was ready. Still he pressed the digit inside her to make sure she received the pleasure she deserved. He added a second after a few moments until Lily was lifting her hips to urge him on.

He waited, it was hard. Oh God how hard he was, but he didn't stop until Lily was pleading.

"Garrett, please."

He drew away and settled between her legs. He grasped his cock with his right hand while pushing her legs farther open with his left. He pumped himself a few times, watching as Lily licked her lips.

He pushed inside her in one smooth, strong, thrust.

Lily raised her arms before letting them fall onto the cushions above her head. Garrett wrapped his left hand around her wrists and held them tightly. Lily shuddered and he withdrew before plunging back in.

Next time he would take his time. Would really give Lily the attention that she deserved but right now he had to claim her. Had to mark her as his own. He drove himself into her over and over again until she was screaming. When she climaxed and her inner muscles clamped down on his cock he grunted and came as well.

It was good, so very perfect.

He dropped down on her. "I think I'm blind," he managed to mumble. He was exhausted and sated.

Lily giggled.

Perfect. Had he said how perfect she was?

PACK LAW

Dedication

For the fans, the readers, and those who believe. It's been an awesome ride and I've enjoyed every minute of it. Thanks for your support.

Chapter One

Shelby Holt slammed her front door as hard as she could. The decorative windowpanes shook but she didn't give a damn. With a scream, she launched her purse from the hall into the living room as she stomped farther into her home. A lamp crashed to the floor and she smiled. If she wanted to wreck her entire place, she would and no one could stop her.

"I hardly think throwing a temper tantrum is going to help anything."

She whirled around, shocked at the audacity of the man who had followed her. Of course he wasn't going to let their argument go. She should have paid attention as she'd driven home, and why hadn't she locked the front door? Hands on hips, she glared at him. "I didn't invite you in," she snapped.

Mike Riley grinned—a wide grin with perfectly straight white teeth, which never failed to make her stomach flutter. Even as pissed off as she was at him, he still affected her. He stalked forward, and like prey caught by the big, bad wolf—because wasn't that an accurate description?—she backed up slowly.

"Unlike vampires, I don't have to be invited in but even if I did, you've done that plenty of times."

Like she needed to be reminded! Shelby had no problem admitting her role in the disaster of their relationship, or whatever the hell was going on between them. Until now she'd enjoyed every minute of her time spent with Mike.

The only light came from the kitchen. She didn't like coming home to a dark house, so every morning she left one room lit. In the dim glow, she could still see the scorching need in his gaze. Shit, just one look from him and she wanted to forget their fight and climb up his hard body. Mike was so damn solid and strong. At six foot one, with a body built from lots of hours at the gym—and his soft blond hair and bright blue eyes—he called to every part of her. But she wouldn't give in so easily this time.

"Stop." She pointed one perfectly manicured nail at him.

Mike raised an eyebrow then took another step.

"I mean it, Mike."

"No, you don't," he said smoothly.

Christ, he was right. As angry as she was, Shelby still wanted him. "You should have told me." It was a weak argument but she wasn't going down without a fight.

"That's not our deal," he reminded. "Your rules. We get together whenever one of us wants but we don't share the details of our lives."

Shelby knew the agreement and didn't appreciate him throwing it back in her face. "Well, you still should have told me!" she yelled.

Mike strode closer while Shelby backed up until she had run out of space. She either had to stop or sit in the large overstuffed chair. Shelby stopped—there was no way that she'd drop low enough to have his cock anywhere near her mouth. Not yet anyway.

"I'm just obeying your rules," Mike said. He reached out and placed his palms on the sides of her neck.

She repressed a shudder. The heat from his touch warmed Shelby from the outside in. It was always like this when Mike had his hands on her. She closed her eyes as she fought herself.

Had it only been two months since they'd started sleeping together? Shelby had known Mike through their professions but it wasn't until two mutual friends had started dating that Shelby had really gotten to know the handsome wolf shifter. He'd given her quotes and once an exclusive interview, but before her best friend Julie had mated with Mike's buddy they'd never spoken of anything other than the law or his firm.

"My rules?" she asked.

"You know the way you try to keep business and pleasure separate," he said.

Of course, Mike was right. It was important to her career to always put her best foot forward and he did the same. "I know I do that. I thought you didn't mind," she said.

As a reporter with the local news station, Shelby had covered a lot of Mike's cases during her work in the last several years.

"I didn't," Mike replied. "That doesn't mean things don't evolve."

They'd sure evolved, hadn't they? "Yeah," she agreed.

A week later they'd run into each other at a bar and had gone back to her place together. It had been amazing, so she'd suggested a deal. Mutual satisfaction that they didn't tell anyone about and kept all feelings out of.

Shelby had plans and any romantic entanglement could throw off what she'd worked years to accomplish. But her feelings had been changing and she didn't know what to do about them. That was probably why she was so mad about his big case which she'd known nothing about.

She huffed before peering up at Mike. "Why didn't you give me a heads-up? This is going to be the most important case we've ever seen in Clear Creek."

"Because my job is to protect my client. You saw the circus today after the news got out," he told her.

Mike had a point.

"But it was going to get out eventually," she argued.

"Yes," he agreed. "I wanted to give my client as much privacy as I could. We don't talk about any of the cases I'm working on or what you're doing, so if I'd brought it up, even just as a hint, you'd have known something major was happening."

Shelby was still stinging from her producer's accusation that she wasn't doing her job and that he could easily replace her. Jake was always an ass and she knew better than to let his words bother her but if Mike had given her *something* she wouldn't be in this mess in the first place. No, she wasn't going to let his betrayal go.

"This is bigger than me and you," Mike said.

Frustration started to build again. "It's my job…"

"No!" Mike barked. "Don't do that. You chose the terms of our relationship and I've gone along with them so far but I won't allow you to use your career against me. I won't put my case or my law firm in jeopardy, and you shouldn't ask me to."

Christ! Shelby dropped her head against his chest. Was that what she was asking Mike to do? Put everything he'd worked for on the line so she'd get a jump on the other reporters? Yes, that was exactly what she'd expected. Even though they never talked about work when together, Shelby was asking that Mike change things between them and that wasn't fair. She blew out a breath. Maybe she was wrong and it would be better to just let it go.

"I'm sorry," she whispered. Mike was a good man, and as much as she wanted to yell, he was right.

"I don't need you to apologize. You can be mad and I understand. But I would still handle the press conference today the same," he told her. His deep voice was calm and soothing.

She wasn't sure if it was due to his shifter side that he was able to remain unruffled or if it was just part of his personality. Shelby envied how he always came across with a steady composure. She was highly strung and she knew it.

Mike reached out and grasped her arms, pulling her in close. Shelby melted against him.

"That's better," he murmured before he kissed her.

Unlike some of their rushed and hard kisses when they were short of time, now Mike gently moved his lips over hers. Shelby opened for him, and he swept his tongue inside, which made her shudder. She pressed her fingers into the muscles of his back and held on tight. With Mike, she was able to just let go and allow him to be in control. Since she spent every minute of every day fighting for top-dog status, the only time she could truly be herself was in these rare, intimate times.

He cupped her ass with his strong hands and lifted her off her feet. Shelby wrapped her legs around his waist as she gripped the back of his head and released every feeling she had into the kiss.

A rumble grew in the back of his throat but Shelby wasn't afraid. Mike might be a wolf shifter but he was also one of the calmest men she'd ever met. As he carried her toward the couch, she rocked against him, letting his erection press close. She wanted him—hell, it seemed she always did these days.

Mike laid her gently on the soft fabric of the sofa as he loomed above her. He'd arrived without his usual suit jacket and tie, so he stood in just his trousers with his white button-down shirt. The top buttons were already loose and his sleeves rolled up. He was one sexy beast.

While Mike began to remove his shirt, Shelby removed her jewelry. Since she'd been on the air earlier she was still in full wardrobe. Mike's gaze never left her as she removed item after item. By the time he'd tossed his shirt and tank onto the chair, she'd also kicked off her heels and reached back for the zipper of her dress.

"No," he said.

Shelby froze. Mike grinned before he bent and removed his dress shoes and silk socks, leaving him just in his slacks. She had no problem at all having to watch him take off that last piece of clothing. She dreamed about his long, hard cock. She licked her lips in anticipation.

He chuckled while reaching for her. Confused, she allowed him to grasp her shoulder until he turned her over onto her stomach.

"Mike?"

"Shh," he whispered as he unzipped her dress. The sound was loud in the quiet of the house.

Goosebumps rose all over her body as he bared her flesh to the cool air. His lips trailed down her spine as he exposed each inch. Shelby arched her back, pressing into his lips.

"That's right," he urged. Mike opened the ends of her dress before he pulled the smooth fabric down her body.

When he climbed between her legs, she pushed back against him. Mike gripped her hips as he rolled his. Why the hell wasn't he buried inside her yet?

"Please," she murmured.

"I'll take my time," he said.

"Come on," Shelby whined.

He nibbled on the back of her neck instead of responding verbally. His cock pressed against her as she pushed back. Mike didn't stop her, so she moved faster. His nips grew sharper.

"I know you want inside me," she said. "Just take me."

"When I'm ready," he replied.

Very rarely, Mike would make her wait like this. Because of their busy schedules, most of the time they had to meet in his office for a quickie or one of them had to rush out after they were finished. Shelby enjoyed the times that Mike had her begging and pleading in need.

She dropped her head back on his shoulder as Mike dragged his right hand down her stomach to the edge of her panties. He slipped his fingers inside the silk to brush through her wet folds over her clit. He slid a finger inside, and she moaned.

"Make all the noises you want," he told her. "I'm not going to stop until you're screaming my name." He added a second finger then plunged both digits in deep.

"Yes!" she cried.

Mike moved his body in the same tempo as his fingers. As much as she enjoyed what he was doing, she needed more.

She lifted one hand to circle his wrist and squeezed. Mike licked the shell of her ear. The assault of so much pleasure all over her body was still just a tease. Shelby groaned in frustration.

"Better," he said before he pushed her back down.

She didn't have time to do more than brace her palms on the couch as Mike ripped off the last piece of clothing. At least now they were getting somewhere.

Shelby lifted onto her hands and knees as she felt Mike fumbling to undo his slacks. When his bare cock pressed against her pussy, she'd never been happier that they didn't have to use condoms.

At the beginning of their relationship they'd discussed their options. Mike couldn't get or pass on human diseases. And since she was on birth control, they didn't have to worry about pregnancy.

She could just enjoy the feel of his cock filling her with no barrier in the way. He was so hard as he pushed in. Shelby helped by pressing back so that he slid in deep with his first thrust. Mike gripped her hard, and Shelby clawed at the cushions under her. He withdrew as gently as he'd entered.

Growling, Shelby might not have sounded like a shifter but her human sounds still got her point across. Mike laughed then plunged deep.

"Yes!" she shouted.

Mike pulled out then thrust in again. Over and over until Shelby had a faint layer of sweat covering her and she was panting hard. Mike's rhythm faltered, and from experience she knew that he was close to coming.

A little more, just another something harder and she'd be able to… There! Mike ran his finger over her clit then pinched. She screamed as she climaxed. Her vision actually darkened around the edges for a moment. She could hear Mike's howl in the background as he also reached orgasm.

Shelby collapsed onto the couch with Mike still buried deep. She wiped her bangs from her face as the sweat had made them cling to her damp skin. Mike's weight pinned her but she wasn't going to complain. It felt good to have him covering every inch of her.

"That was fantastic," he murmured.

She would have laughed if she'd had the energy. Instead she just nodded. Mike kissed her temple, and she decided to just enjoy the few minutes of post-coital pleasure before she'd be alone again. She closed her eyes as the events of the day floated away.

There was nothing she could do to change what had happened. Mike was involved in the biggest high-profile case that the county was ever going to see. A case of a wolf shifter suing his employer for terminating his contract without cause. Or, as Mike claimed, because the employer had found out that the employee was a shifter.

With the laws for the newly public shifters still unclear, what Mike was trying to do could define their generation. If all went as planned, Mike would be a part of the law team who fought for and won equal rights for all shifters. Shelby would be there every step of the way, reporting all the details to the public.

Sure, the bigger networks would send their own correspondents, but Shelby had an edge. Not only had she lived in Clear Creek her entire life, but these were her neighbors and friends. She'd find a way to get any lead possible.

Mike might not be able to help her but there were other ways for an intelligent and determined woman to get ahead.

* * * *

Mike closed the door quietly behind him. Shelby had passed out on the couch not long after he'd pulled out and cuddled her against his chest. She'd been furious earlier but he'd known that Shelby wouldn't hold his secret against him for long. She was a woman full of passion but she was also fair.

He'd have loved to stay with her longer but that was against her rules. Mike glanced over his shoulder at the dark house. When he'd first run into Shelby at his buddy Cooper's house he'd immediately been attracted to her. Her coffee-colored skin and dark eyes were alluring and he'd gotten hard just seeing her. He'd seen her before when she'd reported on one of his cases but it wasn't until he really paid attention that he'd seen past the reporter to the beautiful woman. Their previous meetings had always been in a professional setting, so it had been nice to see her around their mutual friends.

Shelby's best friend, Julie, was mated with his Pack member Cooper, and the more time that Mike and Shelby had found themselves in each other's company, the more Mike had noticed the little things about her. Shelby put up a tough front but she cared deeply for those around her. She was also extremely smart, passionate and funny. The perfect combination wrapped up in a gorgeous package. She was also just as career-minded as he.

Shelby had a plan, being the best and most well-known reporter in the world, and she wasn't going to let anyone or anything stop her. Her future was bright and he had no doubt that she'd succeed. As many times as Mike had tried to maneuver their relationship into a more serious stage, Shelby had backed off. He didn't like her running from him but Mike was a patient man. He wanted Shelby and he would eventually claim her as his own.

As much as he wished he could turn around and carry Shelby to her bed and stay there for the rest of the night, Mike was far from being done with his duties. He really shouldn't have taken the time to follow Shelby home or make love to her but he hadn't been able to resist. When she'd confronted him as he'd been leaving his office, she had been gorgeous in all her fury. She'd made his blood pump harder, and his wolf had risen close to the surface.

Yes, he had to come to see Shelby but now he had Pack business to take care of. His Alpha had ordered him to the main house where they had visitors. Alpha Jeremy was the only other person who had known about the upcoming lawsuit that Mike and his law partner Randy were handling. Jody Norman was a Pack member and it was with Jeremy's urging that Jody had decided to fight back.

Mike didn't know if they'd win but he was sure going to fight for Jody and all the shifters in the world. He was glad he had his Alpha's support. Not only his support, but Jeremy was also bringing some of the most powerful wolf shifters to town to witness the trial. It was a lot of pressure but Mike knew that this was the most important time of his life.

With a sigh, he turned back toward the street where he'd parked his BMW then headed toward it. He wished he had time to change clothes but he was already running behind.

His cell rang as he reached the driver door. He was definitely running behind. He pulled his phone from his back pocket. Instead of his Alpha's name, the caller ID read Cooper Grainger.

"Hey, man," Mike greeted after he'd swiped his finger over the screen to answer.

"Please tell me you're on your way," Cooper spoke quietly.

"Yeah, I just had to make a stop," he said.

Cooper chuckled. "I'm sure." Cooper was one of the few people who knew about him and Shelby.

Mike climbed inside his car and started it up. "I'll be there in less than fifteen minutes. What's wrong?"

"Nothing," Cooper answered quickly. Too quickly.

"Coop?" Mike pressed.

His friend cleared his throat. "Really nothing, it's just…"

"The visitors?" Mike guessed.

"Yeah," Cooper said. "I knew as an Alpha that Jeremy was tough but these guys are just so much more."

"Well, when you bring in the most powerful Alpha and the strongest Enforcer, it would be natural to be a little intimidated," Mike told him.

"Sure," Cooper said sarcastically.

Mike laughed. "I'll be there soon."

"Okay." Cooper hung up before Mike could say anything else.

Unlike his friend, Mike was looking forward to meeting Gage and Cain. The stories about the two men and their Packs were like fairytales to other shifters. There was a reason they were the very first who had come out to the world and why Texas and Oklahoma, where their Packs lived, were the two safest states for shifters.

When Jeremy had told Mike that Gage and Cain were coming to the trials, Mike hadn't believed that it'd ever actually happen. Who cared about some small town in Missouri? But as word spread throughout the Packs around the States of what Jody was doing, Jeremy had been approached by a lot of shifters who wanted permission to enter their territory. A request was technically only a formality, but it showed respect for the Alpha of the area.

Out of everyone who planned to come to town, Mike was most interested in meeting Gage and Cain.

As he sped down the highway that led to the Pack lands, Mike couldn't help the excitement growing inside him. He pressed his foot harder on the gas pedal. He'd bought his car so that he could enjoy the open road. He was going to take full advantage now.

The trees flew by at breakneck speed but Mike didn't slow until he reached the last curve before the turn-off to Jeremy's house. The road went from smooth tarmac to dirt as he entered Pack territory.

Mike hit the button to roll down his window and let the fresh air in. It smelled like home, family and comfort. The familiar aroma of where he belonged. He enjoyed living in the middle of Clear Creek but he did miss the freedom of Pack territory. The fresh grass, trees and quiet. But Mike didn't want to make the drive from Pack lands to his office every day. Maybe he'd finally buy one of the cabins and spend his weekends there. He loved being an attorney but it was a profession full of stress.

He hadn't become a lawyer for riches or fame. He'd only followed in his father's footsteps so that he could take over the small-town law office. There weren't many criminal cases around here, so Mike and Randy spent most of their time on family law. Now, taking on the biggest corporation in the city, Mike wasn't ever going to be able to go back to what he'd done before. His life was changing and there was nothing he could do about it. That was the number one reason he'd gone after Shelby earlier. With so much happening, he needed Shelby to calm both him and his wolf down. Being with her was like a balm that soothed him.

"Shelby," he whispered her name into the night. Would she ever accept him and his wolf and want to settle down? He didn't know, but sooner or later he was going to have to confess the fact that he wanted her for more than just a few nights a month.

There were more vehicles parked around the main house than normal. Even on Pack runs not this many people showed up. He chuckled as he parked to the left away from the majority of the other cars. He didn't want to get boxed in and unable to leave after his Alpha dismissed him. He had an early morning and needed rest. Plus, he hoped to get a workout in first thing tomorrow and for the immediate future he didn't know when he'd have another free moment.

He rolled up the window before he turned off the car and took a deep breath. He'd go in and see if he could speak to Gage and Cain then try to get out of there. Decision made, he pushed open the door.

Music carried from the back yard along with laughter and screeches. It sounded like the Pack was having a great time. Mike walked up the drive and around the side of the house. The first person he spotted as he turned the corner was Cooper.

His friend was standing at one of the large grills flipping burgers. Mike could smell the mouthwatering scent of sizzling meat. His stomach growled. He'd been so busy that day that the only thing he'd eaten was a bagel with his morning breakfast. Lunch hadn't even crossed his mind.

Mike headed over to Cooper to grab a plate before he got pulled away for something else. Cooper spotted him and grinned then waved the spatula at Mike.

"'Bout time," Cooper bitched.

"Man, I hope one of those is ready because I'm starving," Mike replied.

"Not yet, but the ones on the table are," Cooper told him.

"Here." Garrett Sullivan, Cooper's brother-in-law, handed him a plate. "Julie gave this to me as soon as she spotted you. Randy told her that the two of you hadn't eaten lunch."

"Oh God!" Mike grabbed the plate. There was a fat burger between two toasted buns, potato salad and chips. "I love your mate," Mike told Cooper before he took a huge bite.

"Well, she's taken so you'll have to get your own," Cooper said with a smile.

Mike nodded. He didn't even stop chewing to joke back. Garrett was staring at him as he wolfed down his dinner. Mike didn't blame Garrett, though. As a human, Garrett didn't need as much sustenance as shifters and Mike was really fucking hungry.

"Here." Alpha Jeremy handed him a beer. "Take a drink and slow down."

Mike finished chewing the bite he had in his mouth. "Sorry," he said as he ducked his head at his Alpha.

"It's quite all right," Jeremy said. "Let's sit so you can enjoy your food."

Mike followed Jeremy over to one of the folding tables that had been set up around the yard.

"You had a busy day," Jeremy said while he sat across from him. "You doing okay?"

Now that Mike had finished half his burger, he could think about something other than food. He took a deep drink of his beer as he glanced around. He didn't spot their two guests.

"Gage needed to call home and check on his kids and Cain went to the bathroom. You have a few minutes to finish your dinner," Jeremy told him.

"Thanks." Mike was sure that his Alpha had managed to get him the few minutes he needed.

Jeremy smiled. "Just eat."

Sensing that he didn't have much time, Mike bent over his plate and cleaned it in only a few minutes. Cooper passed by and set down another beer but didn't stop. Mike had really good people in his corner and he needed to remember that.

Mike finished his first bottle before he pushed it and the empty plate to the side. With his stomach full, he leaned back in his chair as he held the fresh beer between his hands.

"Here they come," Jeremy said with a nod toward the house.

He took another drink then set his beer down. Mike wiped his hands on his slacks before he stood. The first man was tall but that wasn't what Mike noticed most. The power that flowed from him was almost too much. This had to be Alpha Gage Wolf.

"Mr. Riley." The Alpha held out his hand.

"Call me Mike, please," he said as he shook hands and gave the dominant wolf a small bow.

"It's nice to meet you, Mike. Please call me Gage, and this is Cain," Gage said.

Mike turned to Cain, who was just as intimidating as Gage but in an entirely different way. Cain was the most muscular guy that Mike had ever seen. On top of that, Mike got the impression that if he said one wrong word or did anything that Cain might pick up as a threat, Mike would be on the ground in a pool of his own blood. Instead of offering his hand, he dipped his head in respect.

Both Gage and Cain laughed.

"He really won't bite," Gage said, giving Cain a playful shove.

Mike didn't know what to say or how to act.

"Tone it down," Gage said to Cain.

"Sorry." Cain ducked his head. "Being around all these strange shifters is sometimes difficult."

"Sure," Mike agreed even if he didn't have a clue what Cain meant. There were times when Mike had been uncomfortable around shifters he didn't know, but never enough to attack.

Cain smiled before he offered his hand. "I'm pleased to meet you."

Mike took a deep breath but finally managed to put his palm in Cain's. It was weird that he was more fearful of Cain than he was Gage. How strange was that? "I've heard a lot about both of you," Mike said.

"Don't believe all the stories." Cain released his hand and slapped his back. "We're really just regular shifters like you."

"Well..." Gage winked. "We might be a little special."

And Mike was able to relax and laugh. "Join me for a beer?"

"Sure," Cain agreed.

Jeremy returned, holding a couple of bottles. Mike hadn't even noticed that he'd stepped away. As they settled back at the table that Mike had eaten at, he watched the way the Pack kept glancing over at them. Mike held back a smile.

"You sure have a lot of people around here interested in you," Mike commented.

"And you have even more wanting to meet you," Gage said. "Are you ready for all this?"

Mike barked out a laugh. "You know, Randy and I had to decide who would take first chair in this case, and to protect his boy we chose me. I had no idea what I was agreeing to."

"The Boltons have been through a lot already," Jeremy agreed.

"I read about the kidnapping and assault," Cain said. "You've had a busy year here. It was one of the reasons that we wanted to come and show our support."

"We appreciate it," Jeremy told him. "The hotels are already filling up, and some of the Pack are even opening their homes."

"The Wolf Council is sending some representatives that can help protect and police the city since there will be so many new people, humans and shifters, here. I've already spoken to the local police department, and they're happy for the help. Luckily, we have a head start so there should be enough of us to help," Gage said.

"You expect trouble." Mike just realized.

"There are quite a few human organizations that will come pouring into this town when they hear about the case. Not everyone is happy about us. We need to be ready," Cain told him.

And that was why the Council had sent these two powerful shifters. Mike finished off the rest of his beer with a gulp. He decided he needed something a lot stronger as the realization of what he was doing and how this trial could affect more than just their small piece of the world started to sink in.

"We need to make sure Jody has protection." He sat up straight. "If there are people coming, someone might try to go after him."

"We have it covered," Jeremy said. He nodded at Gage.

"I have some friends that have military training. They arrived earlier today and will keep him safe. You'll meet them tomorrow at your office," Gage said.

Mike nodded. "It seems like you have everything under control."

"We'll watch your back," Cain said. "You concentrate on winning the case and making sure the entire world sees that shifters deserve the same rights as any human."

"No pressure," Mike joked.

"You can handle this," Jeremy said. "We'll do this together."

Chapter Two

Shelby pulled her best dress suit out of the closet and laid it on her bed. It was going to be a big day for the town of Clear Creek, and Shelby planned on having her face in front of the camera as much as possible.

There was a good chance that she'd get picked up for national news, at least for the first few hours. She glanced at the alarm clock on the side of the bed. It was only five in the morning but she planned on getting to the station early so she could meet up with her cameraman.

As soon as everyone started to arrive at the courthouse, she would be there to capture it. Shelby had no idea how Mike had managed to get the court papers filed, a judge assigned, and the entire start of the process going without anyone catching wind of the case. It didn't really matter, though.

She'd made the decision the night before that she would not use Mike. No matter how much she wanted to get ahead she wouldn't step on the people that she cared about. When she'd woken up on the couch, covered by a blanket, she'd felt warm and cared for.

Mike never said much about their relationship but when they were together he did small things that showed that he did have feelings for her. The blanket was only one example. He also remembered when she was working on an important story, gave her small trinkets he'd tell her he just picked up, and would simply sit with her after a long day. The realization made her feel like shit. She'd been taking what she wanted from Mike but only on her terms. That wasn't the kind of woman that she wanted to be.

So she was going to do her job and do it well.

She ran her hand over the red jacket that went along with her dress.

"I like the color."

Shelby screeched and jumped. "What are you doing sneaking up on me like that?"

Mike grinned. "I thought I'd come over and make sure you were okay."

"I am," she said as she took in his appearance. He was dressed in faded jeans and an old sweatshirt, and looked even better than when he was in his full suit. There was just something about him when he was dressed down that made her want to tackle him to get down and dirty. "Don't you have court today, Counselor?"

"I'm on my way to the gym. My suit is in the car along with my workout bag," he told her.

"And you ended up here because?"

"I saw your light on," Mike said.

Shelby bit her lip. "Why don't you come closer?"

He took a step. "Like this?"

"Another," she ordered.

Mike walked halfway to her then stopped. "How about here?"

Shelby untied her robe and allowed it to fall from her shoulders. "Are you sure that's as far as you want to come?"

"On second thought." Mike pounced her, lifting her off her feet and swinging her around.

She giggled. "Put me down, you weirdo!"

They were both laughing by the time Mike put her back on her feet. Before she could catch her breath his mouth was on hers. Shelby gripped his shoulders as she leaned into him.

"I should get going," Mike said against her lips.

"Already?" she teased.

"I really was on the way to the gym. I have a meeting at my office at six-thirty," he told her.

"I know a great cardio workout?" she suggested.

Mike ran his hands down her back to cup her ass. "What would that be?"

"Let me show you," she said before she shoved him.

Mike was caught off guard and stumbled. Shelby followed through and tackled him.

"Jeez," he muttered as he hit the ground.

She knew that she wouldn't hurt him. There were a lot of good aspects of having a shifter as a lover. Shelby straddled him and pushed up his sweatshirt. He had a smooth, strong chest that she loved to feel. So she did just that. She spread her hands over his skin while looking into his clear, blue eyes.

Mike was letting her do whatever, and she liked that. She bent her head then ran her tongue over his right nipple. He jumped as he moaned.

"Oh, I forgot how much you like that," she teased.

"You're right," he said. "And you like this." He lifted his hips so that his erection rubbed against her.

"I do," she agreed. With her robe gone she had no clothes but his to keep them from going any further. "But it won't work with you wearing so many clothes."

"So take them off me," he ordered.

Shelby lifted up so she could unbutton his jeans. Mike squirmed around and together they managed to get his jeans and boxers to his ankles. She should have taken off his shoes and socks. Next time he surprised her in her bedroom she needed a better plan. And there had to be a next time. Shelby found herself missing Mike more and more when he wasn't around. It seemed to her that Mike felt the same way.

Oh well, at least she had access to his cock. She grasped his erection and pumped him a few times. Mike bucked into her hold, groaning. Shelby scooted back up his body to hover over his cock. She positioned the head of his penis at her entrance before slowly lowering herself.

Mike held her tight around the waist then lifted himself up into a sitting position. He kissed her roughly, and she submitted to his aggressive manhandling. Even when she was on top, Mike still had the ability to make her forget everything but him. Shelby rocked her hips as she rode him fast and hard. Each time she slammed down on his cock Mike thrust up. It was going to be a quick session for the two of them but Mike had said that they were on a short timeframe.

She panted and dropped her head back as she felt the edge of climax coming fast. Mike's teeth on her throat added a sweet little sting that was enough to push her into orgasm. Shelby scored her nails down his back and screamed. Mike growled loudly against her flesh then was filling her with cum.

"Damn," he muttered as he fell back to the ground.

Shelby smiled as she laid her head on his chest. "Maybe you should stop by more often before work."

Under her, Mike stiffened then wrapped his arms around her tightly. "I might just do that."

She had clearly surprised him with her comment and she hid her smile in his neck. She was glad that she was able to catch him off guard.

"I don't want to get in the shower but I have to start getting ready," she told him once she had calmed down.

"I know," he said while running his hand over her hair.

Shelby eased off him, and Mike rolled onto his knees. He peered over at her, and she was surprised by the sweet look of adoration on his face. She leaned over and kissed him gently.

When they pulled away, Mike grasped her hands and helped her to her feet.

"Go ahead and get in the shower," Mike said. "I'll show myself out."

"Hey!" That reminded her. "How'd you even get in?" She knew that her house was locked up tight.

Mike laughed. "I have some secrets still."

Shelby shook her head as she made her way into the bathroom. She'd figure it out later but at the moment she was still flying from being with him. She could hear Mike re-dressing behind her.

As she passed the mirror, she caught sight of the smile on her face. She looked well tumbled. What a great start to the day. She strolled over to the shower and turned on the faucets.

"Hey."

"Huh?" She glanced over her shoulder.

Mike leaned against the frame. "I want you to be careful around town," he said quietly.

"Careful?"

"There's going to be a lot of strangers in town. Your face is going to recognizable to everyone who is interested in the trial," Mike said.

That was her plan so she couldn't really argue with him. "Okay?"

"Just be aware of your surroundings and don't trust anyone you don't know," Mike told her.

There was no smile on his face and he appeared more serious than she'd ever seen him.

"Have you been threatened?"

"No." He shook his head quickly. "But it is a concern."

Shelby figured there was probably a little more to it than what Mike was saying but he did need to be careful about what he told her. Still, even if he wasn't supposed to be telling her anything, Mike wanted her safe. She crossed back over to him and placed her palms against his chest. Too bad he'd already pulled his sweatshirt back on. "I will be careful as long as you promise the same."

"I promise," he told her with a smile.

"Good. Now I really do have to get ready," Shelby said.

Mike laughed as he stepped back. "I'll try to see you later."

She nodded. Mike was going to be busy and she understood that. "See you soon."

* * * *

As Mike pushed the papers he'd been going over into a manila folder, someone knocked on his office door. He took a quick sniff and smelled shifters on the other side, including Jody.

There wasn't much of a chance that anyone would be able to sneak back here since they'd have to go through the reception area and Randy's office first but he was taking his Alpha's warning seriously. He was on the lookout for trouble. That was why he'd mentioned earlier for Shelby to be careful.

He stood up and strolled to the door, before opening it up with a smile.

Jody stood behind two large men and next to a pretty female. It looked like Jody's guards were also being cautious, as they all scented him as soon as he opened the door.

"Come in, please," he offered as he stepped back.

The first man who entered gave off a similar wave of power to Gage's. If Mike wasn't mistaken, he was an Alpha. The second man appeared a little friendlier, since he smiled at Mike as he passed. The woman remained beside Jody the entire time.

Mike closed the door behind the group and turned. The Alpha was doing a sweep around his office but Mike knew no one else was in there with them. There weren't many places anyone could be hiding.

"How are you doing, Jody?" Mike asked.

"Good." Jody's head bobbed. "Good."

He was nervous but Mike had expected that. "Why don't you sit down? Would you like some water or coffee?"

"No, thank you," Jody said but he did sit in one of the comfortable chairs in front of Mike's desk.

The Alpha had circled back around to him. "Austin Winters." He held out his hand. "It's nice to meet you."

The name didn't sound familiar but he was sure he could get additional information from Jeremy if he needed it. Mike shook his hand. "Nice to meet you too."

"I'd like to introduce you to Gray Mason and my mate Kiley Palmer." Austin motioned to the two other guards.

Mike dipped his head respectfully. Gray grinned and waved, but Kiley only nodded similarly as he'd done.

"Is there anything I can get any of you?" he offered.

"We're good. Thanks," Gray answered.

Mike strolled back to his desk and turned his attention to Jody. Austin sat next to Jody while Kiley moved to stand by the door and Gray settled with his back to the window on the other side of the room.

"I just wanted to talk to you a little more about what to expect for the next couple of days," he said to Jody. "Remember if you have any questions, I'll be happy to answer them." Mike glanced to Austin. "Is there anything you'd like to know?"

Austin nodded. "We'd like to go over security in and out of the courthouse."

"Let's start there and then we can talk about the legal parts," Mike suggested.

"Sounds good," Austin agreed. "As you know, the three of us will be with Jody at all times. No humans know who we are and, since my Pack is not out in the open, no one is aware that we're shifters. If asked, we'd like for you to say that you hired us as security."

"I can do that," Mike said. "You don't think that will look strange? Three bodyguards?"

Gray laughed. "Three visible," he said. "You won't see the rest of the team unless there's a problem."

"The rest?" Mike asked. Just how many guards were needed?

"Gray is not part of my Pack but he and Kiley were once under the same Alpha before Kiley and I mated and Gray found his mate in New Mexico. Our security company has offices in Colorado, where I'm Alpha, and another division in New Mexico, where Gray lives. Gray's side of the business handles more covert operations," Austin said.

The night before, Jeremy had said something about the military training of the guards. "How many guards are there out there?"

"Five, in addition to us," Austin replied.

"You have eight shifters watching Jody?" Mike was really becoming uncomfortable. If Jody was in this much danger, maybe he should move into the Alpha house. He knew that Jeremy had a lot of the Alphas staying with him so the place was full but surely there was room for Jody.

"Eight divided between Jody, you and your law partner," Kiley spoke for the first time.

"What?" Mike barked. He was being watched.

"Two guys have been on you since we arrived yesterday," Gray told him.

That meant they'd seen him at Shelby's twice in a twenty-four-hour period. "I..." Mike ran his hands roughly over his face. What could he say to that? "I would have scented them." There that sounded reasonable. He was a damn good shifter. He would have known.

"These are highly trained special ops shifters," Gray said. "I wouldn't even know if they were following me."

Jeez, Mike couldn't believe this. No one knew about him and Shelby.

"Anything they see is kept strictly confidential," Austin assured him.

That didn't make Mike feel any better. If he'd known he was being followed, would he have still gone to Shelby's? Yeah probably, and what did that say about him? Shelby was human and didn't deserve to have her privacy violated. But if they were watching him when he was with Shelby, that meant she was protected as well. He didn't expect her to encounter any trouble, but he still liked that she was safe.

"If there is anyone else you'd like to add to the protection order we'd be happy to help," Austin said as if he was reading Mike's thoughts. "Human or shifter."

Yep, Austin knew what Mike was thinking. "Not right now," Mike replied but nodded a little to himself. If anything did happen to worry him, he might take the Alpha up on his suggestion. Shelby didn't really have to know, did she? "I guess I just wasn't expecting more than just the guards for Jody. Jeremy told me about you but didn't say anything about hiring anyone for me or Randy."

"We'll be discreet and you'll hopefully forget we're there," Gray promised.

Mike sat back in his chair and looked around at the other shifters in the room. He liked them already, even if he didn't know why. He just felt comfortable in their presences. Even Austin, who was obviously a powerful Alpha. As much as he'd enjoy meeting Gage and Cain, he wouldn't like to be around them too much since they did intimidate him.

However, he could see inviting these three shifters over for dinner or out to a drink. He relaxed. "I appreciate all you're doing. I won't make your jobs any harder and will be as careful as I can."

Austin nodded in approval, and like a young pup, Mike felt warmth flood his system. It'd been a long time since he'd sought approval from an Alpha. Jeremy was so close to family their relationship felt different to Mike.

"Kiley, why don't you go over our plans for entering and exiting the courthouse?" Austin said.

The young woman stepped forward as she pulled out a map from a bag she carried. She set it down in front of Mike on the desk and pointed to the front entrance. "Today we'll go in the front but we do have two other plans if we feel there is a danger to any of you," she said.

Mike listened as she explained alternative routes and situations that might arise and was wowed. If he ever needed a security company in the future, he knew who to call.

It took half an hour for them to iron out all the details. They already had most of everything they needed but since they were working off blueprints and hadn't actually been inside the courthouse, Mike had pointed out a few trouble spots for them.

All in all, he was extremely happy about how protected Jody would be.

Once Kiley had retaken her spot by the door, Mike turned to Jody. "Did you have any questions or anything to add?" He wanted Jody to feel as comfortable as possible.

"No," Jody told him. "They went over all this with me last night. I don't think this is all necessary. I just wanted my old boss to understand he can't treat people the way he does. I did good work."

Mike felt for the guy. Even if they won the case, Jody wouldn't be able to return to the company. And taking on the biggest corporation in the area was going to make finding another job difficult. Jody was currently doing freelance IT work but Mike knew the younger shifter was struggling. "I know. Hopefully this will help other shifters so that they don't suffer the injustice you did."

Jody nodded but looked sad. "Thanks, Mike."

"Of course," Mike said. "Today is jury selection so you won't have to do a thing."

"Good," Jody said in relief. "I wouldn't mind another day of normal."

Mike laughed. "One more, at least." The entire time that Mike and Jody had worked on putting together the case was all now coming down to the next few days or weeks. Late hours and weekends where they'd given up their only free time had been worth it. At least he hoped so. He was confident that the trial would bring to light how important equal rights for shifters were. His hope was that other shifters would see Jody's example and fight back against shifter prejudice.

"Is there anything else we need to do before court this morning?" Austin questioned.

"I think we're all set. If you want to go next door and get some coffee and maybe a little breakfast, I'll finish up in here," Mike said. "We'll arrive at the courthouse together."

"Sounds good to me." Gray pushed away from the wall. He clamped a hand on Jody's shoulder and guided him out of the office.

"I'm going to take a look around the neighborhood," Kiley said. Her gaze was on Austin, not him.

Austin sighed as he stood. "I'm sure Casey has it covered."

Kiley didn't say anything, just continued to stare at Austin. Austin eventually strolled over to her and cupped her face. Mike felt like an intruder witnessing their intimate moment.

"Be careful," Austin whispered.

"Always," Kiley told him. She leaned up and kissed him quickly before she spun on her heels and left.

Austin shook his head then looked back over at Mike. "Do you have a mate yet?"

Mike smiled. "Not yet."

"When you do she'll keep you on your toes," Austin predicted.

"I can only hope," Mike said honestly.

Austin dipped his head before he also left. Mike sat back at his desk. He hadn't really thought about having a mate in a long time. When his mom was still alive, she used to ask him weekly when he would settle down. For six years now, no one had even brought up him finding a mate. Before he'd met Shelby, Mike had only dated a few women a couple of times before he'd moved on. He spent his time on his job, with friends or Pack. Shelby was the first to get him thinking about a more serious relationship.

She would make one hell of a mate. Shelby already knew about shifters and accepted them. With her high intelligence and passionate drive, she was amazing and he would be lucky if she ever agreed to stay with him for that lasting commitment.

"Crap." Mike shook all mating thoughts from his head. He did not need to be thinking about that. He had to get ready to go to court. This was an important morning. The right jury had to be chosen. If there was one person who had something against shifters, the entire case could be tainted.

At least Clear Creek was a city that had a good combination of humans and shifters. There was a good chance that at least some of the jury would be shifter. That would be to their benefit.

A knock sounded on his door before Randy opened it up. "You almost ready?"

"Yep." Mike stood up and transferred his files into his bag before he slid his laptop in to join them.

"I ran into Austin. They'll meet us in the parking lot," Randy told him.

"Great," Mike said. He swung his bag onto his shoulder. "Let's go."

Mike followed behind Randy as they strolled through the office. He waved at the receptionist, and Carley smiled back. As they left by the front door, he spotted Austin standing next to a dark, luxury SUV. The passenger side and back seat were already filled.

"Are you riding with me?" Mike asked his partner.

"Yes," Randy answered as he headed to the other side of Mike's BMW.

Mike hit the unlock button on his key fob before he opened the back door. He glanced over the roof of his car and saw Austin was climbing into the driver side of the SUV.

This was it.

* * * *

The chants were loud and Shelby still couldn't figure out how the anti-shifter protesters had organized so fast. They'd already done a short report on them, and Shelby could admit that while the leader had been speaking to the camera she had really, *really* wanted to hit him.

It had been tough to stay professional but Shelby had managed to do her job. She had even texted Julie, her best friend, to see if they could grab lunch and talk. If anyone would understand how difficult it was to be a human on the shifter side of things it would be a human who loved a shifter.

Luckily, Julie was free, since she was on the night shift that week for the Clear Creek Fire Department as an EMT. Shelby had a lot of questions that she hoped Julie wouldn't have a problem answering. Not only was Julie mated to a shifter but her brother was also dating a shifter woman. The café that they were going to meet at was across the street from the courthouse, so Shelby felt comfortable that she wouldn't miss anything by stepping away.

Her producer had assigned her to cover the courthouse for the day to catch any information coming out. The actual trial hadn't even started yet but word had gotten around. There were strangers everywhere and it wasn't even eight o'clock yet.

She spotted a familiar car and motioned for her cameraman, Pete. Mike and Randy climbed out of the car as a dark SUV parked next to them.

"Stay on the SUV," she ordered Pete.

"On it," Pete replied.

Mike strolled to the SUV and stood. Damn, he was so good-looking in his dark-charcoal suit. While she preferred Mike in the more laid-back clothing he'd been in earlier that morning, there had to be something said about a suit like he was currently wearing.

"Yum," she mumbled under her breath.

Pete snorted while lifting the camera to his shoulder, so he must have heard. *Well, shit!* Pete was a shifter, so of course he had. She always forgot about the enhanced hearing the shifters had. But having Pete stationed at the courthouse with her gave Shelby another source of information. He'd have first-hand knowledge about how the shifters felt the case was going if Shelby needed the information.

"As soon as the back door opens, start rolling," she said.

"Yep," Pete returned. He was a man of few words.

The back door opened, and Mike stepped aside. Shelby narrowed her eyes, trying to see what Mike was doing. Mike reached out and helped the young man from his seat. *Bingo!* Jody Norman just arrived.

Pete was working the camera, focusing in on the vehicle that Jody and three other people were exiting. She wondered if they were all shifters. While they were still dressed nicely, they didn't appear to be lawyers.

A pretty blonde wearing all black walked around the vehicle and placed her hand on Jody's shoulder to guide him forward.

Shelby held her thumb up, telling Pete to cut when he was finished.

"Got them." Pete lowered the camera before he turned toward her. "Now what?"

"I'll do a short lead-in and then we'll send it to the station so they can edit and play it a couple of times this morning. It should look good against the protester's interview," Shelby said.

"Bunch of ignorant assholes, if you ask me," Pete mumbled.

Shelby grinned. "I couldn't agree more." She moved over so that the courthouse steps were in the background. The edge of the shot would pick up the growing crowd.

"Ready?" Pete asked.

"Count me in," she said with a nod.

Shelby kept her report short but sweet before Pete stopped recording.

"Would you like a drink?" she asked Pete as they started back to the news van.

"That'd be good," Pete answered.

"If you don't mind getting started, I'll go grab us some refreshments," she said. "Sprite?"

"Yes, please." Pete seemed surprised.

"Be right there," she promised. She always tried to pay attention to the people that worked with her. Pete was fairly new to the station but he was a hard worker and had a talent for picking the perfect shots.

Shelby strolled over to one of the food trucks parked on the side of the road. Someone must have heard about all the people gathering there and figured they could make some extra money. Normally, the food trucks rotated throughout the downtown area for the businessmen and women. Since five of them were already parked there, hours before lunch, Shelby was not looking forward to how many more protesters they had to be expecting.

She headed to a purple and gold truck that she knew well. Rosa Martinez made the absolute best Chile Verde. If Shelby had known Rosa would be there she'd have made a plan to meet Julie there. Instead, she'd be stuck eating something healthy at the café across the street. But they'd have more privacy inside than sitting on the lawn.

The walk did not make her feet feel any better in her high-heels. She hated having to wear them but they did make her legs look fabulous. If she remained in her heels all day, she'd probably be limping later. At least at the office, she could kick her shoes off and put on some flats.

"Hi, Rosa," she greeted as she approached.

"Shelby!" Rosa was a beautiful Spanish American who had a smart mind for business and a kind heart. Shelby really liked her. "I knew you'd be here."

Shelby laughed. "Of course."

"So how about one of my breakfast burritos?" Rosa suggested.

"Well." Shelby glanced back at Pete. They had started early and she was going to be working all day. Plus, if she had a salad at lunch, a burrito now wouldn't be too bad. She grinned. "I'll take two."

"Great!" Rosa started to assemble Shelby's breakfast. "So how's it going this morning?" Rosa asked waving toward the courthouse.

"I thought we'd have a little more time before we were invaded," Shelby commented.

"That's exactly what it seems like, isn't it?" Rosa said.

"Yeah," Shelby agreed.

"I heard about it on Twitter," Rosa told her. "My grandson made me an account where I could announce where I'd be any day of the week."

"I know," Shelby said. "I've tracked you down that way before."

"It's crazy," Rosa said. "I just type a few words and anyone can find me."

"Or you can go to the masses," Shelby added.

Rosa rolled the tortillas into foil and held them up. "Drink?"

"A Sprite, water and large coffee, please," Shelby ordered.

"Coming right up."

As Rosa finished, Shelby turned back to look around the town square. The crowd had grown even more, which surprised her. The actual trial was not starting today but that didn't seem to stop the gathering. She frowned, noticing that there was a definite change in the atmosphere. The same people she'd interviewed were on the left side of the main sidewalk and another group was gathering on the right.

"That's interesting," she mumbled.

"Here you go."

Shelby returned her attention to Rosa. She accepted the large coffee cup and a bag with the burritos and other drinks. "How much?"

"Seven dollars, even," Rosa said.

She put the bag's handle around her wrist as she pulled a ten from her purse. Shelby passed over the bill. "Keep the change."

Rosa beamed at her. "See you for lunch?"

"No." Shelby shook her head. "But I'll probably need something an hour later."

"I'll keep something aside for you," Rosa promised.

"You're the best," Shelby told her. She stepped back to rejoin Pete.

"Hey, Shelby," Rosa called.

"Yes." She turned her head.

"Be careful. There will be a lot of crazies out there."

"Yes, I think I already met a few earlier," she admitted. With one last wave, Shelby strolled to Pete and more work.

Chapter Three

Julie looked cute in her jeans and T-shirt. Shelby envied her friend being comfortable, since she was dying to take off her shoes and put on a pair of sweatpants. The busy morning had turned into a chaotic afternoon.

The new group that had gathered while Shelby had been grabbing some burritos had turned out to be an assembly of shifters. As soon as the human protesters had spotted them they'd started to shout insults.

Shelby had reported twice more before other news vans had started arriving. Her exclusives were over and she was going to have to share her space. But this was her town and it didn't matter how many big station reporters showed up, she was going to be right there giving them a run for their money.

"Earth to Shelby." Julie ran her hand in front of Shelby's face.

"Oh, sorry!" Shelby laughed. She gave her friend a hug. "It's good to see you."

"You too," Julie said. They walked inside the small café and grabbed one of the few empty tables. Since it was after two, they'd managed to miss the lunch crowd.

"I was surprised to get your text about lunch. I figured you'd be swamped as long as the trial is going on."

"I will be," Shelby agreed. "I just needed to talk to you."

"About shifters?" Julie questioned. "You know I won't say anything on record."

"Yeah." Shelby waved that off. "You never will. What I wanted to ask you about is a little more…personal."

"Personal?" Julie repeated. "Maybe about a certain wolf?"

Shelby's head snapped up. "What?"

Julie laughed. "I know about you and Mike."

"How?" Shelby lowered her voice as she leaned across the table toward Julie.

"My brother," Julie said.

"Garrett? How does Garrett know?" Shelby asked.

"Well." Julie winked. "He stopped by Mike's office when he was investigating the series of arsons with Lieutenant Haas, remember?"

"Crap!" Shelby did remember that morning. It had been at the very beginning of her and Mike's relationship. She'd stopped by his office to return a jacket he'd left behind the night before, and one thing had led to another and they'd made love on his desk.

At least she'd been re-dressed by the time Garrett had knocked on Mike's door. She'd have died of embarrassment if her best friend's brother had walked in on her and Mike.

"Why didn't you say anything?" Shelby asked.

"I figured you'd tell me when you were ready," Julie replied.

"Hello, ladies, my name's Tony and I'll be taking care of you today."

Shelby glanced up at the cute young waiter.

He passed them each a thin menu. "Can I get you started with something to drink?"

Shelby really wished she could order an alcoholic drink but she still had more work to do. "I'll take an iced tea please."

"Same for me," Julie added.

"I'll be right back with your drinks. If you have any questions about the menu, please let me know," he said before he left them.

"He's cute," Julie commented when they were alone again.

"Yes," Shelby agreed, not really paying attention. "What are you going to get?"

"Shelby?" Julie placed her hand on top of Shelby's menu.

"What?"

"You didn't even check out the waiter. You always check out the waiter," Julie said. "Or at least mention how hot he is."

"He's a little young for me, don't you think?" Shelby questioned.

"Yes, but that's never stopped you before," Julie said. "You're really interested in Mike, aren't you?"

Of course she was! Wasn't that why she was sitting in front of her best friend when she should only be thinking about the next report? "Yes."

Julie squealed. "That is so awesome!"

There wasn't much she could say to that. For Shelby, Mike was a complication that her career didn't need. It was her heart that wanted him. "I think you're a little ahead of me," Shelby admitted. "I'm still getting used to the idea of wanting Mike more than just to warm my bed."

"I can't believe I missed it," Julie said. "You need to tell me everything."

"I will," Shelby promised. "But first I have some questions."

"Hold on." Julie pointed at her.

The waiter walked up from behind Shelby before he placed their drink down.

"Thanks," Julie and Shelby said at the same time.

"Have you had time to decide?" he asked.

"I'll have the grilled chicken salad, please," Shelby told him. She had promised herself that she'd eat a healthy lunch.

"Can I get a cheeseburger and fries?" Julie requested.

Shelby glared at her.

Tony smiled. "I'll have your food to you as soon as possible."

"Thanks," Shelby and Julie said together.

"You're a brat," Shelby told her.

"What?" Julie shrugged. "I don't have to look good on camera."

"I hate you."

"No," Julie said. "You really don't."

"Anyway," Shelby drawled out. "I was wondering if you had any issues at work when everyone found out about you and Cooper."

"You mean because I was dating a shifter?" Julie asked.

"Yes," Shelby said.

"No, but then, I work around a lot of shifters, so I didn't expect any trouble," Julie told her. "But you do?"

"I don't know," Shelby admitted. "There are only a few shifters at the station and they seem to be treated equally."

"But?" Julie questioned.

"But I may not always be at the station. If I ever want to move up, I'll have to eventually move to a bigger city where I'll get more exposure," Shelby said.

"You're going to move?" Julie frowned.

"One day, yes, and the decisions I make now will affect where I can go," Shelby said.

"And Mike is one of those decisions," Julie said.

"Yes," Shelby admitted. "He is."

They sat there at the table for several moments in silence. Shelby figured she'd caught her friend off guard and that Julie didn't understand how the business Shelby was in worked.

"I'm sorry," Julie finally said.

"What?" That wasn't the response Shelby had been expecting.

"You find a guy that you're completely interested in and you think of him as a sacrifice. So you can have the career you want but might not have the man who is perfect for you," Julie said.

"I don't know about that," Shelby replied. "I've been sleeping with him for months, so I'm not going to all of a sudden declare my love and decide I want to settle down and have kids."

"But you could," Julie said.

Shelby had picked up her tea and taken a drink when Julie spoke and she ended up choking. "Are you serious?" she managed.

"Why not?" Julie asked. "You love Clear Creek and are happy here. Mike is a great guy, a successful lawyer, and a good friend to us all. If you didn't have some sort of feelings for him, you would never have slept with him to begin with. So why isn't that enough?"

"First of all, I started sleeping with Mike before I even knew him well. It was supposed to be purely physical," Shelby told her.

Julie scoffed. "Yeah, right."

"That was our arrangement and it was my idea," Shelby snapped.

"You thought he was hot the first time you met him at my house," Julie pointed out.

"Technically, I'd interviewed and talked to Mike before that night at your house," Shelby corrected.

"And always thought he was hot," Julie said with a smile. "Then you actually saw him out in a social setting and the chemistry between the two of you was obvious to us all."

"It was not," Shelby argued.

Julie nodded. "I thought you hated each other but Cooper told me that there was a thin line between love and hate and that the two of you just needed to continue to be around one another."

"So you played matchmaker and kept inviting us over for barbecues," Shelby accused.

"Not that my 'matchmaking', as you call it, was needed, was it?" Julie teased.

"No, it wasn't," Shelby said. "And it was my idea."

Julie just shook her head. "You're still in denial but that's okay. The fact that you're here today just proves my point."

"Here you go, ladies," Tony said as he walked up with their lunches.

"Yum!" Julie cried. "This looks great."

Shelby glanced from her bowl to Julie's plate. Ugh, why had she eaten that burrito earlier? "Yes, thank you," she told Tony.

"Just let me know if you ladies need anything else," he responded.

Shelby picked up her fork and took a bite of her salad. Her conversation with Julie hadn't gone exactly as planned. "Can we get back to my questions?"

"Of course." Julie picked up a fry and waved it at her. "You wanted to know if I worried that my job could have been affected by Cooper being a shifter. My answer is no. Do I think it will affect yours? Probably."

Not the answer she'd wanted but in all honesty, it was the truth. "I can't have both." It hurt to realize that.

"What are you talking about?" Julie leaned close.

"Mike is an out shifter," Shelby said. "I can't date him and try to hide our relationship too. It wouldn't be fair to him and I doubt he'd put up with it for long. Plus, it would seem dishonest."

"True," Julie agreed. "But I still don't see how that matters."

"As a reporter, I have to be unbiased," Shelby said. "It's hard enough hiding how I feel with idiots like those damn protesters. If I'm dating a shifter, I won't be given any assignment that has anything to do with shifters. And nowadays everything has to do with shifters."

"Oh." Julie sat back with a sigh.

"Yeah, so if I decide to take the next step with Mike, I may be throwing everything I've worked so hard on away," Shelby said.

"Damn," Julie replied. "So now what?"

"Now I want to ask some more questions," Shelby told her.

Julie picked up her burger. "Okay, shoot." She took a large bite, humming in appreciation.

Shelby almost kicked her friend.

* * * *

"Just to warn you, the crowd has grown since this morning," Austin said quietly in Mike's ear.

They were still sitting in the courtroom waiting until the hall cleared out so they could avoid Jody running into anyone.

"Even more than it had at lunch?" Mike asked.

They'd decided to stay inside for the day since Jody was still nervous being around other people. Austin had picked up some food from the local deli for lunch and they'd eaten in one of the rooms that was available.

"Yeah," Austin agreed. "But Kiley just told me that the numbers have doubled since then."

"Shit." Mike glanced around the empty courtroom. It had been a hell of a day and he just wanted to go home and have a strong drink. The defense counsel had tried to have any shifter excused from the jury. Mike had pointed out that since they weren't required to admit their shifter status publicly, the law couldn't force them to.

The day had gone downhill from there. The defense attorney Melvin Parks was a sleaze. He did everything he could to try to trick or get the potential jury members to say whether or not they were shifters.

Luckily, Mike didn't need anyone to admit to being a shifter, since he could smell it on them. He'd managed to get two wolf shifters, a lion shifter and a fox shifter, on the jury. That was the only good thing that had come from the day. He'd already written his opening statement for the next day but he had some changes to make. It was going to be a long night.

First, they had to get out of the courthouse. "Should we go out the back?"

"I don't know," Randy said as he joined them. "Will that look like we're hiding him? We want Jody to appear sincere and open. We can't have anyone thinking he's hiding something."

His partner had a point. "True."

"I'd also like to keep our emergency exits available, in case we need to get away from a particular threat," Austin added.

Mike glanced over at Jody, who sat with his head bent. "Give me a minute with him, please."

Randy nodded, and Austin patted his back.

"We'll be right outside the doors," Austin told him.

"Thanks," Mike said before he strolled over to his client. Jody didn't even look up as he approached. Mike sat beside him. "How are you doing?"

Jody shook his head but finally looked at him. "I didn't ask for all this. I liked my job and when I was fired it shocked me. I was good at it and did everything I was asked."

"I know." Mike placed his hand on Jody's shoulder for support.

"Then I couldn't get on anywhere else because that prick lied and told everyone I was screwing things up," Jody said.

"We'll take care of him. He'll pay for what he's done," Mike promised. He knew better than to get emotionally involved in a case but he couldn't help it this time. What Jody had gone through could have happened to him or one of his close friends. The fact that it had happened to a fellow Pack member was bad enough in and of itself.

"Will it even matter in the end?" Jody asked.

"What?" Mike asked.

"He's not going to lose his business. He might have to pay some money and admit he did wrong. And I said *might* there. In the end, he'll go back to running his multi-million-dollar company and I'll still be scrounging around for work. Now, there's a crowd of people outside here yelling slurs about me. Why? Because I can shift into a wolf?"

"That's right," Mike told him. "This is all because you're a shifter."

Jody nodded. "It's not fair."

"No, it's not," Mike agreed. "And you don't have to go through with this."

"After all the time you spent on my case?" Jody asked.

"Yes," Mike assured him. "Whatever is best for you is what I'm willing to do."

Jody sighed. "And the next shifter who gets fired only because they are a shifter, what happens to them?"

"They'll go through the same thing you are," Mike said.

"So I can't just give this up," Jody told him.

"It's up to you," Mike reminded him.

"I'll be okay," Jody said. "I just want to go home and rest."

Mike patted him. "Let's go." He stood and slung his laptop bag over his shoulder. Jody rose and together they walked to the door. Mike stepped in front of Jody so that he would exit first.

"Right here," Austin called out. He stood against the wall with his arms crossed.

Austin appeared at ease, but Mike could see that Gray and Kiley had taken position in front of the outside doors keeping everyone else out.

"Are we ready?" Austin asked.

"Yes," Mike answered. He motioned for Jody to follow him. He passed Austin with Jody at his heels. When they got to the glass entrance, Mike peered out. "Shit!" The lawn was packed.

"Where did all these people come from?" Jody asked.

"Hell, most likely," Gray muttered. "Did you see how many anti-shifter protesters there are out there?"

"This is crazy," Mike murmured.

"The number of shifter supporters is really growing too," Kiley said. "As long as the two groups stay on their own side, hopefully there won't be any trouble."

"I don't see that happening," Austin said. "The longer the trial takes, the more tempers are going to flare."

"Yeah," Mike agreed. He took a deep breath. "Let's get this over with." He pushed open the door and the noise level was astonishing. The anti-shifter protesters were screaming while the shifters stood around talking and laughing. Mike spotted Shelby standing in the small divide between the two sides holding a microphone with a camera on her. He started toward her before he remembered where his priorities had to lie. He had to look after Jody, even with the bodyguards there. He couldn't do anything to protect her if a riot or something happened.

"Let's get Jody to the car," Austin said. "Gray and Kiley, stay beside him. No one gets a hand on him. Mike, lead him out and I'll bring up the rear. We move as a unit. Our guys are spread out throughout the crowd and will step in if there's any trouble."

"Be quick and don't let anyone stop you," Kiley advised.

Mike took the first step down. Shelby's cameraman had turned and was now broadcasting their exit. He kept his gaze straight and didn't give the camera any attention. The closer he walked to Shelby, the harder it was to not look at her. Thankfully as he led the way down the sidewalk she and her cameraman moved out of the way. He nodded slightly in appreciation.

He only took a couple more steps before another reporter was shoving a microphone in his face. Mike shouldered the piece of equipment out of the way but the woman was persistent. She bumped into him, forcing him to slow down.

"Excuse me, we have no comment at this time," he said politely.

Another reporter rushed forward, and light flashed all around him. Mike placed a hand on his bag to make sure it remained at his side as he tried to push on. The taunts grew louder. He could hear the words 'animals', 'abominations' and 'sinners' shouted at them.

It was getting harder to try to muscle his way through the crowd. Mike could put his full strength into it but he didn't want to start any trouble either. Where the hell were the cops? With the amount of people out there, someone should be doing crowd control.

"Let them pass."

Mike glanced over as two men stepped in front of him facing the reporters. The blond guy had been the one who had spoken, but the other glanced over his shoulder at Mike.

"Stay close and we'll get you through," he said.

Mike nodded.

It was easier with the two shifters pushing the reporters out of the way. They didn't use force, just shouldered past. Once they'd walked a dozen feet or so it was easier.

They picked up speed until they were in the parking lot. A dark SUV was idling.

"That's us," Kiley said. "We just need to get Jody inside."

Mike zeroed in on the vehicle. That was his goal. As soon as Jody was inside and off to his house, Mike could get himself home. The two shifters broke away, and Mike rushed forward to pull open the back door. He helped Jody in before he slammed it shut. Kiley jumped in the passenger seat while Gray ran around to the other side of the SUV. As soon as Gray was inside, the vehicle was pulling away. Mike jumped back.

"My guy called and said that reporters are all around Jody's place. I spoke to your Alpha and he has a house that we can move Jody to," Austin said facing him.

"That's a good idea," Mike said.

"You might want to find a place to stay tonight also," Austin advised.

"Fuck! My house too?"

"Yeah." Austin shrugged. "We should have expected this but even I'm surprised by the amount of people that showed up. Do you have somewhere you can stay?"

Mike waved him off. "I'll get a hotel or something."

"Every place is sold out, from what we hear," Austin told him.

Damn, he'd forgotten that.

"You can come with us," Austin offered.

But Mike needed a break. He had work to do and needed peace and quiet. "I got a buddy I can stay with."

"Is there anything you need from your place?" Austin asked.

"A suit?" Mike said with a laugh. "All I have is my gym bag at the office."

"You might want to avoid that place too."

Mike turned to see the two shifters who had helped earlier.

"I'm not avoiding my office," Mike told them.

The blond nodded. "I understand."

"Mike, let me introduce you to Clint Price" —he indicated to the blond—"and Kurt Moore. The shifters the Wolf Council sent to help," Austin introduced.

"Thanks for your help." Mike shook hands with Clint.

"No problem," Clint said. "I think I stepped on a few toes but I kind of enjoyed it."

Kurt laughed and slapped Clint's back. "We don't let him out much so he has to have his fun when he can."

Mike laughed and it felt good. "Yeah, I get it," he told Kurt as they shook hands.

"I'll have a few days' worth of clothing picked up from your house," Austin said, drawing Mike's attention again. "Why don't you sort out your arrangements and call me with the address of where you're staying?"

"I'd appreciate it. Do you need a ride?" Mike asked.

"I'm set," Austin replied.

Mike waved at the three men then started for his own car. He clicked the unlock button and pulled open the door. After dropping his laptop bag onto the passenger seat, he took a look around. It didn't appear the crowd was thinning, and Mike didn't get why. There was nothing else to see.

Oh well, he had bigger problems. He climbed inside his vehicle and slammed the door shut. Blessed quiet.

He took a deep breath and laid his head back. He was exhausted but sleep was a long way away. First, he needed a place to crash.

Mike reached over to his bag and pulled out his cell phone. He'd had it on silent all day and now saw that he had fourteen missed calls and seven text messages. Wow, wasn't he a popular guy.

Instead of listening to the messages, he pulled up his contact list, found Cooper's name and hit dial.

"I just saw your ugly mug on TV," Cooper said as a greeting.

"Oh, don't be that way," Mike joked back. "You know I'm pretty."

"Yeah, yeah, yeah," Cooper said with a laugh. "Since I just saw you live, I'm guessing you're still close to the courthouse."

"Sitting in the parking lot as a matter of fact," Mike replied.

"Why? What's wrong?" Cooper asked, growing serious.

"I hate to ask," Mike said and he really did. "But apparently the reporters have my house staked out and I need a place to stay tonight."

"Oh!" Cooper sounded relieved. "You don't need to even ask. Come over any time."

"Are you sure? I don't want to intrude on you and Julie," Mike said.

"Actually, we're both on nights this week, so you'll have the place to yourself," Cooper told him.

Mike knew that Julie preferred working nights since that was when Cooper was usually on shift. As a detective for the narcotics unit for the Clear Creek Police Department, Cooper needed to be out on the streets late at night and early mornings.

"I can find somewhere else to stay," Mike offered. "You don't have to leave me alone in your house."

"That doesn't even make sense," Cooper replied with a snort. "You can relax and get some quiet time. It's not like I don't trust you. We lived together for four years in college."

"And Julie is okay with this?" Mike questioned.

Heavy sigh. "Yes but I'll ask her if it'll make you feel better. Hang on," Cooper demanded.

Cooper must have put his hand over the phone since Mike couldn't hear the conversation, just muffled voices.

"She said of course and if you wanted to invite anyone over there's leftover lasagna in the fridge," Cooper said once he came back on the line.

"Invite someone over?" he asked.

"A stunningly sexy reporter," Cooper said. "Her words, not mine."

Mike sucked in a sharp breath. How did Julie know about him and Shelby? Damn it, right when he'd felt Shelby was finally getting close to admitting her true feelings for him and now people were finding out. If Shelby panicked and ran, Mike was not going to be happy.

"They had lunch today, by the way," Cooper told him.

"Who?" Had he missed something?

"Julie and Shelby," Cooper answered.

So Shelby had told Julie. That was an interesting turn of events. "I'll think about it," he finally relented.

"You do that," Cooper said.

"I have a few errands to run but I'll be there shortly," Mike told him.

"You know where the spare key is," Cooper said. "Just let yourself in."

"Thanks, man," Mike said.

"No problem," Cooper replied before he disconnected.

Mike shook his head before he dropped his phone back in his bag. He started the car and noticed that the crowd seemed to be getting smaller. He'd have to ask Cooper about some kind of crowd control. They'd gotten lucky with Clint and Kurt earlier but that didn't mean their luck would last. Having some of the Clear Creek Police Department might deter any fights or a direct attack on Jody.

A feeling of unease pricked his awareness, and the hairs on the back of his neck stood up. It was a warning that he'd come to recognize as his wolf growing cautious.

Was someone watching him?

There was no one in his immediate area so he wasn't sure why he had this sudden feeling.

He also couldn't see Shelby, so he put the car in drive and backed up. He didn't really think it would be wise to invite her over to Cooper's, even if he'd suggested it.

The first stop he needed to make was at his Alpha's house. He could call Jeremy but he'd feel better if he could sit down and talk to him. He was growing concerned about Jody. It couldn't be easy for anyone to go through all the aggravation of a trial but Jody was such a kind man that this entire process was really hurting him.

He turned right off the main street toward the outskirts of town where the Pack territory was located. He kept his speed to the limit as he didn't want to draw any undue attention to himself.

Mike pressed the button for the radio and classic rock began to fill the car. As he drove he reached up to loosen his tie. He'd remove it and his jacket when he got to the main house.

It was a lot quieter when he pulled up in front of Jeremy's compared to the last time he'd been there. Mike parked in front of the steps and turned off the car. He grabbed his cell before he pushed open the door and climbed out. He first removed his jacket and tossed it onto the seat then slammed the door closed.

As he started up the stairs, Jeremy stepped out.

"Evening, Mike," Jeremy greeted with a smile. "I didn't expect you to drive all the way out here."

"I wanted to talk. It'll be easier than trying to do this on the phone," Mike said.

"Let's go in the study and I'll pour you a drink." Jeremy motioned Mike into the house.

The dark wall panels that flowed through the hall went well with the wood floors. Mike had spent so much time in the house that he felt at home there. He could hear low talking and laughter farther away. Most likely in the kitchen. Mike glanced at his watch. It was close to dinnertime and he hoped he wasn't interrupting anything.

The third door on the right was Jeremy's study and was open. Mike strolled through and went directly to the large wingback chair in front of the patio window. He heard the door close and Jeremy's soft footsteps as the Alpha walked close to him.

He peered out at the gorgeous garden that he used to run in when he was just a pup. Life used to be so much easier when he was a boy. Even in college, when he had still been trying to figure out his life and what he wanted. He and Cooper used to come out here when exams and stress got too much.

"Drink this." Jeremy handed him a snifter of brandy.

"Thanks." Mike accepted the glass. "I need this."

"I bet," Jeremy commented as he sat across from Mike with his own drink. "Hard day at the office?"

Mike barked out a laugh. "Damn defense attorney is a weasel. I can't stand him but he's the best money can buy."

"You had to expect that," Jeremy said.

"Yeah," Mike agreed. "Still, it irked me how damn cocky he is."

"Run into any problems?" Jeremy asked. His Alpha wouldn't ask any direct questions that could put Mike or his profession in danger.

"Nothing I couldn't take care of." Mike took a sip then sighed. "I'm worried about Jody."

Jeremy smiled. "I know. I wish he didn't have to go through this but Jody deserves something for what he's been through. And in the end, it will help that he fought back."

"He's worried about getting work," Mike told him.

"I know, but it's already being taken care of. A lot of our fellow shifters have already asked about getting in touch with Jody. He'll end up with more work than he'll know what to do with," Jeremy shared.

"That's great." Mike relaxed a little more. "If we can get through this case without anything bad happening, I'll be surprised."

"Has there been a particular threat?" Jeremy leaned forward as he spoke.

"No." Mike waved at him. "It's just a feeling I have. Like as soon as we turn our backs someone is going to try to come at us. I don't know if it's for me or Jody but I just can't get this nagging feeling to go away."

"I can order more protection for the two of you. For Randy and his boy, too." Jeremy was already pulling out his phone.

"I'm certain we have all we need," Mike told him. "Have you met the security detail?"

"Yes, I know Austin from my younger days, so when the Council suggested his firm I was thrilled. But if you don't feel comfortable we can make other arrangements for you and Jody. How about staying here?" Jeremy said.

"We moved Jody due to the reporters at his house," Mike told him.

"Yes, I've already heard."

"I'd like to be in town in case something happens, so I'm staying at Cooper's," Mike said.

"Well, you can't beat staying at a cop's place," Jeremy agreed.

"That was what I was thinking. And like I said I don't know of any danger but I have a bad feeling that this trial is not going to be a simple case."

"Don't discredit your feelings, and keep your eyes open. I'll talk to Gage and Cain and see if they have any suggestions," Jeremy said. "It's the Pack's job to take care of you and we will be there. Just call me if you need anything at all."

"I promise," Mike said.

"Good, now finish your drink so you can get to Cooper's and relax."

Chapter Four

Shelby placed the salad that she'd just finished tossing in the middle of the kitchen table. She'd been surprised and pleased when Julie had called to inform her that Mike would be staying at her and Cooper's house and they both had to work. It had been Julie's suggestion for Shelby to stop by.

After a quick trip home so she could change clothes and put on her most comfortable tennis shoes, she'd hopped in her car and headed over. Julie had let her in while telling her that Mike was expected soon. There was also a large pan of lasagna in the fridge that Julie had said could be warmed up for dinner.

Shelby loved Julie's lasagna and was more than happy to put it in the oven to warm. The house already smelled like mouthwatering marinara sauce and garlic. She hoped Mike showed up soon. Shelby had really expected him at least an hour ago. Julie and Cooper were gone, so it was just her as she prepped the meal.

She took a sniff of an opened wine bottle as she carried it to the table along with two glasses. Everything was almost perfect. She just needed the man she hoped to have a romantic night with sitting in front of her.

Mike had looked so tired when he'd stepped out of the courthouse at the end of the day. The guy he'd been walking in front of, the client, Jody Norman, had appeared terrified. Pete had gotten a good close-up but as Mike had led the way toward her, she'd had Pete step back. Respect, and yes personal feelings, had had her backing off. Unlike the other reporters who'd acted like animals.

Sometimes it shamed her that professional news people acted like they had no class, but that was just natural, she guessed. She'd made a promise to herself a long time ago to act differently. That was what had actually gotten her noticed with KVVT. Her producer had seen her after an interview at her college station. Instead of pushing and screaming at the dean like the others, Shelby had gotten an exclusive by charm and wit. She was still proud of that fact.

The slamming of a car door caught her attention. Shelby rubbed her hands together. She knew that Mike would come in from the back door as that was where the spare key was hidden. It amused Shelby that a cop and an EMT would still place a key outside that could be found by anyone. Shelby could never do that.

She rushed over to the oven to check on the food. As she pulled out the pan, the back door opened.

"Shelby?"

"Hi." She turned still holding the pan. "Hungry?"

He was so cute with the confused but happy look on his face. He stared at her for several minutes as she set the lasagna on the counter and closed the oven.

"I…" He frowned while looking around. "Are you supposed to be here?"

Shelby laughed. "Julie told me that you'd be staying the night and if I wanted to stop by there would be plenty of dinner."

Mike set his bags down next to the door before he grinned. "I was just imagining having dinner with you. Cooper had suggested the same but I got caught up on running errands and didn't think I'd have the energy to entertain."

"You don't have to," Shelby said as she strolled toward him. When she reached him, Shelby pressed close and kissed him lightly.

Mike growled and grabbed her as he deepened their lip lock. Oh, how she loved the taste of him. He'd had some brandy earlier along with a mint or something.

At some time between when Mike had left the courthouse and arrived at Julie and Cooper's, Mike had changed into jeans and a T-shirt. Shelby slipped her hands under the hem of his top to rub his stomach. His flat, muscular stomach.

"God," Mike murmured after he'd pulled back slightly. "I needed that."

Shelby grinned. "There will be more of that after dinner and a glass of wine. For the next half hour there will be no thinking or talking about anything professional."

He blinked at her. Shelby could only take that as a sign she'd caught him off guard and felt proud. "This is new," he finally said.

"Yes," she agreed. "Sit, and I'll pour you a glass of wine and get the rest of the food on the table."

"Okay," Mike said before he moved toward the table.

The way that his ass moved inside those faded jeans made her itch to reach out and give him a squeeze. Once he was sitting, Shelby moved. First, she poured some of the sweet red into two wine glasses and passed one to him. Then she walked to the counter and picked up the pan that was half full of lasagna as well as the cookie sheet with breadsticks.

"I can't thank you enough for this," Mike told her.

She'd only wanted to surprise him but this meal was ending up giving her a chance to come clean as to where her thoughts had been going. "It's really no trouble."

Mike smiled. "It was a hell of a day."

Shelby nodded as she set the food down on the table. "Let it go for now," she advised.

They filled their plates and sat across from each other. Shelby looked over at Mike to find him watching her. "What?"

"This is nice," Mike said.

And he was right. They might order a meal to be delivered after being together every once in a while but even that was rare. Never had they had such an intimate dinner.

"It smells wonderful," Mike commented and took a bite.

Shelby followed suit because she was hungry and she didn't know how to begin the conversation that she wanted to have. So she ate and drank her wine.

He must have been starving because Mike finished the food on his plate then went and got more. Shelby ate slower and kept peering up at him.

"What's on your mind?" he asked when he finally pushed his plate away.

Of course he noticed that she couldn't stop looking at him. "I want to talk to you about something but I'm not sure now's the right time."

"Is it about the case?" he asked.

"No," she assured him quickly. "Not at all."

"Then go ahead. I didn't think about my day the entire time I was eating so any other subject is open for discussion. I want a bit of a break from the case," he told her as he rubbed his stomach. "Damn, Julie makes awesome lasagna."

"She does," Shelby agreed. Now that Mike was aware that there was something she wanted to discuss she couldn't chicken out. Shelby poured them both more to drink.

Mike watched her and his blue eyes shined with what she knew was amusement. She'd caught the look numerous times before.

"Whatever you want to say can't be that bad." He grew serious and frowned. "I take that back. If you want to end our arrangement, I really don't want to hear that."

"Well." Shelby lifted an eyebrow. "I don't want to end things."

"Good," Mike said before he took a drink. "Go ahead."

"I don't want to end things but I do want...need something different," she said.

He sighed before he drained the rest of his wine. Shelby stood to get him a refill, but he waved her off. "I'm okay."

Shelby wasn't so she topped off her own glass. "I've been thinking..." She looked up at him. All amusement had disappeared, and she missed it. "What if I wanted to change things between us? What would you say to that?"

"Depends on the change," he said quietly.

"Something...more...serious," she said.

Mike stiffened. "Serious?"

Oh God! Was that not what he wanted? How had she read his signs wrong? "It's just—"

"You want a relationship instead of sex?" he interrupted.

"Yes, no, yes," she fumbled the words.

Mike held up his hand. "I want more too. If you'd like to date and see where we can go in a relationship, I'd love that."

"Really?" Shelby relaxed back.

"Yes, I thought I'd shown that," Mike said.

"You did," Shelby said.

"So dating?" he asked.

"There's just one thing." Shelby winced as she spoke.

Mike nodded. "Okay."

"I still want to move up with a bigger station," Shelby told him. "My career goals haven't changed."

"Your passion for what you love is one of the reasons that I'm attracted to you," Mike told her.

"I don't want us to hide our relationship," Shelby said. "I'll admit I thought about asking that of you."

"You did?"

"Yes," she said. "But if I ask that of you, I'm not really changing our relationship. It would say that I'm ashamed to be with you in public. I wouldn't expect you to allow that and I'm not that kind of woman. If I care for you I can't hide that away."

"I might have agreed to it at first," Mike told her.

"Really?" She was surprised.

"It's not that I don't understand why you need to be cautious," Mike said. "I'd agree but there is no way that I'd be able to continue like that for long. And if we do try to make it work between us, we won't be able to go back to having just a physical relationship."

"It was never purely physical." She used Julie's words from earlier.

Mike grinned. "It wasn't. I didn't think you'd figured that out yet."

"Sometimes I'm slow," she joked. "And I agree that we wouldn't be able to go back to how things were."

"So we go at this all the way?" Mike asked.

Shelby finished off her drink. "Yes."

Mike nodded. "Yes." He stood with a smile before he circled the table and pulled her onto her feet. He kissed her hard and with urgency.

Shelby wrapped her arms around his neck as she rose to her tiptoes and pushed into him.

"You feel so good," he said when they broke apart to breathe.

"Mmm." She planted her lips back on his while raising one leg around his waist.

Mike lifted her off her feet, and Shelby rocked against him. He was already hard against her stomach and she couldn't wait to get him inside her. She cupped his erection and gave him a little squeeze. He moaned while his hips jerked.

"Shit," Mike muttered. "Not here. I can't take you on my best friend's table."

Shelby laughed. "It would make having dinner here the next time more interesting."

Mike looked like he was considering it but ended up shaking his head. "No," he said. "Bedroom."

"Okay," she agreed. She huffed out a breath in surprise when Mike didn't set her down and instead hiked her up higher and carried her off. Damn shifter strength. Mike surprised her with it every once in a while.

"Just hang on," he advised as he gave her ass a soft smack.

In retaliation, Shelby dropped her mouth to his neck and bit gently. Mike stumbled and groaned.

"You like that," she whispered.

"Do it again," he demanded, voice rough.

So she did. She nibbled and lapped at his neck as he took her into the guest bedroom.

It was just as she remembered it. White walls with just a bed, dresser and two nightstands. The bed was made up with a dark blue comforter and looked comfortable.

She bounced when Mike dropped her down. Before she could move he covered her body with his and kissed her. Shelby gave as good as he did, impatient to have him. She tugged at his shirt until he broke away to yank it over his head. She wriggled out of her own top and bra.

Mike's lips found her nipple, and she arched up while burying her fingers in his short hair. She held him against her breast as she lifted her hips to rub against his erection.

"Slow later," she panted. "I want you so bad."

"Yeah," he agreed. He sat up and pulled on his zipper. "I have just what you need."

She snorted at his cheesy line but then it was a race to get naked. She won since she didn't have to worry about shoes. Once she was undressed, Shelby grasped his hard-on and pumped him a few times.

Mike growled as he continued to fight with his shoes. Since he was still busy, Shelby dipped her head to run her tongue over the tip of his cock. She tasted his pre-cum before she took him in deep.

"Yes," he hissed.

Shelby pulled back and let his cock slide against her tongue before taking him in again. She loved how hard he was, since she knew she had caused the reaction.

With her eyes closed, she enjoyed every second of being in control of his pleasure. She used her right hand to hold him at the base of his erection while with her left she played with his balls. She could tell Mike was struggling not to move with how stiff he was keeping his body. That just wouldn't do.

Humming, she coaxed him into moving. Gently at first, Mike thrust into her mouth. She nodded slightly to show him that was what she wanted. Mike slipped his fingers through her hair as he held her head and withdrew then slid back into her mouth.

Heaven, the taste and feel of him. Shelby sucked harder.

"Oh God," Mike murmured. "So good."

Shelby liked pleasing him. She picked up the pace, sucking him harder.

"You've got to stop," Mike said after several minutes. "I want to come inside you."

Shelby popped off and grinned. "How do you want me?"

"Lie back," he said as he pushed her into position. He ran his fingers through her slick folds. She was already wet and ready.

"Come on," she urged.

Mike lifted her leg and hooked it over his elbow before he edged his cock to the opening of her pussy. He pressed inside, and Shelby sighed. Strong, he was so strong, and she just wanted him to make her forget all her troubles. She could depend on Mike to be true to her, and none of her worries could reach her when she was with him.

He tightened his hand against her hip, and Shelby slid her palm to cover his.

She could feel each plunge throughout her entire body. Her breath came out in harsh pants as she felt like she'd been electrified. Her fingers grew numb as passion turned her mind to a puddle. Shelby opened her eyes, unaware she'd even closed them in the first place. Mike was gazing down at her and the look was full of love and affection.

Had she never watched him at the same time he watched her during sex? No, she guessed she hadn't. With the hand that wasn't linked to his, she cupped his face. Mike blinked and slowed down.

Shelby smiled at him. He'd rubbed his cheek against her palm much like a cat did.

"Keep touching me," he said softly.

"Of course," she murmured.

Gaze locked with his, she placed her other hand on his face. They were making love, maybe not for the first time, but their emotional connection was definitely different from before.

"Mine," he said gently.

"Yes, and you're mine," she said.

Mike thrust harder, and her entire body shook. She hissed then hummed just a little when her clit began to throb. She pressed her hand firmer against his face as she reached climax. She had to work to keep her eyelids open. Mike grunted then came so they finished together.

* * * *

Shelby handed him the last freshly washed plate to dry, and Mike placed a kiss on her neck. After he and Shelby had lain and talked some more for about twenty minutes, Mike had known he had to get out of bed or he'd fall asleep. He still had more work to do before he could call it a night.

He'd told Shelby she could stay in bed but she'd only laughed and said she'd take care of the dishes. But that wasn't fair, since she'd made the dinner. So he'd made her a deal, she could wash but he'd dry before he got to work.

"That's it," Shelby stated as she dried her hands.

"Do you want to stay?" he asked. "I was going to set up at the table if you want to hang around."

She bit her lip and he held his breath then she shrugged. "If you don't mind."

"Of course not," he assured her. "That's why I asked."

"It's just—" She glanced out of the kitchen window before looking back at him. "I feel like we just made this huge commitment to each other and we should be..." She waved her hand around. "At least in the same house."

"I want you here," he said. He liked that Shelby saw their relationship as a commitment. He hadn't wanted to push her, scared that she'd run, so luckily his waiting had paid off.

"I can make some coffee," she offered.

Mike nodded then kissed her gently. "That would be great." He strolled over to the door where he'd dropped his stuff. He'd only thrown on his jeans after he'd gotten back up but he didn't plan to get dressed. After he worked on his statement for the next morning, he would be taking Shelby back to bed.

He pulled his laptop out of his bag and set it on the table before opening the lid. He pushed the power button to wait for it to load. While the computer worked, he peeked over at Shelby. She was at the counter pouring water into the coffee machine. The ease with which she moved around the kitchen told him that she spent enough time here to be comfortable.

In his mind, he could see her doing the same at his house as they both got ready for the day. They hadn't shared that intimacy yet but he now had something to look forward to. He smiled to himself.

A knock on the back door surprised him from his thoughts. He frowned and motioned for Shelby to stay behind the kitchen island. Cautious, he walked over to the door slowly. He pushed aside the yellow curtain that covered the small window in the door.

Clint and Kurt stood on the step. Clint grinned and waved.

Mike laughed and pulled open the door. "Hey, guys," he greeted. "I'm sorry, I was supposed to call and tell Austin where I was."

"Good thing we got guys watching you," Kurt said.

"Got some of your stuff. Don't worry, I broke in without leaving behind any sign." Clint held up a duffle bag, and Kurt held a hanging bag that would no doubt hold a suit or two.

"Come in." He motioned them forward. He wasn't really surprised that Clint had gotten inside his place. One thing he was learning about all these shifters was that they were some talented guys with questionable skills.

Clint entered first followed closely by Kurt. Mike closed the door and reached for his belongings. "I really appreciate it," he told them. There was really no point in stating the fact that he could have given them a key. He got the feeling that Clint had really enjoyed himself.

"No problem," Kurt said. He glanced over at Shelby. "We didn't mean to interrupt."

"Oh no," Shelby spoke up. "We were just going to have some coffee. Would you like to join us? It's about finished brewing."

Clint and Kurt exchanged a look. Mike glanced back at Shelby. There he was in only his jeans and Shelby wore her jeans with his T-shirt. It was obvious that they'd been quite busy earlier.

"Guys, this is Shelby Holt," Mike introduced. "Shelby, this is Clint Price and Kurt Moore. They were sent by the Wolf Council to make sure everything remains safe and in control."

She raised an eyebrow and her eyes twinkled.

"You're off the clock," he said as he pointed a finger at her knowing she would be dying to interview them. "Guys, at least join us for one cup of coffee. I really appreciate this." He held up his bags.

"Thanks," Clint said before he strolled to the table.

Kurt shook his head but followed his friend. "Sorry to interrupt," Kurt whispered to Mike as he passed. "I can smell the hormones in here."

"It's okay," Mike assured him.

"Usually he's not this big of an ass," Kurt said.

Clint laughed. "What can I say? I miss my mate so why should anyone else have any fun."

"Mate?" Shelby walked to the table. "Are you both mated?"

Well, that was easy. He should have known that Shelby would just fit in with a group of shifters. She'd already proved that she was on the shifter side and felt comfortable around them.

"I'm going to take these bags to the guestroom," Mike said.

"Sure," Shelby said as she waved while leaning closer to Clint. "Can I ask how long you've been mated? Shifter or human?"

Mike chuckled as he walked out. Shelby was a reporter in her bones. It didn't matter if she was working a story or just wanted information. He hurried to the room and dropped the duffle on top of the dresser before he continued to the closet so he could hang up his suits.

Instead of going through the bag Clint had brought, he headed back out to the kitchen. Shelby was laughing at something Clint had said but when he walked back in she glanced to him. Her features softened and he felt himself warm from the inside out. There might be two good-looking shifters next to her but she gazed at him like he was the best thing ever.

She started to rise, but he held up his hand. "I'll get the coffee."

Shelby smiled then turned back to Clint. "So you're both mated to humans? Is that usual?"

He half-listened as the three of them talked. The questions that Shelby asked revolved more around the guys' personal lives and she never brought up the trial that had brought them to town. That couldn't be easy for her but she was separating her profession from their relationship.

When he reached the coffee pot, he saw there were already four mugs sitting on the counter next to a canister of sugar and a carton of creamer. Mike filled the mugs then replaced the carafe. He turned with two mugs in his hands and Kurt was standing there holding out his hands. He hadn't heard the other shifter move even with his shifter hearing, which shocked him.

"I thought I'd help," Kurt said. "It seems like Clint and your girl have hit it off."

His girl—Mike liked the sound of that. "Thanks." He tilted his head. He snagged the creamer carton with his finger before he picked up two mugs. He strolled to the table and set one cup in front of Shelby then set the other where he could sit beside her. He placed the creamer in the middle of the table. He preferred his coffee black but knew Shelby liked plenty of creamer and sugar. Kurt joined them, passing one coffee to Clint.

Clint never paused while telling the story about his mate — who owned a coffee shop — and how they'd met. Shelby was nodding along, encouraging Clint, but she did cover Mike's knee with her hand.

Mike sipped his coffee and relaxed in his chair as he listened. Clint's mate sounded like a lot of fun and he wouldn't mind stopping by her coffee shop, which both Clint and Kurt raved about. Maybe he could plan a trip for him and Shelby to visit them. She'd probably love it.

Clint and Kurt both lived and worked for the Council and Mike would love to talk to one of the Council members.

The Wolf Council was an assembly of previous Alphas who helped keep the wolf shifter laws that had been set. Each shifter faction was ruled differently and the wolves depended on Alphas who'd ruled and protected different Packs throughout the states. Since his business brought him into contact with all types of people, Mike had met other shifter species. He knew that the felines followed a royal line. The bears, however, were solitary. The top bear shifter won the position in battle.

Shelby would probably be interested in how shifter species worked. With the spotlight on the shifters due to his case, it might be helpful for humans to see that the shifter world did have a way to police one another. Shelby would be great in charge of getting the information to the humans.

There was even a law enforcement agency called the Shifter Coalition that was made up of shifters and worked like the FBI. Mike even knew one of the shifters who ran one of the selective units.

He rose when he saw that everyone's cups were almost empty. He grabbed the carafe but when he hovered it over Kurt's mug the shifter waved him off.

"We really should be going," Kurt said.

Clint sighed. "He's right. I'd love to visit more," he said to Shelby. "But we do have some more work to do tonight."

"We've contacted the police department and there will be officers at the courthouse to help with crowd control. I don't think they expected the numbers that showed up," Kurt said.

"I'd feel better having them there," Mike said.

Kurt and Clint stood, and Shelby rose as well.

"You'll be around the courthouse tomorrow?" Clint asked Shelby.

"Of course." She grinned. "That's my job."

"I have some friends in town and I think you'd really get along with Nikki," Clint said.

"Oh God!" Kurt laughed. "That's perfect."

Mike glanced between the two guys. "Nikki?" he asked.

"Nikki Stratton," Kurt said. "She's a photo journalist and has written a couple of the shifters books that were released by the Council."

"That's great!" Shelby actually bounced.

"She's a shifter who mated another shifter," Clint added. "So she could give you another view on mated life."

"I'd love to meet her," Shelby said.

"She'll be at the courthouse tomorrow, working on her own article. I'll have her find you," Clint promised.

Kurt walked to the door, and Mike followed.

"Thanks again," Mike said.

"It was our pleasure," Kurt replied.

Clint stepped up and slapped him on the back as he passed. "We'll be seeing you both later."

Mike waited until they'd gotten to their vehicles before he closed and locked the door. He turned and found Shelby cleaning up the table.

"You still have work to do," she said. "More coffee?"

He nodded. "Yes, please."

She smiled before refilling his mug. Mike strolled over to the table where his laptop still sat. He took a seat but when Shelby passed he grabbed her hand.

"Did you enjoy meeting them?" He already knew the answer but asked anyway.

"I did," she said as she gazed at him.

"Good. Maybe before everyone leaves we can get together again," Mike suggested.

"That sounds great," Shelby agreed. She pulled away and took a step before she stopped. "Can I ask you something?"

"Sure," Mike said.

"I know you can't talk about the case, and I understand that. I'm trying to be very careful around your friends so they don't feel like I'm trying to grill them," she said.

"I know and I appreciate it," Mike told her. "But I also don't want you to change. I respect what you do and if you get a chance to ask questions, as long as they don't have anything to do with my actual case, I don't have a problem with it."

"You're awesome," Shelby stated.

"I think you are too," he admitted.

"But what I was thinking is a little different," she said.

"How so?" he asked.

"I was thinking about doing a piece to show the inner workings of shifters. Like how wolf shifters follow an Alpha and what the Pack means to you all," Shelby said. "I've heard how you talk about your Alpha and other Pack members. I'm interested in the dynamics from the inside."

Since he'd been thinking about the same thing earlier he only nodded. "I'll be happy to help. I can even introduce you to people who might be interested also. Other shifter species, perhaps."

"Other...shifters!" Shelby squealed then was in his lap.

Mike managed to keep the legs of his chair on the floor, not letting her knock them over. Shelby was kissing all over his face.

"Okay," he said. "We can discuss this but I have to get some work done."

"Right," Shelby said as she climbed off him. "I'm going to jot down a few thoughts so I don't forget anything."

"Sounds like a plan," he agreed.

Shelby leaned down and kissed him thoroughly. Mike allowed himself to enjoy their lip lock. When she pulled back, Mike had to force himself not to grab her and sit her back on his lap. There would be time for that later.

He really needed to work.

Chapter Five

The opening statement in a case was extremely important. It was the first time he got to state his case and give the jury an idea of who his client was and what had been done to him or her. Mike watched the jury members' faces as he spoke. He was depending on their sympathy to help him. That was one of the reasons that the defense counsel had tried to get a bench trial where there would be no jury and a judge would decide the outcome. Luckily that hadn't happened. Although there had been two judges he could have gotten that were also shifters.

The twelve men and women who'd been chosen all listened intently. Mike appreciated their attention. He felt good about the case. At the end of his speech, he glanced over at the defense table. The attorney was scowling while his client could only be described as bored.

Mike barely kept the smile off his face. The more the defense client acted like an ass, the better things were going to go for Mike's team.

He thanked the jurors then strolled back to his seat. If there was an extra pop in his step, let the other people in the courthouse think it was because he was sure about winning the case.

Of course Mike was damn confident but he knew better than to expect victory. And it was no one's business that he felt so damn good because of how he'd begun his day.

He'd woken up that morning with Shelby in his arms and his morning erection pressed against her. Hoping that she'd be able to sleep a little more, Mike had climbed out of bed trying not to disturb her.

Five minutes later as he'd showered, Shelby had joined him and they'd had another first — shower sex — and he was still buzzing from it. Afterward, he'd made breakfast while Shelby had spoken to her producer about the day's plans.

He'd enjoyed listening to her share all her thoughts about the case and her future projects the night before. It had been after midnight before they'd gone to bed, and Shelby had filled up three pages of her notebook with ideas and things she wanted to follow up on. She'd also made a list of people who might be willing to speak with her.

Mike had been surprised by how many shifters Shelby knew. Really he should have expected it, though. Shelby had been around Clear Creek a long time and she was well liked. Because she was fair and honest, people were willing to talk to her. That, and the fact Shelby had been the reporter who had covered the story when the old mayor had been arrested.

What a scandal that had been. Who would have guessed that the mayor would be accused and later convicted of organized crime, murder, drug trafficking and other assorted offenses? That had been a huge story.

Now she was the face of this trial. Which was another case that highlighted how shifters were targets. It made Mike worry about her. If someone could go after him or Jody, he had to guess that Shelby might also be a target. That thought made his stomach turn.

Damn, he needed to get his mind back on the case. He had friends he could rely on to help watch over Shelby if need be. Mike leaned forward to listen more intently.

The defense attorney was droning on but he wasn't saying anything that Mike hadn't expected. Shoddy work? Then why hadn't there been any write-ups or verbal warnings?

It was obvious that the longer the attorney spoke, the less the jurors were interested. They started to fidget in their seats and look around. Mike leaned forward and peered over at Randy. His law partner discreetly raised his eyebrows and smiled.

Yeah, Randy was feeling the same as he was. Unless something major happened, and Mike doubted it would, the case was going to be a slam-dunk.

Jody had stopped staring at the table and was watching the defense attorney and it was clear the younger shifter just couldn't believe what the attorney was saying.

Several jury members were also glancing at Jody, gauging his reaction. One man nodded slightly, as if to himself.

* * * *

Shelby handed Pete a cold Sprite before she sat down in the passenger seat of the news van. They'd already gone live twice that morning, and so far she was extremely happy with her reports.

"I'm going to work on the interviews you did earlier so we can get them ready for the noon broadcast," Pete said.

"Great." Shelby grinned at him. "I think they went well."

"Are you kidding? It was brilliant. I don't see the others out here taking the same direction or asking the questions you did. The report will be different from what everyone else is doing," Pete said. "And then you have me who is going to edit it all to show the brilliance."

Pete was so much more than just a cameraman. He could edit in the field, then send it on to the station. Shelby was lucky to have him with her again. When they'd met that morning at the station, Pete had even brought her a mocha he'd picked up on his way in.

If these stories worked out, Shelby was going to request him every time she went out in the field. Sure, she would have to share him, but maybe, just maybe he could be her number one technician.

"Shelby Holt?"

She looked up from the water bottle she'd been opening. A young woman about her age was walking up and smiling. She was pretty with tousled blonde hair, along with a cute turned-up nose. Behind her was a good-looking man wearing a motorcycle jacket, black jeans and a black T-shirt. He was glaring at anyone who got close to the blonde.

"Yes?" she asked as she set her water aside and jumped down.

"Hi," the blonde said. "I'm Nikki Stratton, and Clint said it'd be okay if I came over to talk to you."

As Nikki and the guy reached her, Pete straightened and angled himself slightly in front of Shelby. Pete would be able to tell they were shifters right away by their scent. Shelby only knew because Clint had mentioned it the night before.

"It's so nice to meet you," Shelby said as she stuck out her hand. "Clint said he'd introduce us but I'm happy to see you now." She nodded to Pete to let him know she was okay.

"You too." Nikki's voice was soft but there was something in her tone that Shelby recognized as strength. "This is my mate, RJ Cross."

RJ tilted his head but didn't say anything. He was still looking around at the crowd.

"You'll have to excuse him." Nikki waved her hand. "He's a little protective of me at the moment." Nikki placed her hand on her stomach.

"Oh!" Shelby looked between Nikki and the glowing shifter behind her. "Congratulations!"

"Thanks." Nikki beamed. "We only found out a few days ago and I'd already decided to make a trip here. My brothers"—Nikki rolled her eyes—"are also around here somewhere. It was the only way they'd allow me to come."

Shelby opened her mouth, but Nikki was on a roll. She snorted. "'Allow' me, they actually used that word."

"Now, babe," RJ spoke for the first time. "You know that's not what we meant."

His voice was deep and if Shelby hadn't fallen for Mike already she'd have given real thought to finding out more about him. Well, maybe not, because when Nikki glanced back at RJ, his features softened and he brushed his palm over her hair. "We just want you and our baby safe."

"I know." Nikki took his hand. "And I still love you."

Okay, so she would have never had a chance with a man who was obviously deeply in love with another. Plus, as hot as RJ was, she preferred the quiet strength that Mike carried.

"Would you like to sit down?" Shelby offered, motioning to the seat she'd just left.

Nikki laughed. "No! I really am okay. Don't you take their side."

Shelby lifted her hands. "I won't, I promise. Us girls have to stick together."

"Yeah," Nikki agreed as she hooked her arm through Shelby's. "Let's walk and talk. I want to get a better view of all these people."

"Nik," RJ growled.

"It'll be fine," Nikki assured him.

Since Shelby figured arguing with Nikki wouldn't do her any good she went along. Their news van was in the parking lot right by the walkway to the courthouse steps. Barriers had been put up on either side of the sidewalk to keep the two sides separate. She was surprised when Nikki led her to the anti-shifter side instead of the pro-shifter. Shelby had gone back and forth between the two but Nikki was a shifter.

There were small groups that stood in clusters farther away from the middle. The loudest, and usually the ones looking for trouble, would be right at the front of the crowd. This far back, it was quieter and people were actually talking. The subjects that they were discussing ran from the case, losing jobs to shifters, and even how the shifters should be required to register with the government.

Proposing the registration of shifter status had already been tried in Congress and it hadn't gotten very far. Since not every shifter species or faction had come out publicly, there was just no way to force the issue.

Of course, that didn't mean that would be the last that they heard about trying to force shifters to register one way or another.

But she was shocked that these conversations were more civil. Shelby's experience was with the most outspoken of the groups. Even now, as she and Nikki stopped and peered around, they were getting looks that appeared uneasy from the crowd.

"I've already interviewed a couple of the people back here, although none of them would agree to going on record," Nikki said.

"They keep avoiding me," Shelby shared. "But I also haven't seen any other reporters interview them either." She eyed Nikki. "Except you, it seems."

Nikki laughed. "I think it's different since I'm not a reporter. I'm just getting quotes and asking a few questions."

"Did you want to talk to someone or something?" Shelby questioned as she peered around. RJ was still following them but he had dropped back several feet, giving them space. No one else seemed to be paying that much attention to them, other than to move away.

"Yes, actually," Nikki said. "But I think he'll be willing to do it on camera and that's where you come in."

"You want me to interview someone?" she asked. "Really?" That wasn't how things usually worked.

"Like I said, I'm not a reporter. I've found myself writing a lot of articles on shifters but my main job is as a photo journalist. And I'll do that here but I won't have my article complete and submitted for another couple of weeks."

"I need my cameraman," Shelby told him.

"I think it would be better if you met with this guy without him first," Nikki said. "Just trust me on this."

"Okay," Shelby agreed for the moment. She didn't need to do anything she didn't want to but Shelby didn't expect trouble. Clint had seemed like an all right guy and he'd hooked her up with this woman. Also, Mike would not be happy if she was hurt physically or professionally.

"He should be right around here," Nikki said as she started to look around. "Young guy, with brown hair and brown eyes. He was wearing dark jeans and an orange sweatshirt."

"I don't see…" Shelby tried to find the guy Nikki was searching for. "There." She pointed. "Over by the brick building across the street."

"Yes!" Nikki grabbed her hand. "That's him."

She pulled Shelby through the crowd like a woman possessed. Shelby stumbled a little in her four-inch heels. Nikki wore flat black boots so it was easier for her to move.

"Slow down," Shelby muttered. "Or I'm going to tell your man that you need to sit or something." It was desperate but Shelby really didn't feel like breaking her ankle.

Nikki peered over her shoulder but continued to drag Shelby. "I like you. Clint said I would but he can be a little strange sometimes so I wasn't sure. And don't you dare tell RJ anything. I just know I'm going to be wrapped in wool or something and barely let out of his sight."

Damn, Shelby laughed, she couldn't help it. Guess she liked Nikki too.

"Hey, Bryan!" Nikki shouted but thankfully released Shelby's hand and slowed down.

The kid glanced up in surprise. When he saw Nikki calling him, he looked around nervously but didn't move. He seemed jumpy, and Shelby guessed that he wanted to run. Nikki was either oblivious or just good at appearing so.

"Hi," Nikki said as they reached Bryan. "This is my friend. The one that I told you about. Are you still willing to talk to her? Like I said, we don't have to do it here."

Wow! Nikki talked fast.

"I... I'm not...sure," Bryan hedged.

Shelby noticed the coffee shop that they were stood outside was almost empty. "Why don't we go inside and get away from the crowd?" she suggested. "I could use some quiet."

"Please," Bryan sighed.

Shelby motioned Nikki first then Bryan. Inside, the strong scent of rich dark coffee was in the air. The aroma was one that she would never get tired of. "Can I get you a drink?" Shelby asked. "I'm dying for a coffee."

"Me too," Nikki agreed.

A low clear of a throat sounded, and all three of them turned around. Shelby hadn't even noticed that RJ had entered with them. He did move silently for a big guy.

"Tea," Nikki said. "I meant I could use a tea."

"Ah." Shelby laughed. "No caffeine?"

"No caffeine," Nikki repeated.

"What about you, Bryan?" Shelby asked. "I'm thinking about a chocolate mocha."

"With caramel?" he asked softly.

"Of course," Shelby said. "I'll grab the drinks. Why don't you two take that table over there out of the way?"

That table would keep them out of view from the front windows and should help Bryan relax. She didn't know why he was so jittery but Shelby knew how to play things.

Shelby turned to RJ. "Can I get you anything?"

"No, thank you," he said quietly. "I'll stay out of the way and make sure there's no trouble."

Did they need protection in a coffee shop? Either RJ was very suspicious or there was a bigger threat than she knew about. As she walked toward the counter, Shelby glanced around trying to see if there was something or someone she was missing. Nope, they were alone.

"Can I help you?" the barista asked as Shelby reached the counter.

"Can I get two caramel mochas with whipped cream and caramel drizzle, and a cup of tea?" Shelby requested.

"What kind of tea?" the barista, whose name tag read Alice, asked.

"Uh." Shelby glanced over to the table and saw Nikki leaning close to Bryan as they spoke quietly. She then looked for RJ. He was standing close to the door against the wall with his arms crossed over his chest. His gaze was on Nikki and he wasn't paying any attention to her. Shelby sighed and glanced at the woman behind the counter. "I have no idea."

The woman's smile was friendly. "How about the tea that's today's special?"

"Yes," Shelby said, relieved. "But for a pregnant woman."

"No caffeine," Alice said. "Got it." She rang up the order. "Twelve fifteen."

Shelby pulled out a ten and five. "Keep the change."

"Thanks! I'll bring them over to you in just a minute," Alice told her.

"Great." Shelby strolled back over to the table. As she reached it, Nikki looked up and smiled. "Bryan has a story to tell. He wants to help Jody Norman, but is worried about his own job."

That sounded promising. "Well, I'd like to help. I can go on camera with an unnamed source and tell your story. I can put you on camera and shadow you out and change your voice. We'd have to do that at the station, though."

"You'd be willing to do that?" Bryan asked with surprise.

Shelby saw Alice headed over with the tray of drinks. She waited.

"Here you go!" Alice said as she set the cups on the table. Nikki received a dark tea that had an orange scent. The mochas were served in thick, white ceramic mugs and they were piled high with whipped cream and a beautiful caramel design.

"That looks so good," Bryan said, pulling his closer.

"Thanks again," Shelby told Alice.

"Sure thing," Alice said. "Just holler if you need anything."

"We will," Shelby promised.

As Alice walked away, Shelby ran her thumb in the cream and popped it in her mouth.

"That does look really good," Nikki said with a pout.

Shelby just grinned but then she peered over at Bryan. "To answer your earlier question, I will do whatever I can to keep you safe. I don't want to parade you around just for ratings."

"I'd like to do that source thing," Bryan said. "They'll probably know it was me that spoke to you but they wouldn't be able to prove it, would they?"

"No, I would protect you. So would my producer," Shelby said.

"Okay." Bryan nodded.

"Take your time and tell me everything," Shelby said.

* * * *

She was never going to wear heels again. There had to be some sort of shoes that would make her look good and be comfortable as well. She absolutely, positively was never wearing heels again. As she jogged to Pete, she pulled her cell phone out of her purse. Bryan had said he'd be willing to talk to Mike, and Shelby wanted to get him a message as soon as possible. He'd have his phone off but she'd texted a message to him.

Hopefully, when court broke for lunch, Mike would check his messages and get a hold of her.

Pete was still parked in the same spot and she was relieved that she was almost there. He noticed her hurrying over and straightened, looking alarmed.

Shelby smiled so he knew she was okay. "I've got something!" she said as she reached him. "It's an exclusive and we cannot release the name of our source but I got something."

Excitement lit his eyes. "Are we going straight on-air?"

"I've already called Jack and he gave us the green light," Shelby told him. "I'm to give the barest of reports but to get it out there. Then we need to go in the station and really spin it."

"It's that big?" Pete asked.

"It's that big," she said.

"Fix yourself up while I get the camera ready," Pete said.

"Hey, Pete," she called, stopping him from going around the van. "I'm going to give the counsel a heads-up. It's important to the case."

"Important to your man," Pete said.

Shelby jerked back.

He chuckled. "I'm a shifter. You've showered and changed clothes but I can still slightly smell him on your skin."

"Oh." She didn't know what to say.

"He's a good man," Pete said. "He's lucky to have you."

That was nice of Pete to say. "Thanks, I'm pretty lucky myself."

"They should break for lunch soon, so let's get this done so you can get the information to Mike."

"Just give me a sec," she told him. Shelby jumped into the passenger seat and pulled down the mirror before she dug in her bag for her makeup compact. She powdered her face, taking away some of the flush she'd gotten from excitement and her short jog. After, she pulled out her brush and smoothed her hair back.

"I'm set," Pete called.

"Okay," Shelby said. She climbed out of the seat then straightened her dress before she walked over to him. She accepted the microphone and turned to place herself in front of the anti-shifter crowd. They might hear her words but probably not. It wouldn't matter, though. The story would be out soon.

"In five," Pete said then raised his hand to count her down.

He held up one finger, and Shelby noticed movement over his shoulder. Mike moved into her view. Too late to stop now, Shelby began her report.

"This is Shelby Holt reporting live from in front of the Clear Creek courthouse where the biggest case of the country is currently underway. In a time where humans have the ability to shift into animals there is a divide between the two races."

She spoke with a calm clear voice even as she looked right at Mike.

"In interviewing both sides of the case I've been in contact with a source close to both the defendant and Jody Norman. This information was relayed to me by an unnamed source who has already agreed to talk to the attorney for Mr. Norman. This person claims to be present in numerous settings where the accused belittled and threatened Mr. Norman in front of him and other humans."

Shelby peered back into the camera lens. "Join us for our next local broadcast where we'll reveal some critical details that may change the way we all view the dynamics between shifter and human relationships in the work place."

As Shelby ended her live feed, she once again glanced at Mike. This was not going to be fun.

* * * *

Mike dragged Shelby away from the crowd caught between intrigue and anger. He'd seen her text message and had excused himself from the lunch that Austin's people had brought.

He'd almost reached out to her but had seen the light on the camera that was pointed at her so he'd stood to watch.

"Hey." Shelby pulled her arm out of his hold. "I'm in heels."

Mike eased his hold and slowed down. This was what he'd known when he got with her, wasn't it? Shelby was a reporter and it was her job to get information. And she had sent him a message.

They were far enough away from the crowd that they shouldn't be overheard easily. During her live feed, everyone had grown quiet around her. Both sides, the anti-shifters and the pro-shifters, had listened to everything she'd had to say.

Then the pro-shifters had grown angry. Even though they were several yards away, he could still hear shouting. And that pissed him off the most. Standing there in her pretty green dress and sweater, Shelby had put herself directly in the path of danger.

"Okay," he said as he released her. He paced away then strolled closer. "I'm not going to yell," he said, trying to calm himself, but she snorted and drew his attention.

"Yell?" she asked with her arms crossed. She stood stiffly.

"Yes, I'm not going to," he said again.

"I don't see why —"

"Why I'd be mad?" he interrupted.

"I texted you," she said. "It's not like I could just burst into the courtroom and tell you."

"Of course not," he snapped. "So instead you put yourself in the middle of two groups who'd love nothing more than to start trouble and gave them ammunition."

"What?" Shelby squeaked.

Mike stalked to her and grasped her arms, yanking her close. He made sure to keep his hold gentle so he wouldn't hurt her. "What if someone had thrown a punch or attacked?"

"I've been doing this a long time," Shelby said, softer.

"It could have been an accident!" he claimed. "One person knocks you off those damn heels and you'd go down. By the time any of our friends or your cameraman got to you there's a good chance you'd be really hurt."

"Yeah, but aren't you mad about the report?" she asked.

"I'm not happy about it," he admitted. "And I can admit I was pissed off as I watched your live feed, but no, that's not my first concern right now."

She smiled and it caught him off guard.

"Why are you grinning?" he asked.

Shelby lifted her hands even as he rubbed down her arms to grip her wrists. "You really do care for me."

"Of course I do," he said. He leaned forward to simply brush his lips over hers. They were in public after all.

"Then get ready to completely fall for me," she said.

"Why?" He was suspicious.

"My source is willing to talk to you," Shelby announced with a laugh.

"Yeah?"

"He would rather his name stay out of it as much as possible but he does want to help his friend," she told him.

"I can work with that. I might be able to use something that he or she could tell me," Mike said.

"Tonight, after you're done?" she asked.

"That'll work. Cooper and Julie are still working nights so we can use their place. I'll call and let Cooper know, but he won't have a problem with it."

"I'll set it up," she said. "You'll get to meet Nikki Stratton also. She's the one who introduced me to my source, and she's a riot."

"Okay," Mike agreed. "If you can take care of that, I'll grab some dinner on the way to the house so we don't have to worry about it. I'll ask Randy to come with me too. He should hear this info first-hand."

Shelby rose to her tiptoes and kissed him. "I have to go into the station."

Mike glanced over his shoulder at the crowd, which was growing more rowdy. "I'll see you soon, then."

Mike left her where she was standing and strolled back to the courthouse. He walked around the shouting people and knew that someone needed to do something to keep things calm but he didn't know what.

He glanced at his watch. He needed to hurry and get inside before he was late.

"Listen up," Clint Price yelled to the pro-shifter group. At his back, a uniformed cop was facing the anti-shifter protesters.

"For those of you who don't know who I am," Clint shouted, "I work directly for the Wolf Council and we will not allow a riot. We need to let the lawyers do their jobs and if you stay here, you will remain in control."

Mike nodded to himself as he jogged up the steps of the courthouse. The Council had been smart to send representatives. The shifters knew the Council didn't mess around and no one, whether they were wolf shifters or another species, would go against the Council word without knowing that trouble would follow.

"I need to speak to you."

Mike looked up to see the opposing attorney. "I don't have time for you." He continued walking, already planning how to tell Jody the good news.

"Make time. We need to talk about a deal to end the trial."

"He'll admit wrongdoing?" Mike did stop.

"My client does not see the advantage of this trial going on any longer. Since this is a civil case instead of criminal, we can make an agreement to end all this."

"We could," Mike said. "If my client agrees and our terms are met."

"Like I said, we need to talk."

Chapter Six

Mike stepped inside Cooper's kitchen through the back door, holding takeout boxes from the local Italian restaurant. He'd figured that would be the best option since he wasn't one hundred percent sure how many would be there. The family-style pans would feed them all.

The kitchen was warm, and as he closed the door behind him, he saw that there weren't as many there as he'd thought.

Shelby leaned against the counter talking to Clint and another woman who he guessed was Nikki Stratton. Kurt sat with two men at the table as they all drank from beer bottles.

"Hey," Shelby greeted as he walked over.

Mike set the boxes on the island, then kissed her cheek. "Hi."

"You're later than I thought you'd be," she said.

He nodded. "For some reason things were really hopping this afternoon."

Shelby just beamed. "I wonder why." She grabbed his hand and tugged him over to the table. "This is Nikki Stratton and her mate, RJ Cross."

Mike nodded at Nikki then RJ. "Hello."

"And this is Bryan," Shelby finished with a flourish.

The youngest man at the table looked up and winced slightly. He stood, then rubbed his palms against his jeans before he held out his hand.

"I'm very pleased to meet you," Mike said. "You've been a huge help and we really appreciate you being willing to come forward."

"I have been?" Bryan asked as he darted a look to Shelby. "But I haven't told you anything, yet. I still don't want to get involved but I have to try to help Jody."

Mike peered around the room and saw that everyone was listening. He intertwined his fingers with Shelby's before he brought them to his lips. "Thanks to this lovely woman, you don't have to," Mike said. "The trial is over."

"Over?" Shelby and the female shifter repeated together.

He grinned. "It seems the defense decided to accept our terms, including the new ones I added today, and settled out of court with Jody."

"It's over? I don't have to talk to a judge or anything?" Bryan asked, hope tinting his tone.

"They've admitted to violating Jody's civil rights, will pay him an amount I can't share, and must put in a human resource policy and training so this doesn't happen in the future. They've also agreed to donate to a charity of our choosing. Plus, work with shifter policy makers for equal rights in the workplace," Mike announced.

No one in the room said anything for several moments. Bryan dropped down in his seat. "I actually helped, right?"

"Yes," Mike assured him. "And I believe Jody wants to talk to you about going into business with him. It seems he has enough for a small startup company and is getting flooded with requests from shifters for their IT needs."

"Wow," Shelby whispered. "This almost feels anticlimactic."

Mike leaned closer to her. "I can probably help with that feeling later."

"Shit!" Kurt barked out a laugh as RJ choked on his beer. "I heard that."

"What can I say?" Mike commented. "I'm a happy guy who is ready to celebrate."

"We need wine!" Shelby said, waving Nikki over.

"Nice to meet you." Mike dipped his head to both of them.

"I have the alcohol," Nikki said as she joined them around the table. "You need to tell us everything."

"Well, there is a press conference scheduled at eight-fifteen tomorrow morning," Mike shared. He glanced over at Shelby. "That way, if a talented reporter wanted to break the news they could get a jump start."

"Really?" Shelby shouted as she launched herself into his arms.

Mike caught her and whirled her around in a circle, then he kissed her deeply. He could hear the others in the room laughing and cheering. Once he'd put all his feelings into the lip lock, Mike set her back down on her feet. "How about that drink?"

"Yes," she agreed as she wrapped her arm around his waist and snuggled into him.

Since he liked her there, he decided to keep her close. He took one of the free chairs before he pulled her into his lap. Clint had grabbed more beers, and Nikki was pouring wine. He accepted a bottle from Clint.

"Nikki," RJ said.

She laughed. "Sparkling juice." She showed him the bottle. "I found it in the cabinet."

RJ nodded.

So the couple was expecting a child. That was something that Mike had actually never thought about for himself. He could admit that he was considering a future with Shelby, and that maybe down the road they would mate, but no way was he ready for children. He shuddered.

"You okay?" Shelby whispered, leaning close.

Mike draped his arm over her shoulder. "I'm good."

Still, it was nice the way that Nikki sat on RJ's lap and he rubbed her stomach.

"We should probably call in to the Council," Kurt mentioned.

"Ah," Clint whined, making them laugh. "We're drinking. If we call when we're drinking they'll know."

Kurt shook his head. "How?"

"I don't know. They'll use their creepy Council powers," Clint said.

"I'm pretty sure those don't exist," Kurt replied.

"You say that," Clint argued, "but last time I had a drink inside the mansion they totally knew."

"You stole their brandy then tripped over your own feet," Kurt said.

"I had to sit in a meeting for four hours. *Four hours*, man! It was drink or slit my wrists," Clint bitched as he slouched in his chair. "I'm not calling them."

"I'll do it," Kurt said as he stood.

Bryan's phone rang and he jumped before he blushed. Mike thought the kid was cute and hoped everything turned out well for him. "It's Jody," Bryan said before he hopped up and went to the other room.

Mike took a drink as he looked around the kitchen. He wished Cooper and Julie were there but maybe they could get together before everyone left.

"We should have a barbecue," Shelby said.

Once again, their thoughts were aligned, and Mike just stared at her.

"What? Is that a bad idea?" she asked. "I just thought that Cooper, Julie, Garrett and everyone we hang out with would like to meet these guys."

"I was just thinking the same thing," he admitted.

"Cool," Shelby said. "What do you think, Nikki?"

"That'd be great. I think we're leaving tomorrow night, though."

"How about a late lunch? You can leave when you want to and everyone else can hang out. I can host it at my house," Shelby said.

"We'll be there." Clint lifted his beer.

"I'll invite Austin and his friends and see if Gage and Cain want to stop by," Mike said.

"I'll take care of everything," Shelby told him. "I haven't hosted a party in a while."

* * * *

Shelby waited until Mike had returned from taking the trash out before she jumped him. He chuckled as she knocked him against the wall.

"As much as I like our new friends, I couldn't wait for them to leave," she told him.

"I think they got that when you started to nibble on my neck," he teased.

She giggled. "I might have had too much to drink."

"Never," he said. "You deserved it."

"So did you," she said as she ran her hands over his chest. Shelby didn't think she'd ever get tired of touching him.

"It was a good day," he admitted.

"A great day and an even better night," she corrected.

"What do you have planned for the rest of our evening?" he asked.

Instead of answering with words, Shelby reached for the button on his pants and tugged.

He covered her hand with his. "As much as I like your idea, I can just imagine Cooper or Julie coming home early."

"Damn." She backed off. "That would suck and not in the good way. Let's get into the bedroom."

"Yes, ma'am," he said then lifted her off her feet and threw her over his shoulder.

"Mike!"

"Just hang on," he said. "This will be fast."

"I can't wait until we can go back to our houses. Hell, we could have stayed at mine."

"We'll think of it as a little vacation," Mike told her as he stepped into the room and closed the door behind them.

He set her on her feet, and Shelby started to pull off her clothes.

"In a hurry?" he teased.

"I've been wanting you for hours. It's all I could think about," she told him.

"Damn," he groaned then undressed as quickly as she was.

Shelby was naked first and went to him. She pressed her breasts against his chest. "Hurry," she urged.

He kicked off his shoes then yanked his socks away, and finally dropped his slacks and underwear to the ground. Shelby took his hand in hers and brought his fingers to her pussy.

"Feel me," she said quietly. "I'm so ready for you."

"Yes, you are."

Mike turned quickly, and Shelby found herself pressed against the wall. His mouth came down on hers and she let him take control. All she needed was her hands on his body and Mike could take care of the rest.

When he lifted her leg, she wrapped around him.

"Hurry," she demanded, pulling back for air.

He positioned his cock at her entrance and pushed inside with one long thrust. Shelby dropped her head back on the wall. She loved being filled by his thick cock.

Mike grabbed her other leg, holding her against the wall. If he wasn't a shifter she'd probably never trust him to be able to hold her up. But with Mike, she knew he'd never let her fall.

"Harder," she cried as he plunged in deep before withdrawing and slamming back inside. Her entire body trembled as he took her there against the wall and passion ignited throughout her body.

It felt like her blood was boiling and it was way too hot in the room. She clung to him while locking her ankles together behind his back.

His eyes were closed as he thrust over and over and his breathing grew more rapid.

They'd both had a lot to drink so their movements were a little wild and out of control. Did it get much better than this?

She could feel her climax approaching and moaned loudly, letting him know that she was close. Mike picked up the pace even more and was slamming into her. She'd probably have bruises on her back later but she would be proud of them.

"Mike," she panted.

"Mine!" he growled before his mouth came down on her neck and he sucked hard.

Her orgasm hit fast and she couldn't breathe for a second. Then her breath whooshed out as he started to come. Mike plunged into her one last time then stopped moving while buried deep.

"We've got to do that again," she murmured.

"I agree," he said. "It should be a law or something. When we have a good day we must make love like that."

Shelby lifted her head. "Hear, hear."

They laughed as Mike carried her over to the bed, and they fell into it together.

"We will have more good days like this," Shelby told him. "You're going to be a sought-after attorney after this."

"What about you?" he asked. "I bet the offers start pouring in for news anchor jobs all over the country."

Shelby frowned. "I don't think so."

"I do." He rolled her onto her back and lay across her lower body. "And wherever the road takes you, I know you'll be the best."

It was what she had always wanted, what Mike was telling her, but now the thought of leaving Clear Creek made her sad. "I guess we'll have to wait and see."

"What is it?" he asked.

She shrugged.

"Okay." He backed off and lifted her until they were sitting across from each other on the bed. "Talk to me."

"I'm not sure if I even want to get noticed," she confessed.

Mike smiled. Shelby frowned at him. "What?" she asked.

"You're scared," he told her.

"I am not!" she exclaimed.

"All your dreams are on the verge of coming true and it frightens you," he said. "But you don't need to be."

"I just don't know if what I wanted is still what I need," Shelby told him.

"You'll know when it's time." He bent forward to kiss her gently. When he pulled back Shelby reached for him. He captured her hands in his and brought them up to his lips. "You can turn every offer you get away or accept the best one."

"And move away?" she asked.

"Is that what you're worried about?" he questioned.

"It's on my mind," she admitted.

"I may not know what's going to happen but whatever does, we'll be okay. I'll be good, and you'll be great," Mike said. "It may be early in our relationship but I have no doubt we'll find a way to be together."

"Promise?" she asked. Shelby wasn't used to putting her heart on the line but she needed Mike to tell her everything was going to be okay.

"I promise," Mike said. "I'll be taking some time to wrap things up for Jody, then working with the Council on writing some of the Shifter laws they want to try to pass. I don't know what's going to be happening with me either but we'll figure it out."

"Sounds good to me," Shelby said as she crawled into his lap.

"Besides," he said with a laugh, "I'm going to be working with the Shifter Coalition. Just think of all the different shifters you're going to meet."

"There's only one shifter I'm interested in right now," she told him before he pressed his lips to hers. They had some celebrating to do after all.

About the Author

Crissy Smith lives in Texas with her husband, daughter, and three Labrador retrievers. The three dogs love to curl up under her computer desk and nap while she writes. It doesn't leave a lot of room for her but what's a woman to do?

When not writing or reading, she enjoys hunting, camping and shooting. But she has a girly side too and is addicted to pedicures and coffee.

She has been writing since she was a teenager and still loves everything to do with the paranormal. Her stories and characters all have a place in her heart. She loves the alpha male, the dominant werewolf, or the Master vampire which find their way in most of her books.

Learn more about the characters she has created at her website where they have their very own page. It will be updated from time to time to let you know what's going on with them. Also you can find out who will be in the next book.

Crissy Smith loves to hear from readers. You can find her contact information, website details and author profile page at http://www.totallybound.com

.